BLOOD MONEY

♦ Blood Money ♦

Neal Bevans

Bevans Company

Morganton, North Carolina

FIRST BEVANS COMPANY EDITION, SEPTEMBER 2018
Published by Bevans Company, Morganton, North Carolina

BLOOD MONEY.

ISBN: 978-1-7327089-0-7

Printed in the United States of America

i

To my wife, Nilsa Bevans, the love of my life, who encouraged me to write this novel and stood by me every step along the long path of bringing it to life; she is a true inspiration.

♦ ACKNOWLEDGMENTS ♦

I used to wonder why a novelist would have so many people to thank in creating a novel. My image was of a solitary figure, typing away and producing flawless prose on the first try. The truth is something else entirely. Now I understand. Sure, you write, but you rely on a lot of people for help, for the mechanics of bringing a story to life, but also for emotional and psychological support as you grapple with the strange need to tell a story.

As I've written this book, I've met with a lot of people, such as a firearms instructor at the Federal Law Enforcement Center (now retired) who taught me how to shoot everything from handguns to automatic weapons. He prefers to remain anonymous.

But I can name other people who have helped me enormously, including my sister, Lisa Ford, who has been my best friend since we were children and has always cheered me on; my stepdaughter, Tamara Tigani; my friends who gave the first drafts a read-through and came back with honest criticism, including Susan Keller, Eric Abegglen, Mary Charlotte Safford, and Leslie McKesson.

My wife also gave me tremendous emotional support as I doubted that I had both the talent and the will to see this project through.

Finally, no matter how good a writer you think you are, you need a great editor. You need someone who will tell you the truth and give you gut-punch honest opinions about your writing. For me, that person is Sarah Dawson. She gave me suggestions, corrections, and a lot of advice about how to turn a story that I wanted to write into a novel. I owe her a big debt.

◆ PROLOGUE ◆

Friday, March 31, 8:15 a.m.

He sat in the back seat of a stolen van in an empty Atlanta church parking lot and thought about his father. He supposed it was his way of working himself up for the job. Fortunately, his partner, sitting behind the wheel, was always quiet before jobs like this. The driver would smack his gum but didn't like to talk, and that suited the man in the back just fine. He wanted to remember.

Thinking about the old man always made him angry. In his childhood back in Montana, his father would come home some nights, and you could just *tell*. You'd know, *tonight is going to be bad*. Bad for him, bad for his mother, bad for his sister.

He and Christina would try to find somewhere to hide, but there was no hiding from his father on nights like that. He might be distracted by the TV for a while, or he even might go out, but most nights he stayed home and got drunk at the kitchen table, getting meaner with each passing hour.

He'd stand, just out of his father's field of view, and watch as he reached for the first drink. The change came before the alcohol ever touched his lips, at the moment his hand touched the glass.

"Ten minutes," a voice said in the man's earbud, cutting through the memories. He shook himself and raised his walkie-talkie.

"Ten-four," he replied, acknowledging the call, and then he looked at his watch. The armored car would first pass the other van, currently sitting in a McDonald's parking lot, then five minutes later would pass his van. He made eye contact with the man in front, who just nodded curtly.

He returned to his thoughts.

Even as a child, he'd had his hunter's instincts. He'd known that he should never speak when his father was like that. If you spoke, you got hit. You also shouldn't look away. If you looked away, you got hit. But you couldn't look into his father's eyes, either. That was a challenge, and you would get hurt even worse. So, he would stare at a point just above his father's left eyebrow. He would stare and stare and go somewhere else in his mind as the old man ranted and raved.

And sitting there, staring, he would hate his father with every molecule in his body. He would imagine grabbing the bottle and beating his father to death with it, stabbing the old son of a bitch over and over, always with him begging for mercy, blood everywhere. His old man never noticed, couldn't see what was in his son's mind, so he just kept on yelling, and his son would sit across the table from him and imagine stabbing him to death with a broken bottle of Jack Daniel's Black Label.

The accented voice on the radio cut through the man's thoughts again. "I've got package."

It was time.

The man shook himself and put his thoughts away in the padlocked part of his brain where he kept them. It wouldn't help to keep them in his head now that there was work to be done. But his blood was pumping, and his rage was boiling, and it had worked, just the way it always did. Rage always beat out fear. Always.

He tapped the shoulder of the man in front and said, "Good to go." The driver put the van in gear and pulled out of the church parking lot.

◆

The plan was simple. Afterward, he realized that maybe it had been *too* simple. The blonde would pull out in front of the armored car. He and his partner would pull up beside the car, and the Russian would pin the car from behind. As soon as they were stopped, he'd pump a .50-caliber round into the car door's lock, blowing it wide open. Two or three minutes max, and they'd be a whole lot richer.

As his partner gunned the engine, he hefted the big rifle in his hands. He liked the feel of it. Gregor the Russian had gotten it for him from a Ukrainian who owned a bakery and sold guns when he wasn't making bread. If either guard got cute, the man could take them down, but he thought that would be unlikely given the size of the bullet that would blow open their door. Their problem was way more likely to be that both guards would be dead.

Simple.

In and out.

Bullshit.

The whole thing had gone wrong almost from the beginning. The blonde nearly missed her cue and had to scramble to pull out in time. His partner overshot the van and had to back up a little to line up the doors, losing them precious seconds. The man knew the guards would be on the radio or telephone instantly. He realized that he should have brought a signal jammer, but it hadn't occurred to him until that moment. He yanked open the side door of the van and picked up the rifle.

Then the barrel of a shotgun slid out of a gun port on the armored car, and the man knew they were in serious trouble. But he was quick; he always had been. He beat the shotgun to the trigger, and there was a sound like a small bomb going off. The man's ears were ringing so much he couldn't hear anything as he watched the armored car's door fly open, hanging on by a single hinge.

The man pulled his ski mask down all the way and checked to make sure his partner had done the same. The Russian was already at the door, his mask in place, too. The man jumped out of the van and inside the armored car in two big leaps. He felt so pumped he thought he could have jumped right over the car.

Everything was moving slowly and quickly at the same time, the way it always did when you thought you'd be dead in the next few seconds.

"Fuck!" he heard Gregor yell, and that was the precise moment he knew it had gone completely sour. He moved up for a look through the door.

"Where is fucking money?!" he heard the Russian scream.

He scanned the guards. The two in the front seemed stunned; no surprise there. He turned to look past the side door, which was twisted in an almost artistic way. The guard in the back was sprawled in an awkward position with blood pooling under him. The shotgun was at his feet, but the man didn't bother kicking it away. The guard clearly wasn't going to be doing anything with it.

"What the fuck is going on?" the Russian was still screaming.

"What is it?" he asked.

"It's fucking empty!"

He shifted around Gregor to get a better look. There was nothing but a few obviously empty bags lying in the back. Gregor pointed his gun at the driver. "The money! Where is it? Where is money?"

"What?" The driver was obviously stunned.

Gregor looked as though he were going to shoot the guard, but instead he hit the driver on the head with enough force that his jaw slammed shut on his chest. Gregor aimed his 9mm into the driver's right eye. "The money! Where is money?"

"We—" the driver began, but he was clearly coming unglued.

The guard in the passenger seat jumped in. "There isn't any fucking money! Okay? No fucking money! We haven't made our pickup yet. Christ, the bank's right over there. We haven't been there yet."

"You drop off money! You drop it off at bank!" Gregor screamed. "Where the fuck is it?"

"We changed our schedule," the guard explained, sounding desperate. "This week, we pick up."

"What?" Gregor said. "You pick up? You don't deliver today?"

"No. We altered our schedule. This week, we pick up. Another van does the drop-offs." Looking around, he added, "in the afternoons," as though that was helpful.

"Shit," Gregor said. "You are fucking lying."

The man realized that it was a bust. "Nothing here!" he shouted to the Russian. And then, over his shoulder to his partner who was still behind the wheel of the stolen van, "Nothing here! Time to go!"

"I no fucking leave without money!"

"Then stay, tough guy," the man said. "We're out of here."

The man climbed down and ran back to his van. He saw his partner shaking his head and turned to the Russian. Despite what he'd said, Gregor was hustling it back to his van, too. The man motioned to the blonde, but she was already putting her car in gear. He heard a grinding sound, metal on metal, and for one panicked moment thought her car was stuck on the front grill of the armored car, but then she pulled away and drove off.

As they tore from the scene, he punched the seat in front of him.

"Goddamn it!" he screamed. "Goddamn it!"

His partner lifted the ski mask off his face, and despite his anger, the man in the back did the same. He rolled the rifle up in a blanket and tried to calm his breathing. "Slow down," he instructed the driver. "This is no time to get stopped for speeding."

The man up front glanced at him in the rearview mirror and slowed the van. "So much for easy money."

The man's hands shook, and he desperately wanted to grab someone by the throat and choke them to death. It took a few minutes, but he forced himself to calm down. Anger had its place, but it wouldn't do any good here. He had to get his mind clear, and that meant letting go of the panic and the fear.

He took a few deep breaths and watched his hands shake. Even though it wasn't particularly cool outside, he felt his body growing cold.

The adrenaline is wearing off, he thought. It left him feeling jittery and out of sorts.

He took a few more deep breaths, took his gun out of his belt, and shoved it under some rags on the floor of the van. He'd have to ditch it somewhere. He was on the hook for two stolen vans, attempted armed robbery, and quite possibly murder, given the shape of the guard in the back of the armored car. All that, and he didn't have a dime to show for his efforts. He took even more deep breaths and tried to slow his racing heart and *think*.

He already had the bridge overpass picked out and five gallons of gas in the back. They'd park the van, torch it, and hop on two little scooters they'd stored nearby. No cops ever thought that bad men drove around on scooters. He knew he looked ridiculous on it, such a big man on such a tiny thing, but with a plain-looking jacket covering his muscular arms and a helmet, he was virtually invisible. He even had a plastic milk crate secured to the front with bungee cords and might throw some groceries in it before heading home. A motor scooter and a guy bringing home groceries. What could look more innocent?

He'd stash the gun near the overpass, too, but not so close that the police would find it if they thought about doing a search. There was no reason to get rid of it permanently since he hadn't fired it. He'd come back for it later.

With his plan firmly set in his mind, he decided not to think about the whole stupid, failed endeavor.

He had other ways of getting cash.

Sunday, April 9, 8:30 p.m.

When her phone rang, Imogene Resnic was watching television. She wasn't paying much attention to it, though. Her mind kept floating back to the break-in this past week. Harold had often told her that she was crazy to keep that much cash in the house.

"Goddamn it, Imogene," he used to say. "Somebody's going to come along and take it all away from you."

Then God had come along and taken Harold away from her.

The only concession she'd made had been to split it up and store it in different places. Part of it was in the safe, the other part hidden. She'd never even told Tommy where the other part was. She loved her boy, but she wasn't sure that she liked him very much. There wasn't anything of Harold in him, and not much of her either. He was a little, well, *sneaky*. But surely even a sneaky son wouldn't be so greedy as to steal from his own mother…

Regardless, the fact was that someone had broken in, had taken a lot of her money. A stranger had been inside her home. He'd opened her safe and looked at her things—maybe even touched them—then stolen her hard-earned money. It was horrible to ponder.

The ringing phone yanked her out of her thoughts.

"Oh, thank the Lord!" she exclaimed after listening for a few moments. *Thank God*, she thought to herself again while the voice on the other end of the phone kept speaking.

"What, *now?*" she asked, paying closer attention. "Wait, let me get a pencil."

She scribbled instructions. "But—" She waited as the voice cut her off. "Okay, then." She checked her watch. "No more than fifteen minutes, I'd guess."

More scribbling of instructions.

"I will," she said. "And thank you, thank you *so* much." She hung up the phone and breathed a huge sigh of relief. She was going to get her money back, but even more important, a great weight of suspicion had been lifted off her.

The instructions had been clear. She grabbed the rest of her money from its hiding place and dressed quickly, pulling on a raincoat in deference to the threatening clouds.

Before leaving, she made a quick phone call. Esther Jenkins, that nosy next-door neighbor, deserved to know that her suspicions were wrong. Let her simmer on that for a while.

Imogene had a pretty good idea of where she was heading and only had to refer once to her scribbled directions. The place was dark when she pulled in, and she had a moment's anxiety. Maybe she'd gotten the wrong location after all. She looked up at the sign. *Mick's Muffler*. No, that was right. Still…

Then she saw him, standing in the shadows. She sighed and smiled. He motioned for her to park next to his car, directing her with a flashlight. She parked where he indicated and, at another motion from him, stayed inside the car. He walked up, and she put down her window.

"So, you got him?" she began.

"Did you bring the money?" he asked.

"I sure did."

Imogene turned slightly to reach for her purse, and he raised the .38 and shot her twice behind her left ear. Imogene thought she'd been punched before her body stopped listening to its brain and dropped like a stone onto the seat.

He stood quietly for a moment, listening. No sounds. No cars. No lights. No people. He walked around to the passenger door and opened it. Reaching in carefully, he lifted Imogene's purse from beside her body. He was pleased that no blood had gotten onto it. He fished out the thick stack of bills and then put the purse back beside her. He spotted her handwritten directions and picked those up, too.

You had to be careful. You had to be in the moment. His heart was racing just as hard as it had when they'd attacked the armored car, but this felt different somehow. Maybe it was because he was alone. Maybe he was getting better at this kind of thing. He took a few deep breaths, just as he had in the stolen van, and looked around again.

She wasn't going to bleed very much; she was already dead. He stared down at her foolish little body and considered. He cleared his mind and let the impressions wash over him. No fingerprints. Untraceable gun. No witnesses. No tire tracks from his car because he'd made sure to keep it on the cement of the driveway. Should be raining in just a little while to wash away anything else…

Clear. He was clear. He took out his hunting knife and stabbed the left front tire. The hiss seemed obscenely loud, and he glanced around again. Nothing.

A car with a flat tire, he thought. *They'll think she pulled in to get it fixed and then crossed paths with the wrong person.*

He got into his car and drove away, $40,000 richer.

♦ CHAPTER ONE ♦

Monday, April 10, 7:30 a.m.

Sean Turlow had had another night of bad sleep. He'd had disturbing dreams that he couldn't remember, and now he was sprawled in bed, staring at the ceiling after having slapped off the alarm. He finally roused himself enough to climb out of bed and went to the bathroom to splash some water on his face. He closed the door and turned on the light. Wincing at first, his eyes quickly adjusted. His black hair was tousled, and he had that haunted look in his eyes that was always there after a bad night's sleep. He tried shaking it off. He was just over six feet, but he had his father's stocky build, which somehow made him look even taller. Right now he looked like hell, but he decided to cut himself a little slack. Everyone looked like hell first thing in the morning. He turned off the light and let his eyes adjust to the darkness again. Standing there in the doorway of his bathroom, he tried to remember the nightmare, but it had faded. He tried once again to shake it off and started getting ready for the day.

As an Assistant District Attorney, Sean tried cases all the time, but he'd been dreading the one scheduled for today: State v. Winslow. The current wife and the former wife of some loser in Lawrenceville had gotten into a fight at a Hardee's while they were exchanging the children. Sherry Winslow (the old Mrs. Winslow) had taken a chair and cracked Lisa Winslow (the new Mrs. Winslow) over the back and ruptured one her disks. That made it aggravated assault and a felony.

Normally, Sean was able to negotiate plea deals on all his minor cases. But no such luck with State v. Winslow. The Winslows wanted to slog this out through the court system, chewing down to the very last ounce of their pound of flesh. It was a total, ugly mess and a complete waste of time.

Sean had tried to get them to see reason, even arranging an unusual pretrial meeting with the parties, but his "victim" was just as crazy as the defendant. Lisa had been following Sherry around, videotaping her every movement. It was one of the few cases he'd ever heard of where the defendant had taken out a restraining order on the victim.

It was insane. At the pretrial meeting, Sean had tried to explain to them that they were destroying their own lives, not to mention the children's, and then had finally lost his temper and told them that they were both crazy and should be ashamed of themselves.

"I've got plenty of people committing crimes!" he'd yelled. "I've got drug dealers and child molesters and murderers, and then I've got you two who just can't behave like adults!"

Of course, it hadn't worked. So here they were.

He rehearsed his opening statement in the mirror as he shaved and then put on his shirt and tie. He frankly didn't care who won or lost. If he could, he would've put them both in jail. But he didn't have that power, and in a situation like this, that was probably a good thing.

Monday, April 10, 8:00 a.m.

Matt Burton drummed the steering wheel and whistled along with the radio. He had it tuned to a country station. The road was smooth; the sky was clear. It was good driving weather, and he liked to drive. He was a big man, and overweight. Last year, the doctor had told him that he needed to lose at least fifty pounds. Fifty pounds for Chrissake. He knew that he was heavy, but *fifty* pounds? Shit, that would put him at less weight than he was when he'd gotten married. The first time.

He'd been working as a Crimes Against Persons (CAP) detective in Gannett County, Atlanta for nearly twenty years now, and he knew that a lot of people thought of him as something of a legend. He wasn't one for the attention, but he did sometimes find it useful to have a reputation for breaking big cases. It saved time.

"Can we *please* listen to something else?" the man in the back pleaded.

"Just sit tight, Jerry," Matt said, not taking his eyes off the road.

"I'll even take easy listening," Jerry continued through the grill. "Relaxation station. Enya. Even Gospel. Just no more of this fucking country bullshit. 'I ain't got my truck; I ain't got my girl; I married my goat, and she done run off with my best friend.' Goddamn. Please. Anything else."

"Jerry, you need to sit back and shut up," Matt said without any anger in his voice.

"What have we got, like another couple of hours 'til we hit Georgia? Can we *please* just try some other kind of music?"

Matt saw a roadside tourist stand with baskets and shawls hanging on hooks. He thought about his wife, Angela, and decided to pull over. He turned to the man in the back seat. "What I'm going to do is handcuff you to the front grill of this car," he explained, "while I go inside here and buy my wife a present."

"Say what now?"

"You heard me. I'm going inside and getting her one of those dream catcher things, and I'm going to look out at you every so often, and when I do, you'd better be right where I left you or I'll have to come out and shoot you."

"Hey, look, the music thing was just, you know, no big deal."

Matt climbed out and opened the back door. "C'mon, Jerry." He led Jerry around to the front of the patrol car and handcuffed him to the steel-reinforced grill there. "Now, don't go running off," he warned.

"You're really going to buy a present for your wife in this tourist trap?"

"Yes."

"Why didn't you just leave me in the car?"

"You might have died of the heat."

"So, this is better?"

"At least you don't have to listen to country music."

As Matt roamed through the shop, he took out his small digital recorder and dictated some notes. It was an old habit, stretching all the way back to the days of cassettes and tape recorders the size of books, but he'd always liked the system. He'd play the tape later and record the information in his notebooks, and maybe turn part of it over to Judy for transcription.

"April 10," he began, holding the device close to his mouth as he looked at some Comanche blankets. "Jerry mentioned that a guy named Slice has a meth lab somewhere in Buford. I should follow up on that, or at least pass it along to Narcotics…"

Monday, April 10, 8:15 a.m.

Bernie Cassis was pissed off. He kept replaying the phone conversation in his head, and every time he did, it made him angrier. He'd been at his desk in the CAP division, working up a report about a guy found dead in a crack house near Copper Street, when his phone had rung.

"Bernie." It was Chief Black. You couldn't mistake that voice anywhere. He was one of the few people who could call you and not identify himself.

"Hiya, Chief."

"Matt's still out of town, right?"

"Matt? Yeah. Utah or something."

"New Mexico, Bernie. He's bringing some shitheel in from Santa Fe."

"Yeah, that's right."

"I've got Doug on that Mexican drug gang killing," the chief continued, "and Hanson's got a pile of shit to move through."

"Yeah, Chief?"

There had been a long pause. "Well."

"Well, Chief?"

"I got a dead lady over at Mick's Muffler on Barton Street. I need you over there."

"Are we talking a murder here?"

"She's been shot. It could be suicide, but someone there opened the door and saw two bullet wounds, so who knows? The fire marshal is over there, the one from Sweeten Creek who's always sticking his nose in where it doesn't belong. He radioed in and said that there was no gun, but what the fuck does a fire marshal know about a crime scene?"

"Is this one mine, Chief?" Bernie asked. This was important. If it was a murder, it could be something big, and it would be all his. He needed to hear the words.

There was another pause. "Yeah, with Matt out of town…yeah, this one is yours."

"Thanks, Chief. I won't let you down."

I won't let you down, Bernie thought as he drove to Barton Street. Jesus, the chief sounded like he didn't want him to have it at all. *With Matt out of town…* Like the whole world revolved around that fat, old fucker. *Matt's bringing some dipshit back from Utah—New Mexico*, he corrected himself—*and that's the only reason I get a solid murder instead of some fuckup crack house drug killing.*

Bernie had been with the department for eight years. He'd started out as a patrol officer and gotten sick to death of people asking him where he was from. Finally he'd had it and had made the mistake of letting his anger show. "I'm from Jersey, Fuck-o," he'd shot back at some redneck peckerhead working the midnight shift. He should have known better.

The next day, he was greeted in the locker room with, "Hey, everybody! It's Jersey Fuck-o! How you doin', Jersey Fuck-o?"

It had gone on for months, and Bernie had thought about turning in his badge and gun and just getting the hell out of the South completely. But he'd stuck it out, and they'd eventually dropped the "Fuck-o" part. Now he was just "Jersey," and he could live with that.

After working the long, quiet nights on patrol, slowly getting time behind him and better schedules, better assignments, he'd gone to Property Crimes, then Narcotics, and now CAP. He'd worked hard. He'd made some mistakes, but he'd still worked hard. And he'd wanted CAP for a long time. Gannett County didn't really have a homicide division; it just handled murders with the rest of the aggravated assaults, batteries, and other violent things people did to one another. But Bernie liked to tell people that he was in Homicide, even if his business card just said, "Bernie Cassis, Detective, Crimes Against Persons."

Now he wanted to show what he could do. But of course, there was

Matt Burton. You couldn't go anywhere in Gannett County or even downtown Atlanta without hearing some shit about Matt. He'd been around forever and had broken some big cases—in his day. Bernie suspected that a lot of the Matt stories had grown bigger over the years, but Matt was on his way out and it was Bernie's time. He wanted them to start telling Bernie stories, and maybe this murder was the first step toward creating his own legend.

Bernie found Barton Street and turned left. It wasn't hard to find Mick's Muffler. It was on a deserted stretch of the road, and there were about five hundred police cars sitting in front of it. Bernie spotted the green and white lettering of several Gannett County patrol cars, two ambulances with a couple of EMTs standing between them, and the garish colors of the Sweeten Creek City fire marshal's car.

Here we go, he thought. *First order of business, dump the fire marshal. Second, take charge.*

Bernie climbed out of his car with a grim yet determined look on his face. He'd practiced it many times. It was the look of a man facing an unpleasant task but very much in charge, in control. Someone to be reckoned with. He'd even said that to himself in front of the mirror in the bathroom, glaring at his reflection: "I'm a man to be reckoned with." Bernie walked over to a gaggle of cops, some of whom were sipping coffee and deliberately not looking inside the Lincoln housing the dead body. He recognized several of the officers: Jimmy Bennett, Steve Morningside, and Lee Church, all of them with muscles so pumped they looked like their uniforms might split open. Lee owned his own gym—though how he could afford that on a cop's salary was anybody's guess—which was probably why they were all so buff.

"Okay, guys," Bernie began. "Who found her? Who's touched anything even remotely connected with the murder? And where'd you guys find the coffee?"

A couple of the uniforms looked at one another, and Jimmy decided to answer the last question first.

"The guy inside, the guy who owns the garage, he's the one with the coffee. It's pretty good, too."

"All right," Bernie said to Jimmy, "get me a cup, will ya?" He turned to the others and slapped his hands together. "What have we got? Who was first on the scene?"

A man in a red uniform with gold trim stepped forward. *The fucking fire marshal*, Bernie thought with a mental sigh.

"You on this one, Jersey?"

"It's Marshal Deane, right?"

"Chuck Deane, Sweeten Creek Fire Department."

Sweeten Creek was a small community about five minutes outside of Gannett County. Atlanta was full of places like it. Thirty years ago, it had been a million miles from the city, but now it was a suburb of the huge, growing thing Atlanta had become. There were little towns like Lawrenceville and Buford and Sweeten Creek that had somehow become part of Atlanta but still had their own police departments…and fire departments. Fire Marshal Deane was known for monitoring the police bands and showing up at crime scenes even when they had nothing to do with fires. Bernie wished he'd start horning in on Fulton County murders instead.

Bernie established that Deane had arrived within a few minutes of the call and had actually beaten the responding Gannett County officer by five minutes. Bernie also found out that Marshal Deane had opened the passenger door, ostensibly to see if the woman was dead, although it was clear even from a distance that she was not among the living.

Bernie thanked Deane and told him that he'd get one of his men to write up a supplemental on what Deane had found. He shuffled Deane off with one of the uniforms and asked them to work it up together.

"Okay, and who's the responding officer on this?" he asked, turning back to the group of uniforms.

Jimmy, standing with the others near the Lincoln again, raised his hand.

"Okay," Bernie said, "I want the rest of you guys going over this whole place. I want to know if you find anything out of the ordinary, okay?

"Jimmy, lay it out for me."

"I got the call, but the fire marshal—"

"Yeah, I know all about the fucking fire marshal," Bernie sighed. "Okay, what happened after you got here?"

"Well, the marshal was by the car. He told me he'd opened the door and confirmed that the vic was dead, so I did my best to scoot him away from the car and secure the scene. Then I called it in and started looking for a weapon…"

Once he'd finished with Jimmy, Bernie walked up to the Lincoln and stood at the driver's-side window. He stared down at the woman's body and prayed that the gun wasn't inside the car. If this was a suicide, it wouldn't do his career one bit of good.

After he'd looked the scene over without touching anything, Bernie stepped back and debated what to do next. The decision was made for him when Kathy Whisnant pulled up in her Suburban and began unloading. She was the best crime scene tech they had. She could find fingerprints or blood in the most unusual places. She was thorough, imaginative, and a true professional.

Kathy staggered up, carrying a heavy plastic case. She was fortyish with streaks of blonde in her short brown hair, a no-nonsense attitude, and a little too much makeup.

"Hey, Kathy," Bernie greeted her.

"Hey, Bernie." Kathy nodded toward the car. "Anybody been inside? Anyone touch the glass or the door handles?"

"Not since I've been here, but the Sweeten Creek fire marshal was the first man on the scene."

"Funny. I don't smell a fire."

"Yeah, neither do I," he replied with a mirthless laugh.

He watched for a moment as Kathy walked around the car, forming a spiral pattern as she circled it, going a bit farther on each successive turn until she was satisfied. Then she brought out a big measuring tape. Later, he knew, she'd do photos and then move on to fingerprints.

Detective Art Swinson from Property Crimes ambled up to him. Art was blond-haired and blue-eyed and could once have been a model, but he was starting to go to seed. His belly stuck out a little, and he had lines on his throat and around his eyes.

"I've got something I need to talk to you about," he announced.

"Well, I'm a little busy at the moment," Bernie snapped. "Can it wait?"

Art sighed. "I guess I can talk to you about it later."

"Fine. Anything else?"

"How about I get some of these uniforms to control access from the street? The press'll be here before you know it. Those guys monitor the police bands, too. I'm surprised a news truck isn't here already."

"Fine. Nobody gets in unless I say so," Bernie instructed.

"That include the chief?" Art bounced back.

"Wise ass."

"Hey, have you called the DA's office yet?"

Bernie started a little. That was one of the first things he should have done. "Yeah, I'm on it," he replied, trying to sound relaxed.

"Because they're gonna want to know—" Art began again.

"I said I'm on it, Art, okay?" Bernie snapped.

Art shrugged and walked away again.

Bernie yanked out his cell phone and made a call to the DA's office. He spoke with the Chief ADA, Bill Shepherd, who said he'd send over a couple of his own investigators right away. Bernie clicked off and decided to look the place over himself, doing his own walk around the car and up and down the driveway.

◆

At just shy of nine o'clock, the medical examiner arrived in his black station wagon. Dr. Henderson never seemed to be in a hurry.

Maybe it's 'cause all of his patients are dead, Bernie mused. The ME fished a toothpick out of his front pocket, adjusted his glasses, and shuffled over to the Lincoln.

Just then, a Crown Victoria pulled up, and Bernie recognized Tracy Alastair and Rick Gartman, DA investigators, as they climbed out. At least they were moving faster than Henderson. Tracy was tall and lean. Rick was short but as bulked up as any patrol officer. Bernie idly wondered where he worked out. Once a cop left patrol, they tended to let themselves go. That was especially true of the investigators who worked for the DA, but Rick looked like he had six-pack abs under his shirt and tie. Bernie watched as Rick veered off to exchange a few words with Lee while Tracy trudged up and started looking over the scene.

Bernie was pulled from his musings as Henderson finally walked up to stand next to him.

"Mornin', Bernie," the ME said. "Who's doling out the coffee?"

"Guy inside. Supposed to be a goddamn impresario when it comes to coffee. Anyway, don't suppose you could take a look at the murder victim, could you, Doc?"

"Still dead, right?"

Henderson lumbered over to the Lincoln and started talking with Kathy. Rolling his eyes, Bernie approached Tracy and Rick and filled them in on what had happened. "How's about you guys head over to the victim's home and take a look around? Maybe canvass the neighborhood. Take a couple of uniforms with you; they can help do the door-to-door."

"What's the address?" Rick asked.

Bernie gave it to them, and they left.

Jimmy walked up and nodded at Bernie. "Something feel off to you about this one, Bern?"

"How do you mean?"

Jimmy shrugged. "Nothing smashed. Shot in the head. Purse still in the car. If it was personal, you'd expect more violence. If it was random, you'd expect no purse, but you don't even have to open it to see her credit cards are still inside."

"Where are you heading with this?" Bernie asked.

"Just feels off is all," Jimmy answered, and shrugged again.

Monday, April 10, 9:00 a.m.

Sean got to work early but just couldn't bring himself to look over the file for the Winslow case. Instead, he went to the break room, grabbed a cup of coffee, and started looking through the other files he had with him. He usually only tried cases for one week a month, but this month the court had decided to add an extra week to catch up on the backlog. He had a handful of cases other than the Winslow one to deal with this morning, but most of them had already pled out. He'd handle those first and then turn his attention to the matter of State v. Winslow.

"You hear about the murder?" Eddie Barnes asked. He was a paunchy man with a red face who'd been an investigator with the DA's office for years. He'd also been a police officer once, but that had been a long time ago.

"Which murder?" Sean asked.

"Old lady got plugged at a chiropractor's office," Eddie replied, looking through the pile of sweetener packets. "Or maybe it was a garage. Anyway, someone blew the top of her head off. You see any Splenda over there?"

"No. Are they sure it isn't a suicide?" Sean asked.

"Not unless she killed herself and then disposed of the gun." Eddie turned back to him. "What's one Hebrew more or less?"

"Please," Sean said. "*Miller's Crossing*. At least go for something a bit more obscure, and maybe a bit more politically correct. Nobody says 'Hebrew' anymore."

"How do you remember those lines?"

"I just do," Sean shrugged.

"Losers always whine about their best," Eddie began, but Sean cut him off.

"*The Rock*," he answered quickly. "Eddie, you're not even a challenge today."

Sean sighed. He wished he'd never gotten this started. Somewhere along the way the staff had learned that he had this amazing memory for lines from movies, and now they liked to challenge him all the time.

"Goddamn, you really got that down." Eddie was beaming like a kid who'd just gotten a lollipop. He turned to his coffee, found a yellow packet, and poured it in. "Well, I do have one you won't get," he winked. "You seen the new defense attorney? Blonde hair. Blue eyes. About six feet tall. Legs all the way down to the ground."

"I'm assuming it's a woman," Sean interjected dryly.

"Of course," Eddie said, then paused. "Hey, what are you saying?"

"Me?" Sean feigned innocence. "I'm not saying anything. I'm not here to judge you, Eddie. Live and let live; that's my motto. Love is love, that's all. It's not a choice; it's an alternate lifestyle."

"Hey, fuck you."

Sean just smiled.

"You're doing maggot court on Friday, aren't you?" Eddie suddenly asked. "Maggot court" was really Magistrate Court, located at the jail, where all the preliminary hearings for criminal cases took place.

"Yeah. Why?"

"If they make an arrest in this murder, the case'll be yours."

"Have they made an arrest?"

"Not so's I've heard," Eddie said.

"Well, I've got no shortage of business, so maybe it'll end up in someone else's lap."

"Hey, baby. You know murder brings the press. This could be your ticket to Court TV."

"They don't call it that anymore. And the last thing I want is to be on TV."

"Sure," Eddie said. "I know all you guys feel that way. You're bashful.

Just working it for the team. Who needs press coverage and a six-figure offer from a big firm?"

"You watch too much TV," Sean retorted.

"Now *that's* true."

John Lemon, another DA investigator, walked in. He was also an ex-cop and, unlike a lot of them, liked to stay in shape. Although he was pushing fifty, he had huge, broad shoulders and bulging biceps with a big vein running down the outside of the muscle. He turned to Eddie.

"I thought you were going to keep working out with us. Remember? Lean; mean; you, me, and Rick; all fighting machines? Does this ring a bell for you?"

"I was there yesterday," Eddie shot back. "It was closed."

"You were there?"

"Yeah, and you obviously weren't. Try that on for size, Mr. Biceps."

"Why was it closed?" John asked.

Eddie shrugged. "I hear Lee's going under."

"Really? He's had a lot of people there. It's a regular cop flop house. How could he be going under?" John's surprise was evident.

"Beats me. But I'll bet those new machines weren't cheap. Next time you see him, ask him." Eddie shrugged again.

Sean checked his watch and realized he was going to be late. "See you guys later," he said.

"Trial?" Eddie asked.

"Bullshit," Sean answered.

"There's a lot of that going around."

Monday, April 10, 9:25 a.m.

Bernie watched as Merle Portman drove right past the officer waving at him to stop and parked behind a police car.

Oh, shit.

When the officer ran up to tell him to move, Merle gave him a big smile and announced, "Merle Portman, City Council."

"Sir, you'll have to leave. This is a murder investigation," Bernie could hear the officer saying as he walked up.

"Son, I authorize the police department budget, and I've got some info on this murder. I think that allows me to park here for a while."

"Thanks, Rodriguez, but I can handle this," Bernie dismissed the officer, who double-timed it back to his post, looking relieved.

"Detective...uh?"

"Detective Cassis, Councilman. What can I do for you?"

"I've got some information for you on this case."

"How'd you hear about the case this fast?"

"City councilmen hear everything. I mean *everything*."

Portman explained that he'd driven by the muffler shop around midnight the previous evening and had seen the Lincoln and a white car.

"I thought that was strange, and I even thought about stopping. I said to my wife, when I got home, I said, 'That was strange.'"

Bernie doubted that Portman had thought anything about the Lincoln or it being strange until he'd heard the news—probably from a damn police scanner, just like the fire marshal—and realized he'd driven by.

"Maybe if I'd stopped, this terrible thing wouldn't have happened," Portman said dramatically, staring off into the distance.

"Why do you say that, Mr. Portman?"

"Well, it's obvious, isn't it? That's probably when this poor lady was getting herself killed."

Bernie gave Portman a calm, reassuring smile. "Mr. Portman, this *is* important. We're going to need to get your statement in writing as soon as possible. I'm going to work this up myself. Come on over here. The guy who runs this place makes some great coffee. Would you like some?"

"No, but…can I take a look?" Portman asked, flashing a winning smile.

"You mean at the body?"

Portman gave him a sly look. "Yeah. Just a peek."

Bernie looked around. No one was nearby or paying them any attention. He lifted the crime scene tape and escorted Portman up to the Lincoln, let him take a long look, and then brought him back out.

"Now, Councilman, about that statement…"

Monday, April 10, 10:30 a.m.

Sean had worked through five cases that morning, mostly drug charges, and now there was nothing left on the docket but the Winslow case. Sherry Winslow was sitting, arms folded, in the back of the courtroom next to her lawyer. Lisa Winslow was on the other side of the courtroom with about five family members and Kenny Winslow, who was really the cause of this whole thing. It was the first time Sean had seen Kenny, and he couldn't imagine anyone wanting to fight over this guy. He was fat and bald and wore a golf shirt that was too tight around his wobbly chest.

"The last item on the calendar for today," Sean sighed to the judge, "is State v. Winslow."

"Is the defendant present?" Judge Vinhorten asked.

"Defendant is present," Larry Deacon announced, standing. He was an old-school attorney who had probably been a member of the bar for at least thirty years. "We're ready to defend this lady's honor."

"I don't know anything about her *honor*," Vinhorten said, adjusting his glasses, "but I do see that she's charged with aggravated assault."

"Not guilty, Your Honor," Larry chimed.

"Have there been any plea negotiations, Mr. Turlow?"

"No, Your Honor," Sean answered.

"Why not?"

"I can answer that, Your Honor," Larry jumped in. "This case—"

"I wasn't asking you, Mr. Deacon; I was asking the prosecutor. Why no plea negotiations?"

Sean chose his words carefully. "The parties are somewhat…intractable, Your Honor."

"Okay," Vinhorten said. "Ms. Winslow, uh, *Mrs.* Winslow is charged with aggravated assault on, let's see, Lisa Winslow. Sisters?" he asked, looking up.

"No, Your Honor. Lisa Winslow is the current wife of Mr. Winslow, and Sherry Winslow is the ex-wife."

Vinhorten sighed. "Attorneys approach."

Sean and Larry crowded close to the bench, and Vinhorten covered the microphone with his hand. "What's going on here?" he asked.

"Judge, this is a case of injustice—"

"Larry," Vinhorten cut in, "cut the crap. What's going on?"

"My client says she won't plead to anything, Your Honor," Larry explained.

"What have you offered, Sean?"

"I am prepared to offer probation to a plea of simple battery."

"And your lady won't go along with that?" Vinhorten asked Larry.

"My client wishes to assert her full Constitutional rights to—"

"Larry, please. She won't go along?"

"No. She wants her day in court."

"I see. Step back, gentlemen."

Sean took his place behind the State's table, and Larry stood behind the defense table. He motioned for Sherry Winslow to join him.

"Let's see," Vinhorten began. "I understand there haven't been any plea negotiations in this case. I instruct the State and defense to take ten minutes to see if they can reach an accommodation of some kind."

Sherry began to say something, but Larry restrained her.

"Mr. Turlow, what is the maximum sentence on a charge of aggravated assault?"

"Twenty years, Your Honor."

"I see from the indictment that the defendant is charged with using a deadly weapon in the assault."

"It was a chair, Your Honor," Larry jumped in.

"Assault with a deadly weapon," Vinhorten repeated purposefully, staring daggers at Larry. "That's a very serious charge. I don't know what Mr. Turlow would recommend after a guilty verdict in this case, but I would be inclined to give out some serious prison time on such a charge. I can't prejudge, but I have given others facing similar charges five years to serve in the state penitentiary."

Sherry paled at the words.

"Of course, if it should turn out that the defendant was found not guilty and the charge was trumped up by a vindictive person, then I think Mr. Turlow would be authorized to bring a charge of giving false information to the police. What is the sentence for that, Mr. Turlow?"

"One year."

"Oh, I'd definitely give such a person that sentence, if there were a guilty verdict in that case."

Sean couldn't see Lisa, but the significance of the words couldn't have been lost on her.

The judge sat back in his chair. "We'll be in recess for ten minutes. In that time, I strongly suggest to the people involved in this case that they attempt to work out a plea deal, or things might get very serious indeed."

Sean sighed. He didn't like Vinhorten very much, but there was nothing like a judge threatening major jail time to get defendants to start seeing reason.

They worked up a recommendation for a one-year probation, a $1,000 fine, and no contact with the victim on a simple battery misdemeanor, and Vinhorten took it.

Thank God, Sean thought as he walked out of the courtroom. He'd cleared away all of his crappy cases for the month, and things looked great for next month. *No more screwy cases*, he thought.

He would remember that later.

◆ Chapter Two ◆

Monday, April 10, 11:00 a.m.

Bernie had taken down Portman's statement himself and then, finally, had gotten the man away from the scene. As soon as Portman pulled away, Dr. Henderson appeared again.

"No signs of a struggle," he drawled, "but you could see that for yourself. No defensive wounds. No cuts. No scrapes. No bruises. Looks like two shots to the skull, but I'll have to get her back to my place before I can know for sure. That'll have to do you until I get the autopsy done."

"Thanks, Doc."

"I've processed as much as I can here," Kathy said, stepping up as soon as Henderson left. "I've called for a tow truck, and I'll take it to the hangar to finish it."

The Gannett County PD had an airplane hangar off Tara Road where they did mechanical work on their two helicopters. It also made an ideal place to process a car.

"Anything preliminary I can use?"

"Not much. I didn't even get any prints off the passenger-side door. And that's kind of strange, in a way."

"Why's that?"

"C'mon, Bernie. No mess. No obvious signs of a struggle. The passenger door handle looks like it's been wiped clean. I mean, this is almost like a hit or something."

"Somebody's gonna execute an old lady?"

"It's just odd, that's what I'm saying. Jesus, you're testy, Bernie."

Bernie's cell rang, and he answered. "No shit," he said after a moment, smiling a little. He hung up and instructed the remaining uniforms to keep the place under wraps. "We may have a break."

◆

At half past eleven, the press finally arrived. Bernie was back by then, grinning, and there was no doubt in his mind that his star was on the rise. God, it had all fallen together so perfectly. This would be a legend in the police department: the fastest arrest ever on a murder.

While the Channel 3 crew was still unloading their equipment, the reporter strolled up to Bernie to ask some preliminary questions.

"You want a real story?" Bernie cut him off.

"Sure. What've you got?"

"Get the camera rolling and put a microphone up here. I've got something you guys will love."

Once the cameraman and a guy holding a boom mic came forward, the reporter got everything rolling. "I'm here at the scene of a murder," he began. "The victim, whose identity has not yet been disclosed, was found this morning, lying in the front seat of her car with a bullet wound to the head. We have Detective Bernard Cassis with us to explain the rest of the details. Detective Cassis, what can you tell us about this murder?"

"The victim was shot at close range," Bernie said, resisting the urge to rub his hands together with glee. "There were no signs of a struggle, and I immediately thought that was significant. After a thorough on-site investigation, I proceeded to the victim's home and was able to make an arrest."

"Are you saying you have a suspect in custody at this time?"

"Yes, Steve. I made the arrest myself only moments ago."

"Who is the suspect, Detective Cassis?"

"The victim's son, Tommy Resnic."

Monday, April 10, 12:00 p.m.

Sean was sitting in the break room eating his sandwich when the news came on. Someone turned up the volume when the anchor mentioned a murder. After the preliminaries, the anchor said, "We now turn to our field reporter, Steve Matthews, for on-scene coverage. Steve, can you hear me?"

"Yes, I can, Holden. It's been an eventful morning here in Atlanta. Gannett police officers responded to the call of a woman found dead here at Mick's Muffler on Barton Street. They found the body of an elderly woman who had been shot in the head while seated in her car. I had a chance to speak with one of the officers earlier, and he had a major announcement in the case."

Then they played the segment with Bernie.

Sean threw his sandwich down in disgust. While the anchor and reporter exchanged more questions and answers, Sean said, "Tell me I didn't hear what I just heard."

"You fucking heard it. Bernie just blew it," Eddie confirmed.

"You don't tell the whole world you've got the right guy until you're *sure* you've got the right guy!" Sean moaned. "And you sure as hell don't do it without talking it over with Chief Black and Shepherd." Sean threw away his sandwich, appetite gone.

"And there's no way they would have let him say that, not yet." Eddie shook his head, looking disgusted.

"Yeah, Bernie screwed up all right, and I get the feeling that this is going to be my problem, too."

Monday, April 10, 1:45 p.m.

Matt was humming to himself when his cell phone rang. He'd temporarily lost the country music station, to the great relief of the man still in the back of the police car.

"Matt Burton," he said.

"Matt. How far are you from home?"

"Hey, Chief. A couple of hours or thereabouts. We're making good time. Why?"

"You know that feeling you get when you do something you shouldn't have done and it comes back to bite you?"

"Yeah."

"Well, I did that today, and now it's biting right through my ass."

"What's going on, Chief?"

"I gave Bernie a murder, and he fucked it up faster than you can blink." The chief described the morning's events in quick sentences. "I want you to take this thing over," he concluded. "Bernie hasn't got it, not for this."

"Bernie's okay. He just needs a bit more experience."

"Well, he can get it on some other fucking case. First thing, you take this puppy over, and no more fucking statements to the press."

"No problem there," Matt said. "I hate talking to the press."

"Anything that goes out gets cleared through us."

"Chief, I know that. You're talking to the wrong guy."

"I know, I know. I've got a meeting with Bernie at two, and I'm going to ream him a new one."

"Don't be too hard on him, Boss," Matt said. "Maybe he just got a bit carried away."

"Fuck him. You don't get carried away on a murder investigation."

The chief hung up with an abrupt *click*, and Matt sighed and kept driving. This wasn't going to be pretty.

Monday, April 10, 2:15 p.m.

Bernie swaggered into the main room of Gannett Police Department headquarters. He gave a smile to Judy Pontus, a short blonde with an amazing chest and great tan who worked in Dispatch and did some other secretarial stuff. Bernie had fantasized about her doing lots of things, and not one of them involved filing. Normally, she was pretty cold toward him—rumor had it she was dating someone in patrol—but today, she gave him a kind of secret smile. He could feel it right down to his toes. Jesus, it was great. Even Judy was looking at him in a new light.

It'll be the first of the Bernie Cassis stories, he thought to himself as he smiled at the room and then headed down the hall to the chief's office.

Black's secretary didn't smile at him, but then, she never smiled at anyone. Bernie gave her a little wave as he knocked on the door and then walked in.

"Have you lost your fucking mind?" Chief Black barked.

"Sir?"

"Tell me that you were drinking, that you were high, that you'd temporarily taken leave of your fucking senses. Tell me that, and maybe I'll feel just a tiny fraction of a fuck better about this goddamn mess!"

"I don't—" Bernie began, truly confused.

"You're off this case. You got that? Matt's going to be here in a few hours, and he'll take it."

"Chief, what's going on? I've already done the work. I've made the arrest—"

"You don't make statements to the press without prior approval. You don't announce the name of the perp. You don't release the name of the victim before we've had a fucking chance to tell the family. You don't cowboy a murder investigation. You don't fucking let a city councilman into your crime scene. And you sure as shit don't show up fifteen minutes late for a meeting with *me*."

It took Bernie a minute to say anything. "I didn't let him into the crime scene."

"According to the CST, Merle fucking Portman crossed the yellow tape. Is she wrong? Is she lying?"

"I didn't see the harm," Bernie slowly backpedaled.

"Yeah, Bernie, that's the problem. You didn't see the harm of allowing a city councilman to look in on a murder victim. What's the defense going to do with that?"

"I don't see—"

"You're fucking-A right, you don't see! You're out, Bernie. Go back to the crack house killing and give Matt everything you've got. And if I even think you're holding some shit back or about to talk to the press again, you'll be on administrative leave. Is that crystal fucking clear? *Unpaid* administrative leave. Got it?"

Bernie just nodded and left.

Monday, April 10, 3:45 p.m.

After Matt handed his prisoner over to the day watch commander, he said hello to a bunch of the detectives working in their cubicles on his way to CAP. He found Bernie sitting at his desk, staring at nothing.

"Hey," Matt said, startling Bernie out of his reverie and into an angry tirade.

"So, I'm a fuckup! I don't know how to do an investigation. I should be strung up by my balls at the courthouse."

"Bernie, there ain't any call for that."

"There's plenty of call for that. They're acting like I took a dump on the chief's desk, for Chrissake."

"I don't care about any of that. It's just that this whole thing has put us in a weird position, and I don't like it."

"Well, I'm not too fucking wild about it, either."

"Why don't we put all that to one side for a bit, okay? We got a dead woman, and you were helping with the investigation. I'd like you to keep working it with me. Is that going to be a problem?"

"You want me to work with you? Chief Black said I was off the whole thing."

"I'll clear it with him. It won't be a problem. You were on the scene, you helped get the ball rolling, and I could use what you've learned. Okay?"

Before Bernie could reply, Matt's phone rang. It was Kathy.

"Hey, Matt," Kathy said. "I hear you're in charge now. I've had the car in the hangar for about an hour now, and I've recovered a bullet. Front passenger seat, in a corner under the dashboard."

"What's the caliber?"

".38."

"Okay, Kathy. Get me your report as soon as you can."

"We also recovered some latents. They're probably the old lady's, but still."

"Good job, Kathy. I'll be over in about an hour to take a look at the car, and then I'd like to meet you at the scene."

"You got it, Matt. Just give me a call."

Matt got some coffee, and Bernie followed him to his office, which was cluttered with files and pictures of Matt and Angela on vacation at Dollywood and the Grand Canyon. Before they could get started, Judy knocked on Matt's door. Bernie got his smile ready.

"I transcribed your recording from last week," she announced. "That was one wild case. Attempted murder with a hammer. *Ouch.*" She handed Matt a few typed pages, then turned and looked at Bernie. Whatever had been there before was gone. Judy just looked right through him and walked out the door.

Matt took a sip of his coffee. "Let's start with the motive. Why is this woman dead?"

"Let's get something clear," Bernie said, sidestepping the question. "Am I just a flunky, or are we working this as equals?"

"Bernie. You can call it whatever you want, but this thing is squarely on my shoulders, so I call the shots. The first shot is for you to answer my question."

"Robbery," Bernie replied. "Her son killed her for her money."

"What money?"

"I found out in my canvass that this lady was a bit weird. She kept a large amount of money in her house. She's also got a son who's a total fuckup."

"How'd you find this out?"

"The next-door neighbor knew all about it."

"What's her name?"

"Esther Jenkins. She's the neighborhood busybody and keeps tabs on everybody. She was a gold mine of information."

"So, you canvassed the neighborhood by yourself? You left the scene and canvassed the neighborhood. That's a little strange, Bernie."

"Well, I had help. I had Tracy Alastair and Rick Gartman with me. And then I found the son and he spilled the beans. Case closed."

"You're getting a little ahead of things for me. I'm just an old warhorse, so let me take this step by step. You decided, this morning, to go and canvass the victim's neighborhood?"

"Well, I asked Tracy and Rick to do it." Bernie sounded impatient.

"So, you went along. You left the scene to go door-to-door in her neighborhood?"

"No, no. They called me when they found the son, and I went over. After that, they asked around while I was talking to the son, and they found out about the money, and then the son more or less 'fessed up to taking it."

Matt sat for a moment and looked at Bernie. "I don't like this."

"Hey, look—" Bernie protested.

Matt held up his hand. "Bernie, I'm going to spell it out for you. Like I said, I'm old fashioned. I like to start at A, then go to B, then go to C. I don't like to start at H and then go to A and end up at Z. The first thing out of your mouth was that you canvassed the neighborhood and found out about the money, and now you're saying Tracy and Rick did some stuff and you found the son."

"Hey, I'm just answering your questions. If you don't like the answers—"

"Bullshit, son. I've tried to work this thing to give you a break, but now you're trying to treat me like I'm the enemy.

"Let me get specific. You will write me a detailed, thorough, and accurate report explaining, step by step, exactly what actions you personally took in this case, starting from the moment you got the call up to and including this meeting. You will also detail, point by point, what actions were taken by others. I want that report on my desk in one hour."

"Matt—" Bernie began again.

"Bernie," Matt cut him off, voice still steady and calm, "I've been on the road for hours, and I walk straight back into this mess, and you're trying to treat me like a defense attorney. I don't like it. I don't deserve it. You'll do the report and get it to me in one hour, and I don't want to hear another word from you because I'm getting angry and that's bad for my blood pressure. Go on, now."

Monday, April 10, 4:00 p.m.

Because Sean's trial week was essentially over with the plea in the Winslow case, Chief ADA Shepherd asked Sean if he would take over as Duty DA for the rest of the day. Duty DA was a rotating position that fielded phone calls from the public, answered general questions, and dealt with any non-case-specific queries that came in. When Sean had first come to the DA's office five years ago, he'd been surprised that anyone would call the DA's office with weird inquiries. After working Duty DA more times than he cared to think, he now realized that crazies were drawn to the DA's office almost as much as they were drawn to the police.

He retreated to his office and loosened his tie. It was good to have the trial week over. He had three free days now that he could devote to working on next month's cases before he had to tackle the annoyance of Magistrate Court.

Samantha, the receptionist, called. "Duty DA question," she snapped. She was always snapping at people, frowning, and generally looking miserable. She was the perfect receptionist for the DA's office because she was the first face anyone saw when they came through the double doors. Her unpleasant demeanor usually disposed of any in-person crazies right off the bat.

Sean waited for her to click off and braced himself.

"This is Officer Padgett, Sweeten Creek division," the man on the other end said, and Sean relaxed.

"What can I do for you?"

"I called in earlier today to check on the status of one of my cases, but nobody seems to be able to find it."

"You checked with our filing ladies?" Sean asked. There were two women who handled all new case files as they were transferred to the DA's office.

"Yeah, I spoke with Pam."

"So, what's the problem?"

"The problem is that she can't find any reference to the case."

"You're sure it was assigned here?" Sean asked. "Maybe it never made it out of Records on your side."

"No, I checked. It was transferred over on January 13, but you guys don't have anything."

"Well, that's a little strange, but sometimes numbers get switched around, names mixed up."

"Yeah, that's what I thought, but this guy was such an asshole that I want to make sure he didn't fall through the cracks."

"What was the charge?"

"Reckless driving. DUI. Obstruction. His name is Dennis Earl Quitman. Can you look into it for me?"

"Okay, sure. Give me a number where I can call you back."

Sean wrote down the details, and the officer said goodbye.

He had to field two more Duty DA calls before he could escape his desk to check the files: one from a man who thought his neighbor should be arrested for squirting him with a hose and another from a lady who wanted to know if it was okay to use last year's Percocet for the pain in her leg.

Still rolling his eyes, Sean wandered over to Records and saw Pam Sitner and Molly Rice at their cubicles. Their desks guarded a large file room—and getting by them and into the files wasn't always easy.

When cases were transferred over from the police department, they would first be logged here and given an internal number, and then Molly or Pam would create a digital folder for them on the network to be cross-referenced with the police report number. Any additional materials that ended up in the physical file were supposed to be scanned and put on the network so that everyone inside the office could pull up the files on their computers. Of course, that was in the best possible world. Often there was a delay, and paper reports might languish in the manila folders for months before they got scanned. Pam and Molly had been working Records for as long as anyone could remember. They'd developed some pretty tough skins over the years, probably from people blaming them for anything and everything that went wrong with a file.

But when Sean had first been hired on, he'd come under the tutelage of an older, wiser ADA who'd taught him perhaps the most valuable rule that any attorney can follow: Make friends with the support staff. As a result, he'd gone out of his way to be nice to Pam and Molly over the years, and they liked him for it.

"Hey, Pam," Sean said.

"Hey, Sean. How's things?"

"Paperwork and more paperwork. You know how it goes."

"Sure do."

"I got a call from an officer named Padgett over at Sweeten Creek—"

"Yeah," she cut him off, the curls in her tight perm already bouncing with agitation. "He called me about some case and basically said that we lost it."

"Whoa, there," Sean said, smiling. "I just have to ask so I'll know what I'm talking about when I call him back. No chance this one could have been indexed wrong? I checked, and Sweeten Creek does show a transfer of the file over here."

Pam glared at him. It was obviously a sore subject with her. "Every time something comes up missing, the first thing—"

"Hey, I'm just asking," Sean cut in, shrugging. "I got a Duty DA call, and I have to follow up."

She sighed and looked at him. "There's a chance. A tiny, tiny, remote chance. We're not perfect, you know."

"Oh, now that I don't believe," Sean grinned.

It worked. Pam relaxed.

"Is there any other way to cross-reference the case? Some way to double-check that it never got here?"

Pam thought for a moment. "Well…" she said, drawing the word out. "I guess you could do a search on the police report number and see what comes up. They're supposed to issue specific, non-repeatable numbers to each division so that nobody duplicates the same number on a report. But that's 'supposed to be,' and the real world can be a lot different."

Sean looked down at the legal pad where he'd made some notes during the call. "Can you run this report number for me?"

"I've got a lot to do…" she said, offering token resistance.

"I'd appreciate it." Sean tried for a winning smile.

"Hmm." She jotted down the number. "Chances are," she said as her fingers flew across the keyboard, "that they just forgot to—"

"Hmm," she repeated as she rechecked the number on his legal pad. "There is an entry for that number, but there's no internal file number assigned. Weird."

"How can that be?"

"If the officer calls us and asks for a NAD, we wouldn't bother to assign an internal number, but he'd have to call pretty soon after the case was sent over because, once the number is assigned, an ADA would have to sign off on the NAD. This one was dismissed before it ever got assigned a number; had to be the officer's request."

NAD, Sean thought. *No Accusation Drawn.* That was a designation used for misdemeanor cases that were dismissed before they ever got to arraignment, usually because of some problem with the case. But the DA's office had had a policy in place for years that NADs couldn't be used in DUI cases. There had been some hanky-panky back in the nineties with well-connected people getting their DUIs dismissed that way, and there had been a big press story, a resulting scandal, and some firings. It had been long before Sean's time, but the senior people still brought it up from time to time as an example of how *not* to handle cases.

Sean thought for a moment. "Was the case assigned an investigator on our side? Did it get that far?"

Pam looked again. "Yes. It was assigned to Rick Gartman, but I doubt that he ever saw the actual case. The NAD was filed within twenty-four hours of the arrest. Say, this is a DUI, isn't it? They can't drop a DUI."

Sean shrugged in answer. "Anything else?"

"There's not much meat on the bone here."

"What about the NAD itself? Do you have a scanned copy of that?"

Pam punched some more keys. "Yes," she said, squinting at the screen, "but I can't make out the signature."

"Print it off for me, will ya?"

Once he had the hard copy, Sean saw what Pam was talking about. The signature was a scribble with a twirl at the end. It could be anyone's name.

Monday, April 10, 4:30 p.m.

Late in the afternoon, Matt drove over to the medical examiner's office and parked. He hated this part. He'd never liked autopsies and hadn't developed the cast-iron stomach that cops on TV always seemed to have. It was one thing to see a person lying dead in a house or a car or on the street, but this clinical dissection was somehow more horrible than that. TV detectives were always eating donuts or popping gum while the coroner split open someone's chest. Matt usually only looked at the procedure when he absolutely had to.

Dr. Henderson started the autopsy five minutes after Matt arrived, turning on a microphone and talking his way through the procedure. Matt didn't bother to look at the preliminary external examination, but Henderson called him over when he got to the skull.

"Two entrance wounds," Henderson announced. "One just below the left earlobe and the other two inches away, just at the hairline. There's stippling around the wounds, which indicates that the muzzle of the firearm was close to the skin's surface when it went off."

Henderson confirmed that there were no defensive wounds and no other signs of a struggle. He clipped off the victim's fingernails and sealed them in a plastic bag. He took tape lifts from her jacket, shirt, and pants. He took blood samples, and then he started the dissection. He had an assistant take numerous photos.

Matt was glad when it was over.

"I'll make you a copy of the photos. Flash drive okay? Did you guys get your printer fixed over there?" Henderson asked as he began cleaning up.

"Yeah, I think so." Matt looked at Henderson. "You know the magic question."

"She'd just eaten, and the food hadn't had time to digest. Her core temperature and other factors point to somewhere between six and nine o'clock in the evening as TOD. I don't think it could be much later, but it could have been earlier."

"Any earlier," Matt said, "and the people at the muffler shop would have seen something."

"Unless they were the ones who did it."

"Hmm."

"I hear there's been an arrest already," Henderson said, looking pointedly at Matt.

Matt ignored him. "Anything else that can help me, Doc?"

"Nope. That's about it. I'll have my report to you…let's see, maybe tomorrow afternoon?"

"Thanks, Doc."

◆

As Matt was walking back to his car, his cell phone rang. It was Kathy.

"We took a look at the tire, you know, the one that was flat?"

"I'm playing catch-up here, Kathy, remember?"

"The left front tire was flat when they found the body. Well, I thought we should see if it was legit or not, so I took a closer look at it."

"And was it legit?"

"No. Somebody slit the side wall of the tire with a good-sized knife, maybe a hunting knife. It'll need to go to the crime lab to be sure, though."

"So, the flat tire was staged."

"Sure looks that way."

"I'll get somebody to pick it up and take it to the lab."

"Okay. You still coming over to take a look at the car?"

"I'm on my way now."

◆

Matt drove to the police hanger on Tara Road and found Kathy writing up her report. She filled him in on the basic details of what she'd found and pointed out where the loose round had been recovered.

"What about the second round?" Matt asked.

"We weren't sure if there was one," Kathy explained.

"There is. Two entrance wounds according to the ME. I'm going to need that second slug."

"Okay, we'll find it."

Matt walked around the car and then stopped at the driver's-side window. "So," he said. "I'm the killer. I lure her to the muffler shop. Why?"

"Dunno," Kathy shrugged.

"Am I already there, or do I come after she arrives?"

"The car was parked slightly off the concrete part of the driveway. Her passenger-side tires were actually a little bit in the grass."

"So, she parks next to the killer's car." Matt thought for a moment.

"She put down the window, too," Kathy offered. "There was some light dew on her clothes, meaning the window had been open all night. And it isn't as though the killer could open the window from the outside."

"Okay," Matt said. "Maybe that means she knows the killer, but maybe she's just the kind of lady who puts her window down for anyone." Matt positioned himself next to the window. "The killer is standing here."

Kathy stepped closer. "The angle of trajectory?"

"Yeah. The ME said one went through the left side of her head and came out below her jaw. The second one exited through her cheek, but that could have been because she was already falling over. So, our killer had to be standing at the window."

Matt thought again. "I'm the killer. I stand here. Maybe talk to her, make her feel comfortable, then raise my gun." He raised his right hand, first finger out like a gun barrel. "Blam-blam."

"Funny that she didn't see the gun," Kathy commented. "I mean, if he's right-handed, that side would have been facing her when she pulled in."

"That's assuming the killer was already there. Maybe he came up later. And it was dark. Maybe he chose the muffler shop *because* it was dark. He had the gun hidden. Maybe he was wearing something that could easily conceal it."

Matt thought some more. "Okay, two shots. She's dead. Then what?" Matt turned to Kathy. "Any prints on the driver's-side door handle?"

"Yes. I haven't gone through them completely, but a quick check makes me think they're hers."

"No others?"

"Nope."

"So the killer shoots her, and then what? He doesn't open the driver's-side door. Why not?" Matt paused. "What about the passenger door?"

"Wiped clean."

"Really?"

"Yes. And not only on the top, where you'd expect, but he wiped the underside of the door handle, too."

"Now that *is* strange."

"Yeah, I thought you'd see that. Funny thing is, the fire marshal, he actually opened the passenger door."

"His prints weren't there either?" Matt asked, surprised.

"No. Maybe he used a handkerchief or something."

"Okay, I'll have to ask him about that. Maybe he wiped them away himself. But if he didn't, then you're telling me that the door handle was wiped clean, above and below, by the killer?

"Our killer goes to the passenger door, opens it, does…something, and then keeps himself together enough to wipe the outer door handle, top and bottom? That's playing it pretty cool after killing someone."

Matt went back to the driver's-side window. He aimed his finger again. "The ME said there was stippling. So, our guy was close, his body almost touching the door." He turned to Kathy. "What about blowback?"

"Matt, it's called high-velocity blood spatter."

"Whatever."

"You'd have to check with a firearms guy, but I can't see any way this guy pulls the trigger and doesn't get some blood on his sleeve, maybe even up to the shoulder."

"Okay. I shoot her. Then I walk around to the passenger side and open the door. If I'm right-handed, I'd have to do something with the gun. Tuck it in my waistband and risk shooting my dick off?" He glanced at Kathy. "Uh, sorry."

"Matt, I've heard a lot worse."

"Yeah, well, I'm old-school." He looked at the passenger-side door again and opened it. "Why? Why do this?"

"I may have an answer for you," Kathy said. "I ran luminol over the passenger seat, and there's a clear outline of where her purse was among the blood spatter. The killer moved it and didn't put it back in the same place."

"So, this is a robbery?" Matt asked, unconvinced.

"All I can say is, he moved the purse. There was something else on the seat; you can see an outline with the light. He smeared it picking it up. I didn't see anything that it could be, so maybe he took it with him."

"But he left the purse?"

"Yes."

"No prints on the purse?"

"Nope."

Matt moved back to the passenger door. "I've just shot a lady with a .38. That makes a pretty good pop. I need to get the hell out of there, but I take the time to go around to the passenger side, open the door, pick up her purse, and take something else off the seat. How big was this 'something else'?"

"Can't tell. The smear was pretty small. Maybe a piece of paper, or something like that."

"A piece of paper? What is he doing? He picks up her purse, obviously to take something out of it. What was missing?"

"That's one of the weird things," Kathy said. "Nothing, as far as we can tell."

"Wallet, ID, everything still there?"

"Yeah. There's seventy-two dollars in cash in there, so we have to assume he didn't take any money."

Matt frowned. "Now that *is* weird."

"I can't figure what on earth was in that purse worth killing somebody over."

"Well, she apparently had a lot of money in her house. We haven't searched it yet to know if it's missing, but suppose she brought it with her? Maybe in her purse?"

"But why?"

"That's what I've gotta figure out," Matt sighed.

◆

That evening, Matt called a meeting to discuss what had been learned so far. He outlined what they'd learned and told everyone about the money the victim had had in her house.

"I want that angle worked up immediately," he ordered, "beginning with a full search of her house. Let's see if all of that money she supposedly had is still there."

Matt asked Chief Black for permission to set up a roadblock on Barton Street the following night. He wanted patrol officers to stop everyone coming in both directions and ask if anybody had been there Monday evening between eight o'clock and eleven o'clock, and what they'd seen if they'd been there.

"We might get something," he concluded. "Maybe somebody saw a car; maybe somebody even saw the killer. Who knows?"

"The councilman," Black interjected. "Didn't he say something about a white car?"

"Yes. He told Bernie that he saw a white car there around midnight. But Doc says that was probably too late," Matt explained. "He put the time of death closer to seven or eight than midnight."

"Still, the white car needs follow-up. Bernie, that's yours. We'll convene tomorrow morning at eight o'clock to see what the roadblock turned up. I've got Kathy looking for the second slug, and I'll need the tire taken to the crime lab since Kathy says it was cut, probably to make it look like the victim stopped there because she had a flat."

"And we're sure that's not what happened?" Black asked.

"No, we aren't. So the tire heads to the crime lab, and we'll see what they have to say."

"What about our suspect?" Shepherd wanted to know.

"I'm going to question him right after this meeting."

Once they'd finished wrapping up the remaining details, Matt closed down the meeting. Black and Shepherd lingered in the back, talking quietly, as Art Swinson approached Matt.

"I've got something, Matt," Art said.

"How come you didn't bring it up in the meeting?"

"It's something that's come up before, and I figured I needed to play it on the down-low."

"Okay. I already don't like it. What?"

"I've got someone who puts a patrol car at the scene, maybe even around eight o'clock."

Matt glanced over at Black and Shepherd. They'd heard Art, of course. Black got up and closed the door. "Sit down, Art," he ordered.

They didn't ask Matt to sit, but he did anyway.

"What's this shit?" Black asked Art.

"I spoke to a guy who stopped by the muffler shop this morning, while we were still processing it, and he told me he saw a police car parked at the shop last night with the victim's Lincoln next to it."

Silence.

"How reliable is this?" Black asked after a long pause.

"The guy seemed pretty solid. He's an accountant who went out for chicken last night. The nearest KFC takes him from his house down Barton Street and then to the Lawrenceville highway. I actually drove the route a little while ago, and that part checks out."

"And this guy says it was one of our police cars? Is that what he's saying?" Black demanded.

"No, he didn't identify a particular PD. He just said a car that looked like a police car—"

"Okay, then," Black cut across Art.

"But it had a light bar on top and reflecting words on the side," Art continued. "White with green lettering. He was very specific about that."

That brought everyone up short. Gannett squad cars were white with green striping and green letters on the side doors and back panels.

"This guy say anything else?" Black asked.

"No."

"Okay. Work it up and get it to Matt. That's all, Art."

"Just a sec," Matt said. "How come you didn't bring this up during the meeting?"

Art looked at Black.

"I'll fill him in," Black said. "Thanks, Art."

After Art left, Matt looked at Black and Shepherd. "Somebody want to tell me what's going on?"

Black drummed his fingers on the conference table for a little while without talking. Matt waited.

"Nothing we say now," Black finally began, "nothing at all leaves this room. You don't get to talk it over with any of the others, not your wife, not anyone from the DA's office, not your priest, not your mistress, no one."

"Well, Chief, seeing as how I don't have a priest or a mistress…"

"I'm not fucking around here, Matt."

"Maybe this extra-secret stuff isn't something you should tell me."

"I think you should know."

"I'm not so sure about that, Chief. I'm too old to play one end against the middle. If I learn something that figures in this case, it's going in my report. So maybe I should just walk out and leave you fellows to your secrets."

Black drummed his fingers some more. "You don't make it easy, do you, Matt?"

"No, sir, I don't. I've been playing it one way since I started doing this job, and I'm not gonna change."

"Okay, you win. If what I'm about to tell you becomes part of this investigation, you put it in your report."

Matt sat back and waited.

Black sighed, and Shepherd looked angry. But then, Shepherd was always upset about something, so Matt didn't bother to pay him any attention.

"Standards and Practices came to me a few weeks ago," the chief began. "They had vague complaints about some officers, nothing concrete. One person said that an officer was picking up teenage girls and making porn videos. You know the shit they sling around. I told them, you get something concrete against a specific officer and you can run with it. Until then, vague complaints don't mean shit."

Matt waited some more. "Standards and Practices" was the name that a lot of police departments had gone to after the department's other, older name had gained so much bad press: *Internal Affairs.*

Black looked at Matt, but Matt just kept waiting. This had to be about more than vague porn accusations.

"Okay," Black continued. "Well, there were also reports that some officers, some Gannett officers, were engaged in breaking into drug dealers' homes and stealing their money or their drugs or both. It's the old game: Who's the drug dealer gonna call, the cops?

"Now, I know we hear that kind of shit all the time. But there was more. You know the Russian Mafia has been moving into Atlanta over the last few years. Ever since their economy went to shit, every crook in that country has been coming to the USA to make it rich. They figure we're easy pickings. Anyway, some of the gangs recruit police officers. That gives them tip-offs about pending arrests, access to police files, a way to mess with evidence—all kinds of nightmares.

"After S&P came to me, I decided to talk to the DA's office, and that's where things got a little murky. Well, even murkier."

Shepherd cleared his throat. "We've had some files come up missing," he explained. "Small-time stuff, mostly misdemeanors, but enough cases to make us start wondering. And one of the things that came through Standards and Practices was an allegation that you could pay a specific cop two or three grand and make your case go away. No conviction, no points on your driver's license; the whole thing would just…disappear."

"How many cases are we talking about here?" Matt asked.

"Forty-seven, at last count."

Matt didn't say anything.

"Since most of the missing cases were traffic-related or low-grade thefts," Black cut in, "I asked Art to work with S&P to investigate. We didn't know if this was a problem with the DA's office or the PD or both."

Shepherd looked uncomfortable. "Eleven of these cases involve individuals with Russian names. Now," he continued, shifting in his chair, "just because they're Russian doesn't mean anything. But, well, we ran some of their criminal histories, and at least eight of them have gang-related convictions on their records."

"And now," Black picked up the baton again, sitting forward, "Art's got this one guy saying there may have been a police car parked at the murder scene at or near the time of the murder..." He let his voice trail off.

"You're not asking me what I think you're asking me, are you?" Matt demanded. "I'm not supposed to investigate bad cops for S&P and work a murder at the same time?"

"No. I want you to work the case just like you would any other case, but if you come across some police involvement, then I want you to work with the DA's office to follow up on it. If the cop angle turns out to be bullshit, then great. But if it checks out, then this might be part of something bigger, and it could get awfully fucking messy."

"Why not S&P? What makes me qualified to work this kind of case?" Matt wanted to know.

"There's a couple of things. For one, you've been around for a long time."

"Thanks for reminding me, Chief."

"And S&P didn't have any complaints against CAP, so that's helpful. And, frankly, I need someone I can trust on this thing." Black suddenly looked tired.

"So, you're sure that I'm not on the take?"

"I'm as sure about that as I am about anything."

"I guess I'll take that as a compliment. So, who do you want me to work with through the DA's office? One of their investigators?"

"No," Shepherd answered, sitting forward. "There's some issue about our investigative people, too. I want you to work with an ADA. You may need some legal advice on this one."

"You?" Matt asked.

"No, I want you working with someone more junior."

"Why's that? I would've thought you'd want one of your senior people on this."

"Normally, yes. But there's a chance this missing file stuff could be tied to an ADA just as easily as a DA investigator. I want you working with somebody new, who we know couldn't be involved."

"Okay. So, who do I work with?"

"This case is coming up for Magistrate Court on Friday," Shepherd said. "Sean Turlow will get it. Use him."

"But he's been here, like, five years," Matt protested.

"Exactly. He's perfect."

"Hasn't he been here too long to make him perfect?"

Shepherd shifted uncomfortably. "Some of the missing case files go back several years, back before Sean worked for us. He's got the murder case; he's clear from suspicion on the missing files. He's ready-made for the project. You like him okay, don't you?"

"I don't know him very well," Matt said, thinking. "He doesn't strike me as a cowboy or a glory hound. Am I wrong about that?"

"No," Shepherd confirmed. "I'm not that crazy about him myself, but he's a good ADA and he works hard."

"How come you don't like him?" Black wanted to know.

"Oh, nothing in particular."

"Okay," Matt said, getting up. "I'll follow up on this police car thing. I assume you'll want to see my reports?"

"Yes. As soon as you type them up."

"You got it, Chief. Anything else?"

"No, Matt, that'll do."

After Matt left, Black turned to Shepherd. "We never said shit about working an ADA into this mess. What are you doing?"

"Just what I said. Matt'll need to work with an ADA on this case. Who better than the guy who's already assigned to it?"

"That's bullshit, Bill," Black said, "and you know it. A case like this, one of your fucking egomaniacs would usually take it over. Why not one of the senior assistants? Someone who knows the system inside and out?"

"You heard what I said," Shepherd responded.

"Yeah, I heard what you said, but I didn't buy it, and I don't think Matt did either. He may come across like a hillbilly with a fourth-grade education, but he's as sharp as a fucking tack."

"Turlow is going to get the case anyway."

Black studied him. "If Turlow turns up something, you can swoop in and take credit. That's what you're thinking. If he fucks up and makes the DA's office look bad, then he's your fall guy. That's it, isn't it? You don't want to risk one of your senior people when you've got Turlow, who you don't even like. Jesus, you're a bastard, Shepherd."

"It isn't like that."

"Fuck, yes, it's like that. Well, I'm not hanging Matt Burton out to dry if this goes south. That man's been around forever. He's goddamn near a legend here."

"But he is awfully close to retirement, isn't he?"

"Like I said, you are a shit, Bill. A real shit."

◆

While he waited for the deputies at the jail to bring Tommy Resnic over, Matt read through his file. He noted that Tommy had a few, mostly drug-related, priors, but there was nothing violent. *Hmm.*

The Detention Center deputy stuck his head in. "Somebody order a perp?"

"You got Resnic?"

"Yeah, Resnic."

"Put him in room two, will ya? I'll give you a buzz later to pick him up."

"I'll just hang here and get some coffee."

"This could take a while."

"I doubt it. He's very much a 'yes' and 'no' and 'fuck you' type," the deputy offered.

"Okay," Matt said. "Chill for a while, and let's see what happens."

Interrogation room two was as nondescript as you could get. There was no two-way mirror—in fact, there was no mirror at all, no windows, nothing but beige walls to stare at. There were three chairs and a small table, and that was it.

Matt walked over to the room's surveillance cubicle and settled heavily into the chair. He turned on the small black-and-white monitor and watched Tommy wait.

The suspect was dressed in the typical orange jumpsuit, white slippers, and white socks. He was still handcuffed and was rocking back and forth in his chair.

Nervous, Matt thought. Tommy looked like he was trying to find the cameras and mics—but he wouldn't. No one ever did.

With a sigh, Matt turned and walked through the door.

He introduced himself and explained that he was investigating Tommy's mother's murder.

"Before we get started with anything," Matt began, pulling out some papers, "I've got to tell you, my boss is a real stickler.

"He's always on me about this and that, especially the paperwork. Before I can say anything to you about anything, even what color the sky is or what you had for dinner last night, we have to go through this form. Here," he said, leaning forward, "let me get those cuffs off.

You okay? You comfortable? You need something to drink?"

"No, I'm okay," Tommy answered.

"You need to go to the bathroom or anything? You don't want to sit here listening to me read you some form when you got to take a piss."

"Nah, I ain't gotta go."

Matt went through the Miranda form with him. *You understand you have the right to remain silent? You understand you have the right to an attorney...?* He had Tommy initial each right as he read it off. He asked if Tommy had an attorney yet, and Tommy said no.

"Okay," Matt said, "that takes care of the paperwork end of things. You still okay? Not hungry? Not thirsty?"

"I'm okay."

"Tommy," Matt began. "I can call you Tommy, right? My name's Matt, by the way. Tommy, we've got a problem, a really big one, and I need your help. We have an issue we've got to get resolved here. I think you know what it is."

He let that hang for a moment, waiting for Tommy to fill the dead space.

"Momma," Tommy supplied.

"Yeah, that's right," Matt said, sounding almost reluctant to get into it. "I know this must be painful for you."

Tommy nodded.

"I lost my mother a few years back," Matt continued. "I don't know; I just wasn't prepared. Maybe you're never prepared for something like that. You must be taking it pretty hard right now."

Tommy nodded again. "Yeah."

"Why don't you talk to me about it?" Matt asked. "Tell me about her. What was she like?"

He got Tommy talking about how his mother was very sweet and gentle and made cookies. Getting the suspect talking was always the first hurdle.

"I'll bet she was proud of you," Matt offered.

A cloud passed over Tommy's face. "Yes, she was. For a while."

"For a while?"

"I got into trouble. A lot."

"Well, hell, Tommy, we've all gotten into trouble. I used to throw eggs at the neighbor's house when I was a kid. Is that what we're talking about here?"

Tommy shook his head. "I'm into drugs. I got a drug problem. I...I stole from Momma."

"Oh, I'm sorry to hear that. I know you couldn't have felt good about that. You must have felt there wasn't any other way."

"No, I felt terrible. But I didn't have a job, and that goddamn coke is so fucking expensive. Those guys, they're always jacking up the price, just a little bit more, just a little bit more. They know you need it, so they always jack it up. A bit more. A bit more."

"Those bastards," Matt agreed, without heat. He was waiting. But when Tommy didn't say anything else, Matt prodded. "So, you took things from your mom's house? Little things?"

"Yeah, just little things. At first. DVDs. Momma never watched them. Shit, all she watched was Fox News and the Disney Channel. You can get three bucks apiece for DVDs, if they're good."

"Really? I didn't know that."

"Yeah. Then...well, I took other things. My dad, he's dead and gone, but he had a bunch of real nice fishing poles, real nice. I took those. I pawned them, all for some goddamn coke. I was crazy. I knew what I was doing was wrong, but..."

"But you had to have the stuff? Right?"

"Yeah. You don't understand what it's like. You ache for the shit when you ain't had it for a while. Shit, you need it just to feel normal. I ain't even talking about getting high. Hell, you need some blow just so you feel regular again. Getting high? Shit, that takes four times what you took when you started. Nobody tells you what it's like when you're hooked on that shit. It makes you fucking sick. You puke your guts out. Your hands tremble all the time. Your whole body hurts. You think about it all the time. 'When can I get it? Who's got some? How can I get some money to buy some more?' It's a fucking illness."

"So, after a while, you ran out of stuff to take from your mom? Or you had another idea?" Matt suggested.

Tommy looked down. "Yeah," he said finally. "I had a brilliant fucking idea."

"What was that, Tommy?"

"I don't want to say."

"Hey, I'm not gonna force you to say anything. We're two guys talking. You can shut up right now and not say another thing, but I don't think that's what you want. You want to get this off your chest. Go ahead, tell me I'm wrong. Am I wrong?"

"No," Tommy replied miserably, still looking at his hands. "You ain't wrong."

"So, tell me about the money," Matt suggested.

Tommy hesitated.

"I mean, there it was, right there in the house," Matt prompted.

Tommy still hesitated.

"How about I get you some water? Something to eat? We got a good vending machine here. You need to go to the bathroom?"

"No," Tommy said, but it wasn't clear which question he was answering.

"Is it the money that's bothering you?" Matt asked. "Or is it something else?"

"I don't get what you mean."

"Come on, Tommy. You know exactly what I mean. We aren't just talking about money here, and you know it."

But Tommy seemed genuinely confused.

"Tell me about that night," Matt suggested. "Come on, you know the night I'm talking about."

"I didn't go at night."

"Oh, bullshit," Matt said, but again without much heat. "Don't kid me, Tommy. I know better."

Tommy made a face. "You said I could talk to a lawyer?"

"Whoa!" Matt said, holding up his hands. "What do we need a lawyer for? We're just guys talking."

"I think I need to talk to a lawyer," Tommy repeated.

"Okay," Matt said, sitting back and shrugging his shoulders. "You can go back to the jail until we get you a lawyer. But it might be easier to keep talking just the two of us."

"I want to talk to a lawyer," Tommy repeated yet again.

"Fine," Matt said calmly, though he was frustrated. The interview had left him with far more questions than answers. Tommy Resnic was clearly torn up with guilt over something he'd done to his mother. But whether it was robbery or murder, Matt had no idea.

◆

A little after midnight, Matt trudged out to his car in the nearly deserted parking lot. He was too damned tired to go back to the muffler shop. Instead, he went home, and Angela made him ham and eggs. He didn't care that it was breakfast food; he liked eating ham and eggs after a long day's work.

Angela sat down at the dining room table after she'd handed him the plate and a big glass of milk. The milk went well with the ham and eggs, and he ate quietly for a while, trying not to think about how tired he was. He glanced at Angela. They'd been married almost twelve years now. His second; her third. Police work and marriage didn't always go together. He'd been married to his first wife for almost twenty years, but the last eight or nine had been pretty miserable. Angela's first husband had been a salesman; the second had been a cop. Now she was married to another cop. She was fifty-three and had gained a bit of weight, but she still had the look. With those dark eyes and that dark hair, she had a look that caught you up and made you instantly unsure of yourself. He still felt its impact as much as he'd felt it the first day they'd met.

He'd been at a traffic accident, called out because somebody had claimed that one of the dead people had been dead before the accident. He'd spent a couple of hours there, though he'd been sure as soon as he'd seen the bodies that everyone had been killed in the wreck. He'd called for a radio car to take him back to headquarters, and when the patrol car pulled up, a thin woman with dark hair and dark eyes had climbed out and said, "You Burton? Somebody said you need a ride."

"So, they sent me a lady police officer," he'd quipped. "Is this all you do, give people rides all day?"

It had been a long day, but he still shouldn't have said it.

"That's not the only thing I can do," she'd said. "I can leave your ass standing in the fucking street."

Then she'd gotten back into the car, put it in drive, and—to his astonishment—circled him and driven off. He'd expected her to turn around and come back and apologize, but she hadn't. He'd been angry when he'd had to call for another car, and even angrier when it took forty-five minutes to get to him. But later, he'd had time to think about it and had chuckled.

He'd found out where Angela Dixon worked and sent some flowers and a note with an apology. He'd followed up with a phone call and asked her out. She'd said no. And no again after the next bunch of flowers and another phone call. And a third. After that, he'd given up.

Two months later, he'd been standing on the edge of a ditch, looking down at a little girl's body, naked and bruised, and he had stood there and cried and not cared who was looking at him. Kids were always the hardest. Some of the EMTs had been arguing about who should go down and collect the body.

He'd turned on them in a rare rage, screaming at them to shut up, and then he'd scrambled down the side of the ditch, waded through the putrid water, and bent over to pick her up himself. The EMTs and a bunch of officers had stood there on the edge of the ditch and watched him come back up. When some of them offered to help him up the side, he'd roared at them, "Back off! Back the hell off!"

He'd clambered up with the little girl and laid her gently on the gurney, covering her with his jacket. No one had dared to say anything to him after that. He'd stood there for a while, next to the gurney, looking at her little swollen face as tears streamed down his own. When someone had finally pushed through the crowd, it was Angela.

To this day he didn't remember getting into her squad car or the long ride back to his house. But she'd guided him up to his door, even helped him unlock it. She'd taken him into his bathroom, helped him clean up, and then put him to bed. And that had been that.

She was older now; they both were. But she still had that look, the one he liked so much. Her dark eyes were watching him now.

"Tough day?" she asked.

He drank some milk. "How'd you get to be so pretty?"

"Oh, brother." She rolled her eyes. "What's going on?"

He thought for a moment. "How long have you been at the DA's office now?"

"Why?"

"Just asking."

"You're never 'just' asking." Angela thought for a moment. "About eight years. Why?"

"You ever hear anything about DA case files being made to disappear?"

"What are you talking about?" When he didn't immediately answer, she responded, "No, I haven't."

"No cases on the roster one day that are suddenly gone the next? Maybe cops calling in to check on cases that have been misfiled?"

"Where are you going with this?"

He didn't answer.

"Oh, Matt. You're not saying what I think you're saying, are you?"

"Could be there's something bad happening at your place of work."
Then he sighed. "And mine, too."

She just stared at him.

"There could be a real mess coming."

◆ Chapter Three ◆

Friday, April 14, 1:00 p.m.

Sean hated Magistrate Court. He parked in the employee section outside the jail and climbed out. It wasn't too hot yet, thankfully. In the summer, making this slog was pure misery since there wasn't a scrap of shade in the whole parking lot.

The defense attorneys had already arrived. As he walked to the building, a huge stack of files under his arm, Sean looked out over a sea of BMWs, Lexuses, and even one Porsche. He wondered who owned that one. His little Nissan was six years old, the same one he'd bought the week after he graduated from law school.

He sighed. He had about thirty-five files with him but had only taken a few minutes to glance through them. Thirty-five wasn't a bad number of preliminary hearings, but you never knew. Sometimes you'd be out in less than an hour and could beat the evening traffic home. Sometimes you were there until nine o'clock, cursing the evil gods of crime.

Sean stepped into the cool, dark lobby. There was no one in the public seating, and he was grateful. Sometimes civilian witnesses would wait there and pounce on him as soon as he walked through the door. They didn't understand about prelims and thought they were at a trial or something. Sometimes they even dressed up.

The jail was a little like something from a futuristic movie. The ceiling was about twenty feet above his head, and one wall was pockmarked with little square windows to let in the light. The other walls were a sheer mass of white, stretching floor to ceiling. Beyond the public seating, at the back of the cavern that was the lobby, there was a glassed-in deputy's station with a metal detector on one side. Two deputies sat behind the glass, and one stood next to the metal detector. Sean walked up, not bothering to identify himself. The deputy just waved him through and didn't say anything when the detector beeped.

While there were precious few perks that went with the ADA job, those he had were nice.

After the metal detector, he shifted the weight of the files to his other arm and passed by the elevator in favor of the stairs. It was only three flights up to Magistrate Court, and you never knew who might corner you in the elevator. Besides, climbing the steps felt a little like exercise.

When he got to the third floor, Sean stopped and glanced through the small window in the door that led down the hallway to the courtroom. He caught his breath. There were people everywhere. He heaved a deep sigh and braced himself.

I hate this shit, he thought as he pushed open the door.

A dozen attorneys turned and swarmed over him like hungry predators. The pandemonium always reminded Sean of feeding time at the zoo, or of some poor animal having his flesh stripped by a school of piranha.

First up was a lawyer from the old school, with slicked-back gray hair and an easy manner that disguised a lethal foe. Sean had fallen for the "aw shucks" personality once, but never again.

"My guy's a scumbag named Parquin in on burglary, no priors," he explained, seeming to talk slowly even though the words were coming out fast. "Agree to $10,000 on bond, and I'll get you a waiver."

"Your guy's got four priors, three of which were burglaries," Sean returned. "Ten won't do it."

"Three? Are you sure about that?"

"Very."

"Let me talk with him." Mr. Old School vanished, and three more eager and overpaid attorneys filled his space. *I've got Smith. I've got Jones. I've got Tom, he's got Dick, we've both got Harry.*

Sean worked the crowd, attorney after attorney walking up, some smiling, some snarling, some unsure, some way too damned sure. When there was a brief lull, a youngish, plump attorney stepped forward and offered his hand. Sean took it, immediately wary of the new face.

"I'm Tom Delaney," the new guy introduced himself with an

embarrassed smile.

"Nice to meet you, Tom. What have you got?"

"Got? I don't—"

Sean waved his handful of files. "Which one of these is yours?"

"Oh, uh, no. I'm a third-year. I've been assigned to you."

Sean sighed. "You're part of the Prosecutorial Clinic?"

"Yes," Tom said.

"Nobody told me you were going to be here today. It would have been nice to know."

"Is it going to be a problem?"

Sean sighed again. *Thirty-five cases, and now I'll have to be explaining every little detail to some third-year.*

"No, I suppose not. Okay, uh, Tom, right?"

"Right," Tom said, looking eager.

"Tom, do me a favor? Go and sit at that table, okay?" Sean pointed out the prosecutor's table.

Tom looked unsure. "Don't you want me to do something? I could do one of the hearings—"

"Not yet. There'll be plenty of time for that later. We've got to get to know one another a little first."

A few minutes later, Sean joined Tom at the table. "Okay, Tom, we've got about two minutes before the magistrate comes out. It's Judge Ames. He's a real bastard. Loves golf. Hates prelims. Wants all defendants to rot in hell. Now, that last part is good for us, but the rest isn't. Anything we do to keep this man from a late golf game, he's going to take out on us. Got it?"

"Got it."

"I know you heard about the procedural requirements of a preliminary hearing in law school, but that crap doesn't mean anything here. The real world works different."

An attorney handed Sean a piece of paper, nodding at him, and Sean nodded back. "See this?" Sean asked, holding the paper up for Tom. "This is a waiver. On an afternoon like this, these things are better than gold. I've got thirty-five cases on the calendar this afternoon. If I can get them all to waive, I can get out of here and go home. Even an empty apartment is better than this place."

"What's the waiver for?" Tom asked.

"The waiver is a form that the defendant signs, waiving his right to the preliminary hearing. When he waives it, we don't have to have it."

"Don't we want to have it?"

"No, we absolutely do not. If I have to put a bunch of cops on the stand this afternoon and have them tell the judge about why they arrested these guys, we're going to be here all night."

"But why would the defendant waive a hearing? Maybe the judge will rule in his favor."

"This is a prelim," Sean explained. "All we have to show is preponderance. That's the legal standard. It means that it's more likely than not that he committed the crime."

"I know what preponderance means," Tom said, bristling a little.

Despite himself, Sean was starting to like the kid. He had spunk.

"Good. You got preponderance. That means these hearings are easy. Your chances of losing one, as a prosecutor, are slim to none. Even if the judge goes against us, all we have to do is seek an indictment and get him bound over that way. The defense attorneys all know that, so they negotiate with us: get a lower bond in exchange for a hearing that they'd probably lose anyway."

Tom thought for a moment. "So, this is pretty meaningless."

Sean winked at him, liking him more by the minute. "There are bond recommendations inside the folders. They are deliberately higher than I would normally recommend. That gives me room to negotiate to the bond I actually would have recommended. See? It's like buying a car."

They were interrupted by the appearance of the judge. There was no bailiff, so Sean motioned for Tom to stand up.

Judge Ames was middle-aged and short, with gray hair, broad shoulders, and a substantial gut. He scowled at everything, looking even surlier than usual. He hoisted his robe, squeezed behind the bench, wrestled his chair into position, and finally sat down. Sean briefly considered applauding.

"Be seated," Ames ordered. "Okay, Mr. uh, oh, Mr. Turlow. How are you?"

"I'm fine, Your Honor," Sean replied, standing up again. When Tom moved to stand, too, Sean put a hand on his shoulder and held him in place.

"What have we got today?" Ames asked, with about as much excitement as if he'd been asking when his prostate exam would begin.

Ames began calling the cases listed on the docket for that afternoon. The first five went smoothly, all announcing waivers in exchange for bond reductions, and Sean was beginning to hope that maybe he'd be out of there a little earlier than usual.

"State v. Howard," Ames called.

An attorney whom Sean hadn't seen before stepped up. She was tall and blonde, but he could tell that the blonde wasn't her natural coloring. She had on a crisp suit and carried a messenger bag over her shoulder. He'd never seen her in prelims before, but she walked with sure-footed assurance. She glanced at him, and there was something in that look. For a moment, he forgot his own name, only noticing that her nose was a little off center and her eyebrows were brown, even though her hair was blonde.

He shook himself when she walked up to his table.

"If I may have a moment with the prosecutor, Your Honor?" she said.

The judge nodded and scowled at nothing in particular.

"I'm Diana Baker," she introduced herself. "Howard is my client. What are you recommending for bond?"

Sean opened the file and glanced inside. He'd written $10,000 there, but he knew it was high. "If he'll do $8,000 and no contact with the victim on bail, then we have an agreement."

She stopped and looked at him again. It was a good look. He figured she had to know what that look did to men. Some part of Sean's brain—the part that was actually working—told him he was being manipulated, but the rest of his brain didn't particularly care.

"If you can go six, then he'll sign," she countered. He noticed that her voice was a little huskier than he would have expected. She also didn't have that southern drawl most native Atlantans carried. Where the hell was she from?

Sean's brain kicked back into gear, and he shook his head. "I'm sorry, but $8,000 is as low as I'll go, and don't forget to tell him about the no-contact provision."

"These men are neighbors," she protested. "My client lives across the street from the man he allegedly hit with a baseball bat."

"Even so," Sean said, and immediately thought it had been a stupid thing to say.

"I'll check with my client," she said, slinging the bag over her shoulder and walking away. Sean liked the way she moved.

"What's next?" Tom asked, destroying the mood—though that was probably just as well.

"Oh, uh, Your Honor, the defense needs time to confer with her client. Perhaps we can move on to the next one for now?" Sean asked, snapping back to attention and looking up at Ames.

"Hmmph," was all he got in reply before Ames called another case and another attorney stood and announced a waiver.

Six out of thirty-five. Sean's luck was holding.

"State v. Resnic."

There was a slight whirring of motors, and Sean turned to see Pat Reardon rolling to the front of the courtroom. Pat was a paraplegic as the result of a car wreck twenty years prior. He was overweight, and his ponytail looked particularly idiotic on him.

"Still in discussions with the State," Pat announced. "In fact, if I could have a word with Mr. Turlow, Your Honor?"

"Go ahead."

Pat's stage whisper could be heard in the next county. "My guy's a wing nut. He wants his day in court. I keep telling him that this is a prelim, but so far, no dice."

Sean picked up the file and glanced through it. *Murder.* He showed the file to Tom, pointing at the charge, before turning back to Pat. "He's charged with killing Imogene Resnic. Was that his wife?"

Pat shook his head, and if anything, his whisper got louder. "Mother. Capped her in the head." Pat aimed an imaginary finger. "Allegedly."

Suddenly, it clicked into place. *Oh, shit,* he thought. *The muffler shop murder.* Sean turned to look around the courtroom and saw Bernie Cassis sitting in the third row, holding a file and wearing a brown coat and tie.

"We can't set bond here anyway," Sean said, turning back to Pat. "What does your guy want?"

"He wants to 'make a statement.'" Pat emphasized the last words with his fingers, making air quotes.

"Oh, God," Sean said. "Tell him no. This is a prelim."

"I've tried that."

"Mr. Turlow?" the judge interrupted, sounding impatient.

"Your Honor, we have a situation with Mr. Resnic. Perhaps we should bring him out of the holding cell."

As they brought Tommy out, Tom leaned in close. "Why can't you set bond here?"

Sean answered without looking. "Murder One. Superior-Court-only bond. This is Magistrate Court. A Superior Court judge is the only person who can set bond on that kind of charge."

Tommy came through a door in the back of the courtroom, accompanied by a harried-looking deputy.

Tom whispered, "He looks terrified."

Sean was still reading the file. "Uh-huh."

Tommy took a seat, and Pat rolled up next to him and whispered with him for a few moments. Sean could tell that Pat wasn't making any headway by the way Tommy kept vehemently shaking his head.

"State ready?" Ames asked.

Sean glanced at the warrant and then nodded at Bernie to come forward. "Yes, Your Honor," he said, "the State is ready."

Sean called Bernie to the stand and swore him in.

"Are you the arresting officer in the case of State versus Resnic?"

"Yes, I am."

"Please explain to the court the facts surrounding the charge of murder against Mr. Resnic."

Bernie began. "Sometime on the evening of April 9 or the early morning of April 10, Mrs. Imogene Resnic drove to Mick's Muffler shop on Barton Street and was shot in the side of the head. Employees of the muffler shop discovered her body the next day. The first officer on the scene was Jimmy Bennett, who arrived at 8:20 a.m. He saw that she had been dead for quite a while and called the CAP division. I arrived about twenty minutes after the first officer on the scene. Once the scene was secured, I went to the victim's neighborhood. I wanted to canvass the neighborhood to see if any of the neighbors knew anything about the murder.

"During the canvass, I knocked on the victim's door, on the off chance that someone might be inside, but no one answered. I went around to the backyard and found the defendant asleep in a lawn chair. He wasn't wearing anything but cutoffs, not even a shirt or shoes. This was about half past ten on the morning of April 10. The defendant appeared to be extremely intoxicated. He had a scratch mark on his right cheek that looked pretty fresh, and he was holding a large yellow envelope in his hands. I told him that I was a police officer and asked him who he was. He said it was none of my damn business. I drew my service weapon and told him to lie down on the ground. I had him place his hands behind his back, and I handcuffed him. I patted down his jeans and the envelope. There was a suspicious bulge in the envelope, so I looked inside. It contained $3,812, mostly in hundred-dollar bills. I asked the defendant what he was doing in the backyard, and he told me it was his mother's house and he had every right to be there. I took out my Miranda card and read him his rights. Then I asked him what the money was for. He said he was bringing it back because he had 'done his mother wrong.' He said he hoped she would forgive him. I asked him what she would need to forgive him for, and he answered, 'I've been a bad son to her. I've done things I shouldn't have done. I want to make it up to her, somehow.'

"I asked him to tell me about the previous night, and he said he had had a lot to drink, and the more he'd thought about what he'd done, the worse he felt. I asked him where he'd been drinking, and he said at his trailer, alone. I asked him where the gun was, and he claimed he didn't know. I tried to ask some other questions, but he kept getting more and more upset and was fairly incoherent."

"Did you find out anything about the money the defendant had in his possession?" Sean asked.

"I learned, from talking with neighbors, that the victim was known to keep a large amount of cash in her house. She was afraid of banks or something like that. I secured her home and discovered that the victim did, in fact, have a wall safe. The safe was open and, except for her will, empty. When the safe was dusted for prints, two sets were identified: the victim's and the suspect's."

"Was a gun located?"

"Not yet, but the investigation is continuing."

"No further questions," Sean said and sat down.

Throughout Bernie's testimony, Tommy had sat like a stone, staring straight ahead. Now that Sean wasn't asking questions, he took the opportunity to study Tommy a little more closely. He was about twenty years old, with long hair and a scruffy goatee. He was thin and pale, and when he turned and caught Sean looking at him, Sean thought his eyes looked haunted.

Tom leaned toward Sean and observed, "He doesn't look like a murderer."

"What does a murderer look like?" Sean shot back, but he privately agreed.

After Pat's few questions, which did little more than go back over the testimony, he announced that he had nothing further.

Tommy stood up so quickly that his chair flopped over. "That's it? That's all you're gonna do?" he shouted. The deputies immediately moved in and seized him by both of his arms.

"This ain't right!" he continued. "This ain't right!"

"Mr. Resnic," Ames ordered, "control yourself. Be quiet and sit down, or I'll have you removed from the courtroom."

The deputies shoved Tommy down in his seat and stood on either side of him, unwilling to take any chances since he was still fidgeting.

"Does stuff like this happen a lot?" Tom whispered.

Sean shook his head. "Hardly ever."

"Mr. Resnic, this is not your trial," Ames continued. "I don't make the decision as to whether you are guilty or not. My only function is to confirm that the State has sufficient evidence to bind the case over to the Superior Court. My decision today is that they do."

Tommy again tried to leap to his feet, but this time the deputies were ready for him. They pinned him to the tabletop and handcuffed him. He wriggled his head around and looked directly at Sean. "Mr. Prosecutor! Mr. Prosecutor!" he screamed. "I didn't kill her! I took the money, but I swear to you, I didn't kill her. I wouldn't kill Momma. I wouldn't!" The deputies began dragging him away, but he kept his eyes fixed on Sean. "I didn't kill her. Please. Please!" The door closed behind him, but everyone in the courtroom could still hear his muffled cries as they led him away. There was one last wail of *pleeeeeeeease*, and then he was gone.

Sean sat staring at the closed door. Tom, apparently trying to act like a cynical veteran, smiled and said, "Well, I guess everybody says they're innocent."

Sean didn't answer. He closed the file and tucked it under the rest of the stack, but he knew he'd be looking at it again. There had been something about Tommy's eyes, something about the way he had stared at Sean. *No more screwy cases,* he reminded himself and almost smiled. He already knew this one was going to be tough.

Saturday, April 15, 12:05 a.m.

He watched from the porch overhang as Gregor arrived at the cabin an hour before the scheduled meeting, parking his truck about fifty yards away. Gregor sat there for a moment, apparently letting his eyes get used to the dark before emerging. He watched as Gregor climbed out, hunched down, and listened, a 9mm with a fifteen-bullet clip gripped in his hand. He had to stop himself from chuckling; Gregor obviously suspected something, but neither the gun nor the sturdy Nike running shoes he wore were going to do him a bit of good.

He continued watching in silent amusement as Gregor dashed into the cover of the nearest set of trees and worked slowly through them, making a complete circle around the cabin. He'd known he could get Gregor here by promising him a "bigger, better hit," but he'd also figured it would set off Gregor's alarm bells. So he and his partner had prepared.

They'd figured Gregor would approach the small, one-room building from an unexpected side first, and sure enough, that's what he did. The north side had no door, but Gregor used the tip of his gun to push up the window on the north wall as he shone his flashlight inside. After a moment, the flashlight clicked off.

Now Gregor walked around to the front of the cabin, holstering his gun. The man braced himself for action as Gregor stopped and listened in front of the three short steps to the porch. He watched as Gregor, apparently hearing nothing, shrugged and headed up the steps toward the potted plant in the corner where they kept a key.

And then he slid the barrel of his gun down to press into Gregor's ear. "Freeze," he ordered softly.

Gregor froze. He'd obviously forgotten about the porch overhang. He hadn't realized that, if you'd gotten to the cabin even earlier than Gregor, say two or three hours ago, you could have pried loose some of the ceiling boards and climbed up inside. He hadn't realized that you could wait there, unseen, taking your time, waiting for your target. It would be uncomfortable, but it was the best place to hide. You'd position yourself to drop your arm through the opening you'd made, just as soon as the idiot picked up the key. You could wait, like a jungle cat, for your prey to make a mistake and then attack.

"Raise your hands, Gregor," he instructed, sliding the gun away again. "Interlace your fingers on the back of your head."

He grabbed his radio and muttered into it. In less than a minute, the headlights from a truck were illuminating the front of the cabin as his partner drove up, got out of the truck, and walked up the front steps.

"Hiya, Gregor," he said in an almost friendly tone, pointing his own gun at the Russian while the man climbed down from the roof overhang.

Then they grabbed Gregor together, pushing him roughly against the wall and expertly searching him. They found his ankle holster and the small knife he kept in his back pocket. The man couldn't help but release a dry-throated cackle as he wrapped some duct tape over Gregor's mouth.

Then he unrolled a longer strip of tape and wrapped it around Gregor's nose, all the way around the back of his head. He watched Gregor's eyes reveal horror as he realized they weren't going to stop. Gregor began to fight then, but they dragged him to the steps and laid him down so that his head was jutting out over the top step. His partner pinned Gregor down as he kept cackling and wrapping more and more tape around Gregor's head, smothering him. Gregor tried to suck in air, but it was no good. He began to panic and really fight, but it was too late. It had been too late the minute the gun had pressed into his ear.

They watched in fascination as Gregor's body fought for air and then went still.

Saturday, April 15, 2:00 a.m.

Sean woke up and couldn't get back to sleep. He tossed and turned for a while and then realized it just wasn't going to work. He finally got out of bed and washed his face in the bathroom sink. He stared at his reflection and realized he'd be forty in only five years. Not a great thought. He didn't want to think about the nightmare he'd had, either, so he went to his briefcase and opened it. The Resnic file was right on top, where he'd put it before leaving the office for the day.

He remembered Resnic in the courtroom, and the long wail of *pleeeeeeeeease* echoed in his head. He tried to push it out of his mind, but he couldn't.

It only took ten minutes to read the entire file, front to back. True, it was all still under investigation, but there should have been more, even at this stage. The case was almost entirely circumstantial. Mom got killed; son suddenly had money. Son made a few ambiguous statements and then went to pieces. Son did have a fresh scratch on his face that he wouldn't explain. And the fingerprints in the house all matched mom and son—but there wasn't anything particularly unusual about that. Presumably, he stopped by to visit his mother on a regular basis and touched things. Sean made a note to check. Maybe they didn't get along, and she'd barred him from the house. That would give him something.

Typical Bernie, Sean thought. *He's always in such a damn hurry.* This whole case looked like it had been whipped together in about two hours. Bernie must have made up his mind the son was guilty the minute he saw him in the backyard of the mother's house. Everything else he did was just to support that theory.

Even with the sparse material, Sean had already spotted some anomalies. Bernie had testified the day before that he'd canvassed the victim's neighborhood by himself, but there was a supplemental report in the file from Tracy Alastair about being asked by Bernie to canvass the victim's neighborhood. She'd gone door-to-door with Rick Gartman, who'd also written up a supplemental. According to those reports, *they* were the ones who'd found Tommy Resnic sitting in a chair behind his mother's house.

There was also no mention of the murder weapon. If Tommy had shot his mother, there should have been a gun somewhere. But the police report indicated nobody had found a firearm anywhere on her property or in Tommy's trailer.

Because Sean had handled the preliminary hearing, the case would be assigned to him later, and he was not happy about it. There was something fishy about the whole thing, the way it was thrown together and the way that Bernie had left things out. The case already had a bad taste to it, and he had a feeling it was only going to get worse.

He made some notes and then, feeling as though he might actually be able to get some sleep, climbed back into bed, falling asleep almost immediately.

◆

When Sean woke again, the sun was up. He brushed his teeth, made some coffee, ate a Pop-Tart, and then called the main precinct and asked for CAP. He was in luck; Bernie was there.

"You working on a Saturday?" Bernie asked. "Jesus, that makes me proud."

"I wanted to ask you a couple questions about the Resnic case," Sean began.

"Wasn't that fun yesterday? I love it when they scream and carry on. I went outside right after that and smoked a cigarette. Better than sex. God, it was great."

"Yeah," Sean muttered. "About the case, though. What about the gun?"

"Gone. Probably threw it in a river or dumpster. We'll never find it now."

"Where have you looked?"

"Usual places. Got a search warrant for his trailer. Nice place. I'd like to retire there. Looks like an aluminum box wrapped around a pile of garbage. I spent half the time wondering what the hell I was standing on. Found some DVDs that we might call pornographic, but no gun."

"Did you look anywhere else?"

"Yeah, I tried his scrotum, but when it wasn't there, I gave up."

"Don't get touchy, Bernie."

"What's going on? You call me on a Saturday about some fuckup and want to know where I looked for the gun? The fucker won't say anything about it; it ain't at the scene; it ain't at his trailer. Where else am I supposed to look?"

"What about his mother's place?"

"Why the fuck would he hide it there?"

"Well, you were inside—"

"I searched, but I was looking for the safe, not the gun. If it was there, though, I'd have found it."

"So, we don't have a gun. I assume he hasn't made any more statements?"

"You'll have to check with Detective Matt Burton on that one," Bernie said stiffly.

"Matt? I thought this was yours."

"Past tense. Matt's got it now. He's giving it his magic touch. He did the follow-up interview with Resnic. And as far as I know, he didn't get anything."

"Why the change?" Sean asked. "And why didn't you mention this at the prelim yesterday?"

"There's a lot of shit we don't mention in prelims. You *have* done this job for a while, haven't you?"

"I'd just like some straight answers, Bernie."

"Wake up on the wrong side this morning? Jesus, go back to bed, Counselor."

Sean wanted to ask more questions, but Bernie suddenly said he had to go. The line went dead.

Go back to bed, Counselor.

He wished he could.

Saturday, April 15, 11:30 a.m.

Matt arrived at the abandoned strip mall and drove around back to where all the activity seemed to be centered. He quickly dictated the time into his handheld recorder as he parked near the other squad cars and pulled himself out of his seat. He wasn't supposed to be taking on any new cases yet, but he wasn't one to ignore a call from Dispatch.

He stood for a moment and surveyed the scene. It was a typical strip mall, with about ten empty business units lined up in a neat little row. The last building on the right ended in a small knoll. The other end had a small driveway, currently occupied by two squad cars, with access to the dumpsters and back entrances of the businesses. Someone had already strung yellow crime scene tape from the back corner of the building across the entranceway, effectively blocking anyone from driving into the area.

It was no wonder the place had gone out of business, really. The location was terrible. A large hill rose up from behind the stores and blocked all view of them from westward-approaching traffic. A large complex of office suites blocked the view from the other direction. A rental place; a closed gym; a cell phone distributor. *Bad location*, Matt thought again. This part of the county was getting a lot more affluent. Except maybe for the gym, the people around here didn't need those kinds of services.

Matt walked around the squad cars and stood outside the tape, surveying again. From his vantage point, he could just see the body near the first dumpster, lying on its face. Even from twenty or thirty feet away, Matt could see rope binding the hands behind the back. Oddly enough, though the victim was wearing a nice blue sports jacket and light gray slacks, he had on white socks, but no shoes.

Jimmy Bennett was talking with a civilian, but he excused himself and came over to Matt.

"Hey, Matt."

"Jimmy. Why am I here?"

"Your name's on the rotation; that's what I heard."

"Well, it shouldn't be. I'm off the schedule this week. This should have gone to someone else."

"You want me to call for a replacement?"

Matt thought about it for a second. "Nah, forget it. What have you got?"

"Dead guy, hands tied with rope. They wrapped his fucking face with duct tape. Can you believe it?"

"That the guy who found the body?" Matt nodded toward a slightly green-tinged man standing with some uniforms.

"Yeah. Todd Greaseman. As in grease."

"What's he say?"

"Says the place was auctioned off about two weeks ago. Last owner went bankrupt. This guy, Greaseman, bought the place and has been coming out here almost every day to check on it. He got here around eight o'clock, walked around back, and holy shit, who's this? Called it in on his cell."

Matt glanced over again at the man, now standing off by himself. He looked uncomfortable and nervous.

"Anybody mess with the scene?"

"Nope. Nobody. I checked the guy. Dead as disco. Looks like he's been there for a while. His body's stiff. I mean, goddamn, fucking duct tape? Mouth, nose, eyes, whole goddamn head, except for the top. Must have smothered to death. Jesus, just shoot the fucker."

"Anyone else been near the body?"

"No. Didn't even let my partner near it. When I heard you were on the rotation, I told everybody to stay clear. Funny thing about this place, I used to come here to work out before Lee changed the gym's location."

"Huh. Okay, well, I'll talk to Greaseman first. Send some of the guys across the street and into the office building. I know it's a Saturday, but it's worth a try. See if anybody saw anything."

Matt walked over to the man and smiled. "Hi. I'm Detective Matt Burton. I understand you own this place?"

Greaseman returned the smile. "Yeah. Bought it last month. I've been coming over here every day to check on it. Been trying to get some people to invest in it. It's a great location."

Matt let that one slide. The man's facts about the murder were simple and straightforward. He'd driven over around eight o'clock, poked around out front for a few minutes, walked around back, and found the body. He hadn't touched it, hadn't even walked close to it. Just as Jimmy had said, he stated that he'd called it in on his cell phone. Matt asked to see his phone.

Greaseman paused. "Why?"

"Procedure," Matt lied.

Greaseman shrugged and handed over the phone.

Matt looked at the calls register. Sure enough, one call to 911. Nothing else since the night before.

"Thanks," Matt said, handing it back. He got the man's full name, address, home and cell numbers, and driver's license number before releasing him.

The ME had arrived, and for the first time, Matt lifted the crime scene tape and walked over to the body, where Henderson was making some preliminary notes.

"Hey, Doc."

"Matt."

"Death by smothering?"

"This duct tape has a hundred and one uses," Henderson said. "Can't tell without an autopsy, but there are no other serious wounds."

"Some not so serious?"

"Bruises."

"Where?"

"Where would you expect bruises? Defensive on the arms. Some on the lower face. Not likely to get bruised on his ass, is he?"

"Have you checked?"

"Ha, ha. Tell the EMS boys that I'm ready to take him away."

Matt walked away as Henderson started gathering up his utensils. Kathy had just appeared, a large digital camera around her neck and the big plastic toolbox used to process fingerprints in her hand.

"Hey, Matt," she greeted him. "I hear there's some guy all wrapped in tape around here."

Matt thumbed over his shoulder. "See if you can lift any prints off the tape on his face. That stuff's got a pretty good surface; you should be able to get something."

"Sure, Matt. How's Angela, by the way?"

"She's fine, Kathy. Has to put up with me is all."

"Well, hell, Matt, she's a tough woman."

He laughed and walked away to start dictating information for his report. He listed the witnesses, the physical features of the scene, his impressions. He stood for a moment, without really thinking, letting his eyes roam over the area. Something about it bothered him. It was more than just the method. Smothering somebody to death with duct tape...well, that was a pretty mean way to do somebody in. Jimmy had been right; it would've been kinder to shoot the poor bastard. That meant the victim had really pissed the perp off. Or the perp was a sicko. Matt prayed that wasn't so. The press would be all over it. The last thing he needed was a psycho.

No sense jumping to conclusions, Burton, he told himself. First things first. What was bothering him?

The scene. This was the absolute perfect place to dump a body. The businesses were all closed down, so there was no chance of an early morning cleaning lady or somebody staying late to work on the books. And with the mall hidden from view of the road, no drivers would see anything suspicious. So, they drive around back, dump him out, drive away.

It was all too efficient, and that bothered him.

Who else would know about a place like this? People who made deliveries? But the businesses had been closed up for a while. Telephone repair people? Cable installers? A small tickle brushed the back of his mind. There was an answer there, but it hovered just out of his reach.

Matt took out his recorder again. "Scene is right off the main road but is just about invisible in the back. No way someone could see the perp dump the body. It would be a quick in and out. No surveillance cameras anywhere, but worth checking nearby businesses." He made a note about the cameras and then tried again to bring the answer to the surface of his mind. Who else would know about a place like this?

It just wouldn't come, so he gave up and put his notebook away.

◆

When Matt walked into the morgue at three o'clock that afternoon, one of the attendants waved and motioned him over. Matt recognized the enormous black man in green scrubs.

"Hey, Tiny."

"Matt. Got an ID on your dead guy."

"I didn't think he had a wallet on him."

Tiny smiled. "Didn't. But Jimmy was here when we peeled the tape off his face, and ol' Jimmy says that it's Gregor, uh," and here he checked a notepad, "Itz – Itzvanie?"

"Gregor Itzvanov," Matt corrected, reading from the printout.

"I didn't know big dumb cops could pronounce Russian names."

"His name rings a bell, that's all."

Matt walked into the autopsy room, where Henderson had already cut the body open.

"Hey, Matt. Do you see my iced tea?"

Matt glanced around and found the glass.

"Thanks." Henderson studied the dead man's wrists intently while he sipped his tea. "Take a look at this," he invited after a moment, motioning Matt over.

Matt leaned forward. The ME was pointing to the Russian's wrists, where he had just cut off the ropes.

"Those aren't rope burns," Matt said, surprised.

"Nope. Looks like handcuffs to me. Our fellow here had cuffs on him before he died. See the associated bruising? Probably from rough handling, maybe defensive moves. Raises an interesting question, doesn't it, Matt?"

"Yeah," Matt agreed, frowning. "If he was handcuffed before he died, why take the cuffs off and tie his wrists with rope?"

"Bingo."

"Did he smother to death?"

"Too early to tell," Henderson said, carefully placing the cut rope in an evidence bag. "I made sure the knot is still tied."

"Thanks." Matt knew the way a killer tied a knot was almost like a signature.

"The only thing I can tell you about the cause of death is that there aren't any wounds that would account for it. His mouth and nasal passages were filled with blood and some vomit. It certainly looks like he died of asphyxiation, maybe hemorrhaging, but I'll need more time to be sure."

"How long before I get your report?"

"Oh, two or three days."

"Doc, let me know if you find anything weird."

"Weird?"

"You know, anything out of the ordinary."

"You mean more out of the ordinary than being suffocated with duct tape? Something about this case bothering you, Matt?"

Matt didn't answer for a while, then said, "You've got my cell number, right?"

"Yeah."

"Take it easy, Doc."

♦

The address Dispatch provided for Gregor was a place Matt knew well. Brookshire Apartments was located just off Interstate 85, one of the main corridors through Atlanta, but Matt doubted most of the thousands of commuters who passed by every day had any idea what lay just a few hundred feet away. Brookshire might once have been a nice place to live, but those days were long gone. Now trash lay everywhere, dumpsters overflowed, and several mattresses were strewn through the parking lot. It had become a refuge for the less-desirable elements of society.

Men were milling around in the parking lot. Seeing Matt's Crown Vic, with the obvious police antenna, several of them began sidling away. Matt smiled to himself. He could probably pick up a half dozen of these guys on outstanding warrants, if he knew who they were. Instead, he walked up to 23C and knocked.

A skinny, greasy-looking man opened the door and stood staring at Matt.

"Hello, Lev."

"Hello, Matt."

"Can I come in?"

"Sure, Matt. I'm clean."

Lev was also a Russian. Matt couldn't recall arresting him personally, but he'd come across him once or twice in the past few years.

The apartment was a mess. Clothes and trash and magazines were scattered everywhere. The sofa Matt stood next to was covered in potato chips and popcorn, and he could smell a faint whiff of pot in the air. Lev had probably been in there so long he didn't realize it.

Matt didn't sit down, and Lev didn't offer him a chair.

"How you been holding up, Lev?"

"Same as always," Lev answered, his accent already beginning to show. Lev had worked hard at sounding like an American since he'd come to the United States ten years before, but the accent still shone through.

"'Fraid I got some bad news," Matt announced. "They found Gregor this morning; somebody killed him."

Lev froze. He moved his jaw around for a moment, then pushed some trash off a chair and sat down.

"Who? Who kill him, Matt?"

Matt shook his head. "You okay, Lev?"

"Sons of bitches," Lev muttered. "Rotten motherfucks."

"Who're you talking about?"

Lev hesitated, then looked up. "Whoever kill him."

"Any ideas about that?"

"No," Lev answered, a little too quickly.

"You and Gregor were roommates?"

"*Da*, five years, maybe more. You ever meet him?"

Matt noticed that Lev's accent was getting stronger, perhaps because he was upset. "No. Can't say that I did, least not that I remember."

"Oh, you would remember. Tats all over. He look bad motherfucker, like Russian gangster. You know that word, 'gangster'?"

"Yeah, I know that word."

"They all get these tats, all over. If you know how, you can read it like…like, what you say, story of your life?"

"Biography?" Matt offered.

"That a good word," Lev said, still looking down at his hands. He had some tattoos of his own.

"Gregor have a regular girlfriend these days?"

"Gregor, he like the black stuff. Got a girl on Copper Street named Neeka. You know, near the burned-out trailer park. She live in a single-wide with bushes—that the word?—in front."

"Bushes? You mean flowers?"

"Yeah, yeah. Flowers. She like flowers."

"I can find the place. She got a last name?" Matt fished his pen and notepad out of his pocket.

"Just Neeka, that all I know. I see her couple times. Oo-ee. I know why Gregor like that stuff." Lev thought for a moment, then grew sad. "Past tense now. That what they say for what happens in past, right? *Past tense.* Now we speak of him that way.

"How did he die?"

Matt skipped over the question. "Had he been hanging around with anyone in particular lately?"

Lev looked at the floor while he scratched his crotch. "No. Gregor keep pretty much to himself. Did they shoot him?"

"Lev," Matt warned. "I want to find out who killed him, okay? I don't care what he was into. He's dead; he's not going to jail. So far as I know, neither are you. Not even for those two joints laying over there. So cut the bullshit."

Lev looked at Matt for a long moment. "Cop," he finally said. "Gregor been hanging with some cop for the last few months."

Matt froze. "What cop?"

Lev was already shaking his head. "I don't know. I never see him. I only hear Gregor talk about him. This cop is going to help him make big score."

"What kind of a big score?"

"Gregor never say. Enough money to move to Miami Beach. Gregor always talking about moving to Miami Beach. Have a big condo. Stand on balcony, piss on cars below. Biscayne Boulevard. He going to piss on cars on Biscayne Boulevard. Kind of weird goal, but that what he want. That what he always talking about."

"He never gave you this cop's name? Never described him?"

"No. I think Gregor is just giving me the bullshit. He always talk big like that. He always just this close to big score and live like a king. It was bullshit."

"Know of anyone who'd like to kill Gregor? Maybe this cop?"

"No. People like Gregor. He act like tough guy, but he not bad. Good with guns. Some of his tats," he said in a conspiratorial tone, "some bullshit. Russians, they take serious. Your tats like your, how do you say, your rep?"

"Street rep?" Matt asked. "Some of his tattoos were fake?"

Lev shrugged. "Gregor not even Russian. He Ukrainian. But he always say, 'Russian.' Better street cred, better reputation when people think you Russian mafia."

"And he wasn't Russian mob?"

"Shit," Lev said. "He know some guys who know some guys. You know what I am saying?" He paused. "You still don't say how they kill him."

"I don't know for sure," Matt lied. "I haven't seen the body yet. The only thing I know is that they have a positive ID on him and that whoever it was dumped him behind a strip mall. Somebody found him there this morning."

Lev sat forward, getting angry for the first time. "That not *right*, Matt. Gregor deserve better. Not like trash. I get picked up on bullshit theft charge last year, Gregor, he bail me out. I find out later, it was his, what you call, emergency money. He call it 'mad money.' He saving that money for something, maybe his condo in Miami. What the hell. He use for me. He get most of it back when I go to court, but still. That how Gregor is." Lev paused. "That how Gregor *was*."

Lev suddenly didn't seem to have anything left to say. Matt found that he didn't have any more questions, either.

◆

Copper Street was like a scene from a World War II movie after the fighting stopped. There were burned-out shells of mobile homes here and there and men of every race standing around on the street looking stunned. They shared a universal hatred of Matt's Crown Vic and what it represented. It was not a place he enjoyed visiting, and he patted the 9mm automatic in its holster on his belt without really thinking about it. Matt recognized some faces as he drove slowly down the street, thought *what the hell?*, and waved at a couple.

He was surprised when one or two waved back. Less surprised when two or three others gave him the finger.

You couldn't work in Gannett County as a cop for very long before spending time on Copper, Silver, or Gold Streets. Despite their names, they were examples of the worst of living conditions. Drugs were openly sold on the streets, and the houses were all old and run-down. There were several trailer parks that backed up on woods. The odd thing was that fifty yards into the woods you'd come to a tall fence that backed up on some nice neighborhoods. Matt had often wondered if the people who lived on the other side of the fence knew what was here.

Matt cruised up and down the street a few times, looking for a single-wide mobile home with flowers out front. It was going to get dark soon, and there weren't a lot of streetlights—at least ones that hadn't been broken. He saw a patrol car coming in the opposite direction and waved it to a stop.

When the car pulled up, he saw that it was a friend: Lee. Lee was a big guy and claimed he actually liked to work Copper Street because it helped him keep his "edge."

"Lee," Matt called in greeting.

"Matt. What brings you to my neck of the woods?"

"Looking for someone."

"Me, too," Lee replied, holding up a photo of a young black male. "His name's Tic Tac, and he's my target for the night."

"Your target?"

"You know how it works, Matt," Lee smiled. "I give myself a target every night. Tonight it's Anthony Lew Hart, aka Tic Tac. I'm going to the village elders and telling them to hand over their boy or I'll make their lives a fucking misery."

Lee was talking about the older residents on Copper and Silver Streets who knew everybody's business. They'd seen it go from a low-end neighborhood on the fringe of Atlanta to an absolute hellhole.

"Yeah, well." Matt shifted in his seat. "I'm looking for a girl named Neeka. You know her?"

"Hell, Matt. There's all kinds of girls around here with names like that.

Neekaya, did you say?"

"Neeka," Matt repeated, a little louder.

"Got a last name on her?"

"No. Just that. Neeka."

"I'll keep my ears open. You gonna be around for a while or heading out?"

"I'm heading out. Call me if you come across her, okay?"

"What d'you want her for?"

"You got my cell phone number, right?"

"Yeah, I got it. What'd you say you wanted her for again?"

Matt smiled. "Tupperware party. What else?"

"You kill me," Lee hooted. "You up for some deer hunting this winter? You're overdue for a good-sized buck."

They'd hunted together, on and off, for several years. Matt liked the woods and the cool, clean air, but somehow Lee always ended up with a deer and the only thing Matt ended up with was the feeling he was getting a little bit older and a little bit slower every year.

"Sure," Matt agreed.

"I found a new spot," Lee said. "Some old fart sold me five acres on Hog Mountain. Got a stream and a cabin and everything. It's not even that far out."

"Got a fridge with beer in it?"

"Always."

"Then count me in."

"Well, I better get back on it. Tic Tac ain't gonna just jump into my back seat and say, 'Arrest me officer, I been a bad boy.'"

"You take care, Lee."

"Matt."

Matt looked in his rearview mirror as the patrol car rolled away. He considered his options. He would have liked to track down Neeka, especially before she heard about Gregor. If she knew something, she might blurt it out in the shock of hearing the bad news. He did a U-turn on Copper Street and then, just as he'd made up his mind to let it all go, he saw a single-wide trailer with several rows of geraniums in front. He parked and got out. As he walked along the street running parallel to the trailer, he saw a black woman lifting grocery bags out of the back of an old Volvo. He remembered Lev's description of a pretty woman with large breasts, and this woman certainly fit the bill.

He walked toward her. "Hello. I'm Matt Burton. I'm with the police."

The woman immediately stiffened and stared at him suspiciously.

Matt fished out his badge and showed it to her.

"So you're a cop. What do you want?"

"I'd like to talk with you about Gregor," Matt said. "Can we talk inside? What I have to say is kind of private."

She considered for a moment, shrugged, and then walked up the three steps to the front door of her trailer. He followed her in, standing just inside the front door while she put away her bags of groceries.

"Gregor ain't here," she said quickly.

"I know. Do you know where he was last night?"

"No."

"It's Neeka, isn't it? That's your name?"

"Yeah."

"What's your last name?"

"Tatum."

"You're Gregor's girl, aren't you?"

"Yeah."

"I've got some bad news for you, Neeka. Gregor is dead."

She looked skeptical but stopped putting away groceries and sat down.

"Somebody killed him last night. Wrapped duct tape around his face and smothered him to death. Beat him up some, too."

Neeka shook her head, starting to rock back and forth. She was going to get upset, of course, so Matt just braced himself for it.

"No, uh-uh," she said, "no. No. Gregor ain't dead. He just had some business. He's gone out of town or something."

"Neeka, I'm afraid that he *is* dead. He's down at the morgue now—"

"Gregor ain't dead!" she screamed, face suddenly lit with rage. "Gregor is alive! You get out! You get out of here! Gregor ain't dead, d'ya hear me? He ain't dead!"

"Neeka!" Matt shouted over her. "*You* calm down! All of this screaming isn't gonna change a thing. He really is dead, and I'm sorry about it."

She started crying, curling up into the fetal position on the large recliner. Matt wondered idly if it was Gregor's chair.

"Neeka," Matt soothed. "Do you know who did it? Who could've done it?"

"No, no, no," Neeka sobbed.

"Listen to me," Matt said a little more harshly, trying to snap her out of it. "Do you know who could've done it?"

"No," she repeated, wiping her face and straightening up a bit.

"Maybe somebody he's done a job with lately?"

"I ain't telling you nothing about what Gregor done."

"I'm not asking. He's gone, and I can't arrest him. But I think that Gregor would want you to help me find his killer. Don't you?"

"They ain't never gonna charge the man that done this."

"Why is that?"

"I don't have to talk to you. You ain't got no warrant. You get out."

"Neeka—"

"You got a warrant? You ain't got no warrant, you get out of my house. You get out!"

"All right," Matt said, throwing up his hands. "I'm going. And I really am sorry that your man is dead." He fished a business card out of his wallet and laid it on her coffee table. "If you change your mind about talking to me, you give me a call."

"You go fuck yourself," Neeka muttered.

Matt sighed and stepped outside, pausing for a moment to look around. He could see Lee's patrol car slowly winding its way down Copper Street. He watched as it turned and moved in the direction of Gold Street, thinking for a moment about Lee and his target for the night.

He had just opened the door to his car when Neeka stepped out.

"He's really dead?" she asked, quiet grief in her voice.

"Yeah. I'm afraid so."

"What did you say they did to him?"

"Wrapped his head with duct tape. They smothered him to death and put his body behind a strip mall just a few miles from here."

Neeka sniffed and took a deep breath. "I shouldn't have said what I said."

"What was that?"

"'Bout how you should, you know, go fuck yourself. I was raised better than that."

"You were upset, I get it." He paused. "What did you mean when you said the man who did it wouldn't get caught?"

"I told him," she said, wiping at her nose. "I told him that sonofabitch was no good. But he wouldn't listen. He was all like, 'Don't worry. I'll make a big score and we'll move to the beach.' Did you know he always wanted to go to Miami?"

"No. I didn't know that."

"We was gonna live right on the beach," she said, staring into the distance.

"Who is this other person we're talking about?" Matt asked.

She sniffed again. "No one."

She went back inside her trailer without another word, and he got into his car and drove away. The short interview had left Matt with more questions than he'd had when he'd arrived.

CHAPTER FOUR

Sunday, April 16, 2:30 p.m.

Inventing something to do, Sean drove to the muffler shop where Imogene Resnic's body had been discovered. ADAs rarely visited crime scenes, but this case was bothering him.

He didn't really think he would find anything the police hadn't already found. In fact, he didn't even intend to get out of his car. He just wanted a mental picture of the scene.

On that mild Sunday afternoon, the muffler shop was closed. Sean pulled into the short driveway and noticed immediately that this stretch of road was one of the few on the fringe of Atlanta that wasn't swamped with strip malls and housing developments. The muffler shop was next door to a defunct gas station, the whole setup remote and lonely. Sean sat for a few minutes, noticing there didn't seem to be any traffic going down the road.

It's the perfect place to meet someone you plan on killing, he thought. *You wouldn't have to worry about witnesses or the odd passerby. Any killer could feel pretty confident about not getting caught.*

But Tommy didn't need this setup. Tommy could have killed his mother in her own house.

With that in mind, he drove to Imogene Resnic's house, checking the address once to make sure of where he was going. The house was located on the edge of a township called Lawrenceville. Atlanta was full of these places: little towns that had once had their own character, their own charm, and then had been swallowed up whole by the sprawl of Atlanta. King's Way, where Imogene had lived, was a small subdivision filled with monotonous ranch-style houses. It wasn't hard to locate 1028 Dallas Way. It still had yellow police tape across the front door.

Sean stopped on the street, not wanting to pull into the driveway and attract too much attention. It was a typical street in a typical subdivision. Imogene's was the fifth house down the street from the corner. He could see the backyard, which had some large trees in it, and a lawn chair where Tommy must have been sitting when the cops came calling.

He checked his odometer. Twelve miles from the muffler shop.

Why?

Sean ran it through his mind: Tommy decides to kill his mother, so he lures her out to a closed muffler shop late one night. Why? If he wanted to kill her, why not do it right in her house? The body might not have been found for days. Leaving it at the muffler shop, though, ensured it would be found the next morning.

It just didn't add up.

Sean drove back to his apartment, mulling it over. He didn't normally get this involved in a case, at least not this early in the proceedings. It would be months before it came up for trial. But there was something bothering him about this case, something he just couldn't shake.

Why?

Sunday, April 16, 8:55 p.m.

Matt sat in the dark, balancing a glass on his ample stomach. It was a beautiful night. He had opened the windows and pushed the recliner back to almost full horizontal. The glass contained a healthy portion of Wild Turkey, but he hadn't touched it yet.

"Is there more to what you were telling me earlier?" Angela asked from the doorway.

"Just that."

"Oh, bull. I can see all the signs. Something's on your mind. Something big."

He pushed the recliner to the upright position and set his drink aside. "What signs?"

"You come home on a Sunday afternoon and don't spend any time in your rose bed. You play with your food at dinner. You pull out the bourbon, which you never touch unless you've got something heavy on your mind. Do I really need to go on?"

"Well," he said, "you sound like a trained investigator."

"And you're trying to get me off the point. You didn't answer my question."

"Just some random thoughts."

"Bull, Matt. Tell me."

"I'm worried," he admitted.

"What about?"

"I got assigned another case yesterday. Wasn't supposed to happen. They were supposed to have me off the roster for a while, but I got the call. There's this guy, his head wrapped in duct tape, looked like he'd been smothered to death. Hell of a way to go. Turns out he's Russian, maybe connected to the local mob, maybe not, but he's got a record. Armed robbery, stuff like that. Now he's dead. I have a nasty feeling about it. Then I've got the chief telling me there are rumors about Gannett cops taking money on the side, maybe even working with some Russian mafia types..."

He looked meaningfully at her.

"Oh, Matt," she said. "You're not suggesting..."

"Like I said, I got a bad feeling about it."

Monday, April 17, 6:30 a.m.

Sean woke up early and stared at the ceiling. For some reason, he was thinking about a blonde attorney with a messenger bag and a husky voice. Shaking off the image, he showered and got dressed and, even though it was a bit earlier than he normally left for work, decided he might as well head in.

Pouring himself a cup of coffee in the break room, he sat down for a few minutes to watch the morning news and chat with some of the other staff.

"I'm telling you," Eddie was saying to a table of DA investigators, "my goddamn jaw dropped to the floor."

"Well," Rick replied, "since you're all of three feet tall, that's not saying much."

Eddie ignored him. "It was like—" He fished for a word.

Rick turned to Sean. "Eddie's in love. Again."

"—a miracle," Eddie concluded. "This is beyond love," he corrected, catching the tail end of Rick's comment. "This is worship. This is…"

"A load of crap?" Tracy finished for him, looking up from her magazine. "A horny old cop lusting after an attractive woman? Any of this sounding familiar, Eddie?"

Eddie was hurt. "No, Tracy, this isn't simple lust."

"At your age," Rick cut in, "there's nothing simple about lust."

"This is like when somebody stands in front of a painting in a museum. That's what I'm talking about." Eddie's face was rapturous.

"Eddie," Tracy chuckled, "have you ever been in a museum?"

"This morning," Eddie said, staring into the distance, "I felt as though I was."

"What is he talking about?" Sean asked.

"Some new defense attorney," Rick explained. "She's a nice-looking kid, but to hear Eddie tell it, even her shit don't stink."

"You guys." Tracy shook her head. "I come in here to read my magazine, just to get a quiet moment, and all I hear about is shit and how big some woman's breasts are."

"They're not *that* big," Eddie said. "But they're…"

"Eddie, for God's sake," Rick said, "you get any more excited and I'm gonna have to move away from you."

"You wouldn't have to move very far," Tracy muttered.

"…and she had this smile," Eddie was saying, although no one appeared to be listening to him anymore.

Sean saw Tom Delaney walk by the door, on his way to Sean's office no doubt.

"Who's that?" Rick asked.

"Third-year," Sean explained. "He got assigned to me on Friday at maggot court. You know what they're like."

"Gonna have to beat all that law school stuff out of his head?"

"I wish it were that simple," Sean said. "He's got the bug bad. Wants to be a prosecutor when he grows up."

"Anybody tell him how much it pays?" Rick asked. "That'll kill that bug pronto."

"Say," Sean said, "I hear that you and Tracy were out on that Resnic thing last week. You helped Bernie find the suspect, right?"

Tracy scoffed. "Shit."

"Yeah," Rick said, glancing at her. "That's exactly what we did."

"I don't get it," Sean said.

"Bernie didn't do dick," Tracy growled.

"Weren't you just saying how we should watch our language in front of a lady?" Eddie cut in.

"Fuck that!" Tracy snapped. "Bernie couldn't find his own dick if he had three hands. *We* found the perp. Bernie shows up and then comes off like he did everything. Typical fucking man."

"Hey!" a couple of guys protested.

"Typical. Fucking. Man," Tracy repeated.

"She's right, though," Rick chimed in. "At least about Jersey. He horned right in, scooped up the perp, and we might as well have been trees. Tracy's the one who found the guy, all crying in his momma's backyard. I knocked on the front door; she went around back. Drew down on him and everything. Jesus, I've never been so proud."

"Hmmph," Tracy said, turning a page in her magazine.

"Did he say anything?" Sean asked.

"I Mirandized him while Annie Oakley here cuffed him," Rick explained. "He just kept crying and blubbering about his mother. Then Jersey showed up and asked us to canvass. We left the kid there with Jersey and did a house-to-house. We only got two houses down before Bernie called us back. But we'd already found the old lady by then anyhow."

"What old lady?"

"Uh, Jenkins. Right, Trace?"

"I don't know. You're the one who talked to her. Bernie was all, 'I'm gonna book this fucka,' and, 'This fucka's toast. Gawd, I'm gonna be famous.'"

Rick rolled his eyes. "Needs some work, Trace. He did say he was going to book Resnic. But he didn't say anything about wanting to be famous. And," he directed this to Tracy, "please God don't ever do that impression again."

"That's what he was thinking, though," Tracy disagreed. "And you know it. He wanted to be on the six o'clock news."

"He actually made it on the twelve o'clock," Sean mused.

Tracy glared at him. "Well, whoop-dee-fucking-do."

"Tracy's a little bitter," Rick confided. "He leave you crying at the altar, Trace?"

"He fucking wishes."

With a chuckle, Sean tilted up his mug to drain the last of his coffee. By the time he'd lowered it again, the puppy dog had found him.

Tom was bright-eyed and ready for action. "Where do we start?" he asked, settling across the table from Sean.

Sean stood up. "Paperwork. We start with paperwork."

"And you end with paperwork, too," Rick added as Sean and Tom left the room.

Just to give him something to do, Sean put Tom at a spare desk and had him pore over upcoming arraignment files.

"These cases are all scheduled for arraignment in a couple of weeks," Sean explained. "The arraignment is the first time the defendant hears what he's officially charged with."

"Didn't they hear that at the preliminary hearing?"

"No. Once we get the case, we can change the charges, add new ones, dismiss old ones." Sean cupped his hand and joked, "That is the awesome power of the State."

"You get to decide what to charge these people with?" Tom was clearly enchanted by the idea.

"Yes. The individual ADA makes the choice, but it has to be supported by the facts. We can even order additional investigation if we think it's warranted."

"ADA?" Tom asked.

Sean sighed. *Third-years, my God.* "Assistant District Attorney."

"Oh."

"I want you to go through these files—"

"—and come up with ideas of what to charge them with?"

"No. I want you to see if there's any *Brady* information in there."

Tom knew that much from law school. "*Brady,*" he parroted, "anything that is exculpatory or mitigates the defendant's guilt must be turned over to the defense."

"Very good," Sean said, picturing himself tossing the kid a cracker, "but I follow a more expansive rule. It's always better to give them too much than too little. So, I want you to go through these files and pull out anything that's even *helpful* to the defense. That way, we can't go wrong."

"O-*kay,*" Tom replied with obvious pleasure. "Do we get to go over to the jail later and interrogate some of these guys?"

"No," Sean said, slowly and deliberately. "Let's get this out of the way right now. We don't go to the jail. We *never* go to the jail. First of all, the jail is scary. There are guys over there who would beat the crap out of you if they got even half a chance. I don't want to get the shit kicked out of me, and I'm betting the same is true for you. Second, what do you or I know about interrogating anyone? Cops interrogate people. *They* are trained for it. We aren't.

"And finally, all other issues aside, let's suppose that we did talk with one of those guys. Ethics rules prevent us from speaking directly with anyone who is represented by counsel. But even more important, suppose that the guy we start asking questions of says something like, 'I killed him. I enjoyed it, and if the system sets me free, I'll kill again.' We'd be totally screwed. Why?"

Tom considered this for a moment.

"Because," Sean continued, filling the silence, "an attorney cannot be both a witness and an advocate in the same case. Suppose we get a serial killer who admits to offing someone. Now we're witnesses. I don't want to be a witness. A witness has to be sworn in and take the stand and get cross-examined. I don't want to be cross-examined. I want to *do* the cross-examining. Got it?"

"I wasn't suggesting—" Tom began, but Sean cut him off.

"Sure you were. You've seen it a thousand times on *Law & Order*, where the ADA is watching through a two-way mirror or negotiates a recommendation in the jail with some guy dressed in orange. You can't help it. Those shows have been on for years, and even when some part of your brain tells you that it probably isn't right, you still believe what you see. Well, welcome to the real world.

"Now, have you got the picture of what you're supposed to do with these files?"

"Anything even remotely helpful to the defense gets pulled out and served on them," Tom said, a little deflated.

"I'd give you a cookie, but I don't have any." Sean turned to walk away.

"You had me at hello," Tom called after him.

Sean turned back. "What?"

"I heard that you're really good with movie lines. Know that one?"

"*Jerry Maguire.* That wasn't even hard. And it's a completely useless ability." Sean rounded a corner and just about ran into a woman. "Excuse me," he said and stopped dead.

It was Diana Baker. Again.

"You should watch where you're going," she replied, stepping back.

"I really should," he agreed. "I've been meaning to work on it."

"I see you've met the newest member of the defense bar," Eddie said, walking up behind her.

"What?" It took Sean a minute to focus on anything but Diana.

"Diana Baker. I was talking about you earlier in the break room," Eddie added.

"I can just imagine," she sighed. "I'm in a bit of a hurry."

"But you haven't met one of our most distinguished ADAs," Eddie said, enjoying himself. "This is Sean Turlow."

"Yes, I know. We met at prelims on Friday," Diana informed him.

Eddie visibly deflated, clearly feeling cheated out of the opportunity to introduce the object of his lust to Sean.

"I've got a case on your arraignment calendar next week," she continued. "Do you have time to talk about it now?"

"Diana," Eddie began. "I thought you needed to talk to *me*."

"Sorry, Eddie. Do a girl a favor and hand me off to Mr. Turlow here? I'll make sure that he doesn't get lost."

She obviously knew the office policy: no unaccompanied defense attorneys in the hallways. Everyone who entered had to be escorted by DA staff.

"Okay," Sean agreed. "I'll take Ms. Baker."

He led her back to his office, and they sat down.

"I have to confess something," she began. "Although I really do have a case on your calendar next week, I mostly just wanted to get away from Eddie."

"He can be…" Sean began, searching for the right words.

"A bit of a perv? I've caught him checking out my chest about sixteen times, and I only got here ten minutes ago."

"Well, that's our Eddie. I'd apologize for him, but I think he should apologize for himself."

"The way he was looking at me, I kept expecting him to slide a dollar bill under my jacket."

"Well, since you are here, would you like to discuss the case?"

"Sure. My client's name is Alvin Woodard."

Sean turned for the case files, then remembered he'd left them with Tom. "I'll be right back," he said, sauntering out of the office. As soon as he was out of sight, he broke into a trot, practically ripped the file out of Tom's hands, and raced back to his office.

"Here we are," he said nonchalantly, trying not to breathe heavily. "Let's see. Looks like he got caught red-handed coming through the smashed window of a pawn shop. Had a pillowcase filled with jewelry, watches, and other stuff."

She shifted on her seat, and Sean couldn't help but watch. Diana had nice, athletic legs. Maybe she was a jogger. Her legs were tanned, but not too tanned. The kind of color you get just being outside. Maybe she liked to camp.

"He says he doesn't have any priors," she said, smoothing her skirt. "Is that what your file shows?"

"Prior conviction for narcotics, possession with intent to sell. Less than twenty-eight grams."

"Small time," she said, and Sean changed his position so that the file cut off his view of everything but her face. She was distracting, and he had a feeling she knew the effect she had on men. Although she was nice to look at, Sean didn't like the feeling that someone might be trying to manipulate him.

"True," he agreed, "small time."

"What's your recommendation?"

"Ten years, serve two in custody, $1,000 fine."

She paused and fixed him with a look. It was a good look—and it made him realize that she *absolutely* knew the effect she had on men.

"That's pretty steep," she protested. "Couldn't you just give him probation and send him on his way?"

Ice blue, Sean thought. That was the color of her eyes. Not pale blue or sky blue. Ice blue. *Bedroom eyes.* He'd always thought that was a stupid description, but Diana had changed his mind. She pushed a lock of blonde hair behind her ear in a gesture that made her even more attractive. He could picture her then, as a little girl, roaming through the woods in coveralls, catching toads and fireflies.

Jesus, Sean.

"I'm afraid that probation won't fly," he said aloud. "Have you been in front of Judge Vinhorten before?"

"Uh-uh."

"He wouldn't take anything any lower, even if I was inclined to reduce it."

"But you're not inclined to reduce it?"

"No," he answered without hesitation.

"Well," Diana said, standing up and reaching for her briefcase, "I don't think we have anything else to talk about."

"I guess not."

She swung her shoulders to get the briefcase strap in place. He liked the way she moved.

"I imagine," he began, not knowing exactly what he was going to say next, "that a lot of men ask you out."

She turned to look at him, her eyes flashing. "Not that often. A lot of men find women attorneys…intimidating."

"Well, I don't feel particularly intimidated," he blurted out, surprising himself. "We could meet for drinks…"

He was suddenly out of things to say.

She continued to stare at him, but he couldn't read her expression. "No, I don't think so."

Sean mentally kicked himself. *Smooth, real smooth. Duh, would you like to go out? Me like women. Me make fire.* He silently escorted her back to Eddie's office and handed her off. Eddie looked like Christmas had come early.

Diana looked at him again before he left, but Sean still couldn't read the expression or what was behind it. Did she despise him for being like every man she'd ever met? Did she find him attractive? Did she want to chew him out for mixing work and personal life? He just couldn't tell.

Stymied, he opted for a quick retreat. "Nice meeting you," he mumbled and headed back to his office, feeling like a moron.

◆

"I hear we're working together," Matt said, his sudden looming presence in the doorway pulling Sean out of his musings.

"Did you need to see me?" Sean asked. He'd been going over Tom's work on the arraignment cases.

"Yup."

"You wanna sit down?"

"Not particularly. We need to talk, and it's a pretty day. Why don't we do it outside?"

"Well, I'd love to have a picnic and all, maybe catch some rays, but I've got about a hundred cases to work on."

"Not anymore," Matt replied, and something in his voice made Sean pay more attention. "Resnic," Matt continued, looking around Sean's office, still not sitting, still taking up way too much real estate. Sean didn't like the intimidating effect Matt had on him.

"Resnic," Sean repeated.

"I thought we were going outside." It wasn't a question.

"What do you want, Matt?"

"You and I are going to be working together on the Resnic case." Matt was looking at one of Sean's prints, an Ansel Adams he'd picked up somewhere. "This is nice."

"So you've got the Resnic case. So what?"

"What do you think of it?" Matt asked, and for a moment Sean thought Matt was asking about the print.

"It's got some holes in it. I've been doing some digging, and I already don't like it."

"You don't beat around the bush," Matt said, now looking at the books on Sean's bookcase.

"There are several points that just don't add up," Sean explained.

"Let's go play detective," Matt suggested, straightening up. "How about a door-to-door in King Way's subdivision?"

"Why are we going to Lawrenceville?"

"And he already knows where the dead lady lives."

"I like to do a lot of my own legwork." Sean was feeling defensive and wasn't sure why.

"Yeah, I've heard that from other people." Matt finally turned back to Sean. "Well, then, this should be right up your alley. Let's do some legwork together."

Matt drove the two of them to King's Way subdivision and parked in Imogene Resnic's driveway. Sean moved to climb out, but Matt held up a hand.

"What?" Sean asked.

"You said you had problems with the case."

"I said there were holes," Sean corrected.

"And you want me to spoon-feed you the answers."

"Spoon-feed what answers, exactly? Do you know something I don't?"

"Probably a lot of things. Like how last Monday, your chief and my chief decided that the two of us would make a great partnership. My chief told me to meet with you and pin down the details in this case. Wrap it up in a bow and put it under the Christmas tree."

"What's this all about?" Sean asked, feeling uneasy. "This isn't normal procedure."

"See, not all cops like prosecutors. Did you know that?"

"Yeah. I know that."

"Some cops think you guys are all glory hounds. That you're weak. That all you think about is yourselves. You work nine to five, and nobody ever asks you to put your butt on the line. Nobody ever asks you to pull over some guy at two in the morning, and maybe he comes out of the car with a hand cannon and blows your brains out."

"But thank God you're above all of that," Sean said, voice rich with sarcasm.

Matt shrugged and looked out the window. "I've been checking up on you."

"Is that why it took you a week to tell me our bosses have decided to make us Butch Cassidy and the Sundance Kid?"

"They both died in the end."

Sean sighed. "Okay, moving right along. What is all of this about?"

Matt smiled and seemed to come to some internal decision. "You'll do." He shifted in his seat to open the door. "Let's go investigate a murder."

Once they were out, Matt paused. "You take that side of the street, I'll take this side."

"We're going to canvass the neighborhood? You and me?"

"Yup."

"Why not call out some patrol officers, too? It would take a lot less time."

"Yeah, but you wouldn't get that hands-on feel. I heard somewhere that you like to do your own legwork." Matt grinned.

"You hear a lot of things." Sean paused. "You kind of make it sound like that's a bad thing."

"No, not at all. Very commendable. We'll skip the next-door neighbor, Mrs. Jenkins, and do that one together at the end. Meet back here in forty-five minutes. If you get bogged down, call my cell. It's on this card.

"We'll want to know about anything unusual. Did Mrs. Resnic and her son have fights? Did they scream and yell at each other? Any other—"

"Matt," Sean cut in. "I get it. I have been doing this for a while. I've got a degree and everything."

Sean felt Matt's eyes follow him as he walked across the street. He couldn't help but feel as though Matt wasn't telling him everything, and that made him nervous.

◆

They reconvened in front of the Resnic house about an hour later.

"Anything?" Matt asked.

"I got four people who thought I was a Mormon," Sean reported, wiping at the sweat on his forehead. "One guy wanted me to stay and have tea and watch some movie with him, and there was a woman who swore the Resnics have been giving off 'negative energy' for years. All in all, a pretty productive afternoon. What about you?"

"Nothing. Nobody asked me to stay for tea, and nobody knew much about the Resnics."

"Well, time to tackle the next-door neighbor. How would you like to handle it?"

Matt turned to him. "How would *you* like to handle it?"

Sean thought for a moment. "I'd like you to ask the questions. You're better at it."

"Okay. Let's go."

When the old lady answered, she glared at them before shouting through the storm door. "You're cops, aren't you?"

Sean couldn't help but smile.

Matt stepped forward. "I'm Matt Burton," he said, giving her a reassuring smile. "I'm with the police." He tugged out his worn leather badge case, flipped it open, and pressed it against the door. "Can we ask you a couple of questions?"

"Your name sounds familiar," Mrs. Jenkins said. "It's about Imogene, isn't it? You better come in."

Sean noticed that her eyes were sunken and she had a strong, almost pointed nose. Her hair, although a youthful brown color, was very thin.

She colors her hair, Sean thought. For some reason, he found that touching.

He noticed, as she unlocked the door and motioned them in, that her hands were gnarled with arthritis. She was wearing a faded floral-print housecoat and slippers. The house felt about 90 degrees, and Sean wiped a bead of sweat from his forehead as they followed her to a side room filled with knick-knacks, most of them photos of children at various ages.

"This is quite a place you have here," Matt said. "Don't tell me these are all your children."

She beamed. "Yes. They're grown now, but I keep all of their pictures out. Over here, these are my grandchildren."

Matt put on thick-rimmed black glasses and stooped to look at them. "These are beautiful children."

Mrs. Jenkins went through their names, which Sean promptly forgot. But Matt seemed genuinely interested.

"Do you play?" Matt asked.

"Not anymore," Mrs. Jenkins answered, while Sean looked around to figure out what they were talking about. He realized after a moment that many of the photos were perched on an old upright piano.

She motioned for them to sit and then asked, "Would you like some lemonade?"

Sean was about to refuse, but Matt answered for them both. "Yes, we'd love some. Can I help?"

She waved him away and walked into the kitchen. The tray must have been ready, because she was back in seconds with a pitcher and three glasses. Big as he was, Matt was on his feet in a flash and helping her with the tray. He put it down on the ornate coffee table in front of the huge, floral sofa that he and Sean were sitting on. Mrs. Jenkins' hands were trembling as she poured. Sean thought of his own grandmother who'd lived in a house something like this in Boston. She'd been gone for ten years now.

"Poor Imogene," Mrs. Jenkins said as she sat down, primly repositioning her housecoat and eyeballing them, a shrewd look on her face.

Sean smiled at her, but she didn't smile back. He looked down and sipped his lemonade. He was surprised at how good it was.

"I always said that boy was no good," Mrs. Jenkins continued. "He grew up here, you know. Right on this street. He was a rotten young man. Always telling lies, getting into trouble. She said they'd confirmed it was someone else, but I never believed it. Who did you say you were again?" she asked, directing the question to Sean.

"I'm the prosecutor assigned to the Resnic case," Sean explained.

"Oh." She didn't seem to have any clear idea what that meant.

"I'll bet there's not a lot that goes on around here that you don't know about," Matt began.

"I keep my eyes open. I watched you two go up and down the street knocking on doors. I figured you'd end up here eventually.

"People in this neighborhood carry on just like hoodlums," Mrs. Jenkins continued, sighing. "Parties and carrying on and girls wearing hardly any clothes. Some of the young men are cute, though," she said with a wink.

Sean was beginning to like her.

"Did Tommy and his mother have a lot of fights?" Matt asked, taking out a small notebook. Sean hadn't thought to bring one.

"Fights? No, not really. She used to yell at him something awful when he was younger."

"Any arguments or anything like that lately?"

"No, they haven't fought too much lately. He doesn't come by as much as he used to, though. Would you like some more ice for your drink?"

"No, thank you, ma'am," Matt smiled. "You know it's my job to be nosy."

"A policeman has to ask questions," Mrs. Jenkins said knowingly. "My Earl always wanted to be a police officer."

"Was Earl your husband?"

"Yes. He had rickets, though, when he was a child. People don't get rickets anymore, but Earl had bandy legs. Always looked like he'd been riding a horse." She smiled. "That's what I used to say. Like you've been riding a horse for years. But they wouldn't take him on the force. Wouldn't take him in the military, either."

"What did he end up doing?" Matt asked, and Sean wondered what the hell difference it made.

"Gas company. He was a manager when he retired."

"Has anything out of the ordinary happened over at the Resnics' lately? Has Tommy come by at a strange time of night, or something like that?" Matt asked.

"No, I don't think so. I don't sleep very well, and I hear every noise on this street. But I don't remember anything like that. Are you going to put him in the chair?"

"I don't know. That's not really my decision. The District Attorney decides that."

"Isn't that *you*?" Mrs. Jenkins asked Sean.

"I'm an Assistant District Attorney," Sean explained. "The District Attorney is David Holloway. He makes that decision, not me."

She waved Sean away as though assistant whatevers didn't interest her. "I met him once. David Holloway. He shook my hand. It was some kind of fundraiser. God, it has to be twenty years ago. I hate it that he killed Imogene." She changed subjects with lightning speed, and Sean realized she was talking about Tommy. "But I wouldn't want him to go to the chair. I'm sure he didn't mean to do it. Maybe it was an impulse. He was a drinker, you know?"

"Yes, I'd heard something about that," Matt said. "Did he come by here a lot when he was drinking?"

"Sometimes. A lot more often when he was younger. We just didn't see very much of him in the last few years. I was happy about that. Of course, I'd never have told Imogene, but I didn't care for him. He was always talking big. You know the type? Always just about to get this big job. He was what my late husband called a bull—" she covered her mouth, "artist. I don't like to say that middle word."

"I understand," Matt assured her.

Mrs. Jenkins kept talking, and Sean's mind roamed. Maybe he should just head back to the office and let Matt handle this end of things.

"I guess that won't make much difference now," Mrs. Jenkins was saying.

"I'm sorry; what won't?" Sean asked, suddenly tuning back in.

Matt glanced at him, and Mrs. Jenkins gave him a withering glare.

"The burglary."

Sean was about to ask another question, but Matt shot him a warning look.

"That's one thing we were curious about," Matt said smoothly. "I don't have a lot of details on that."

"Detective, shouldn't you already know about this?"

"Well, there was a bit of a snafu," Matt began. "Paperwork getting misfiled. That sort of thing."

"Probably some new girl in the Records department," Mrs. Jenkins sighed. "This generation, I tell you. No attention to detail. No work ethic." She seemed to be talking about Sean, and he shifted a little uncomfortably.

"Why don't you tell me about the burglary?" Matt prompted.

"It happened about two or three days before Tommy killed Imogene," Mrs. Jenkins said. "I still have a hard time saying that. That she's gone. That he killed her. He took her money, you know."

"You seem pretty sure that Tommy was the burglar."

"She tried to tell me that it was somebody else, but I told her, 'Who else knows you have a safe? Who else knows the combination?' You know, they didn't jimmy it or anything. Somebody just went in, worked the knobby thing, and opened it right up. Who else? That's what I told her, and no matter what she said that night, I still think I was right."

"You say this was just a few days before she was, uh, before she died?" Matt asked.

"Yes, that's right. She was murdered on Sunday night, right? Well, the break-in was Wednesday or Thursday, the week before."

Matt was making notes. "Did he take anything else?"

"Well, he wouldn't need to."

"Why not?"

"After he got the money, he wouldn't need to."

"How much money are we talking about here?" Matt wanted to know.

"Shouldn't you already know all this?" she asked.

"Like I said, paperwork problems. How much did he take?" Matt persisted.

"He got away with something like twenty thousand."

"Twenty thousand dollars?"

Mrs. Jenkins sighed again. "I've been through this. I thought all of this stuff was cross-diddleyed in the computer, or something."

"This is the first I've heard of it, I'm afraid." Matt's face was grave.

"Yes. But Imogene outsmarted him."

"How did she do that?"

"She only put part of her money in the safe. She told me that. She told me she hid the other part of the money somewhere else. She never told me where. I told her it was a bad idea to keep that much money in the house, but Imogene had a thing about banks. You know how old people get some funny ideas."

"Uh-huh. Did Mrs. Resnic tell you about the break-in?"

"Naturally. I went over the next day to ask what all the fuss was about."

"Was she pretty upset?"

"No, not too much. I think she suspected Tommy even then."

"I see," Matt said, making more notes. "Is that why she didn't report it?"

"Didn't report what?"

"Report the burglary. Because she suspected her son?"

Mrs. Jenkins gave him a strange look. "If you're the detective, you should know all of this, shouldn't you?"

Matt sighed. "Well, Mrs. Jenkins, I couldn't have known about this. If she didn't file a report…"

"You could have done some more homework before coming out here," she admonished. "Why didn't you at least ask the officer who came out?"

"A police officer came out here on a burglary call?" Matt's surprise was evident.

"Well, yes. That's what I just said."

Matt excused himself, saying he'd be right back. Sean watched him walk to his car, pick up the radio, and start talking into it.

While they waited, Mrs. Jenkins stared at him.

Finally, just to have something to say, Sean asked, "Did you work with your husband at the gas company?"

"No."

Sean gulped lemonade. "This is delicious," he offered, praying for Matt to get back soon.

Matt knocked again before coming in and sitting down on the sofa. "I understand that no burglary report was filed," he announced.

"Well, you understand wrong," Mrs. Jenkins argued. "The officer did a complete workup. Came back a couple more times. He sat right there, drinking lemonade. He was thorough. He knew how to do a proper investigation."

"Mrs. Jenkins," Sean cut in, "Are you saying a police officer came out here several times *before* the murder?"

"Well, of course he did. I told you the burglary happened before she was killed."

Sean thought for a moment. "You don't happen to remember the officer's name, do you?"

"No, I don't," she said, standing up. "I don't like to be critical, gentlemen, but I really think you could have looked all this up yourself."

They got the hint and stood up, too. "Thank you for your time," Matt said. "You've been very helpful."

◆

Sean waited until they were settled in the car and Matt had started driving. "Okay, Matt, what the hell is going on?"

"What are you talking about?"

"C'mon, Matt."

"So the son broke into his mother's house a few days before he killed her. Seems like a perfect motive to me. What's the best way to keep someone from testifying?"

Sean ignored the question. "I've had a bad feeling about this case for days, ever since I saw that first report on the news. Then Bernie makes an arrest in about an hour. The regular follow-up isn't done. Then you get assigned to the case and Bernie gets taken off of it. Now I find out that there was a call about a break-in a couple of days before Mrs. Resnic was killed. Apparently, the police officer who got called out for that burglary did an extensive follow-up. Hell, he even came out a few times. A *few times!* I haven't seen a report on it; it's not in the file. Who was this cop? And where the hell is his report?"

Matt sighed. "There isn't any report."

"What do you mean?"

"The original call was a 10-24. At least, that's how it's listed in the log."

"What's a 10-24?"

"Assignment complete. No report necessary."

"Yet we have an officer who came out several times and did some follow-up? With no report? Nothing?"

"That's right."

"Do we know who the original officer was? The one who got called out the first time?"

"Yup," Matt said. "That's part of what I was checking on. The officer was Chris Franklin."

"Well, I think we need to talk to him right away."

"Yup." Matt picked up his radio again to call Dispatch. "I'll see if he's on duty and have him meet us at headquarters."

Sean settled back in his seat. Something else was nagging at him, but he couldn't put his finger on it. Something Mrs. Jenkins had said... He tried to remember, but it slipped away. Instead, a different thought popped into his head.

"Uniformed officers aren't authorized to do follow-up investigations."

"Is that a question?" Matt wondered.

"They're not, and we both know it. If Chris did his own investigation, that would be...unusual."

Matt shrugged. "It would be unauthorized and could get him suspended or even fired."

"Well now I'm really curious to hear what he has to say."

"This may not be as straightforward as you'd like," Matt warned.

"Another 'unusual' feature to this case? You know, I'm starting to think you know more than you're telling me. I don't suppose you'd like to give me a clue?"

"This is one of those things you'll have to evaluate yourself."

"How wonderfully helpful."

When it became obvious that Matt wasn't going to say any more, Sean settled into his seat, trying to decide if there was a single thing he liked about this case. After several minutes, he still couldn't think of one.

♦ CHAPTER FIVE ♦

Monday, April 17, 2:30 p.m.

He stood on the edge of the schoolyard, waiting for the bell. He loved to be here when school got out. Elementary school kids were so sweet and innocent. Not like those monsters in high school. By then they were all little pricks. He had no use for them. But here, with these children, he could have an impact. They would see him standing there when they came out, and they would feel safe. He would protect them. The boys and, especially, the girls were in awe of his uniform. They liked to peek at him, steal covert looks at his pistol. He towered over them like a god. Once, a little boy had walked up to him and asked if he'd ever killed anyone. *No,* he'd answered, *but I could.*

That had sunk in. He'd seen it register in the little boy's eyes. The awe. The worship. He'd heard the boy when he ran back to his friends: *He can kill people!* They'd all looked at him then, standing like a tree over them, strength and power and…death. No drug could come close to that feeling; no other moment in his life meant as much to him as when he got that look from the kids as they left school.

The bell rang and he could hear them, their little feet scrambling over the linoleum as they moved toward the exit doors. A finger of pleasure scratched across his lower abdomen when the doors opened and his flock came pouring out.

Look at them, he thought. *Look at them. They're beautiful.*

Monday, April 17, 3:00 p.m.

Sean and Matt drove over to Gannett Police Department headquarters. Matt was greeted warmly as they walked through the halls, but Sean got a cooler reception. It was always like this. At first he'd thought it was just him, but then he'd been here with other ADAs and noticed the same reaction. When he'd first become a prosecutor, fresh out of law school, he'd had a simplistic idea of police and prosecutors. He'd figured they'd all get along great because they were on the same side. But that wasn't true. The real world was more nuanced. Just as Matt had said earlier, there were some police officers who actively disliked prosecutors. They worked with them, sure, but that didn't mean they had to like them. Police officers often saw themselves as doing the real work while the prosecutors got the glory, probably in part because DA prosecutors received badges—even though they didn't have the power to arrest or detain anyone. But having them seemed to inflate quite a few prosecutorial heads.

Prosecutors had mixed feelings about police officers, too, and that contributed to the complexities of the relationship. Most prosecutors had never worked in any form of law enforcement and had only vague notions of what it involved. Law school didn't help. Professors routinely discussed draconian police procedures and often portrayed cops as power-mad, muscle-bound oafs who thought the Constitution got in the way of good police work. There were no courses in law school that actually discussed evidence-gathering techniques, crime scene investigation, interrogation, or anything other than the most rudimentary of police work. As a result, when a new graduate went to work at the DA's office, there was a gulf of ignorance that often took a year or two to bridge. By the time that bridge was built, the new lawyer would have made more than a few mistakes and several enemies on the force.

Then there were some who made it even worse by overcompensating with arrogance for their lack of knowledge. They seemed to think the police worked for them, even though they had no power to order officers around. Cops were only too happy to straighten those types out in a hurry. Fortunately, Sean had never made *that* mistake.

Once he and Matt had found their way back to Matt's office in CAP, Sean took a seat without being asked and waited while Matt listened to his messages.

"Nothing from Chris on my voice mail," Matt reported after a minute. "I asked Katie to give him a call. But so far, nothing."

"Katie Burnett? What does Standards and Practices have to do with this?"

"Nothing," Matt answered. "She transferred out of S&P last week and was assigned to CAP a couple days ago."

Matt got up and retrieved the duty roster from a clipboard hanging above the coffee station. He riffled through a few pages and then checked his watch. "Well, it looks like Chris is just coming off duty. Maybe we can catch him in the duty room."

Matt's phone rang, and he moved back to his office to answer it just as Katie walked up and said hello.

"Hey, Katie," Sean greeted her. "Do you know Chris Franklin?"

"Sure."

"Let's go down to the duty room and see if we can find him. I need to ask him some questions."

"Okay."

Sean waved to Matt to indicate where he was going, and Matt gave him a thumbs-up in reply before returning his focus to his conversation.

The duty room was just off the locker rooms and had ten or fifteen cafeteria-style tables, a smallish counter for coffee, and a couple of vending machines. A lot of uniformed officers were milling around. Some of them were seated at the tables, writing up police reports about incidents that had occurred earlier in their shifts. Others were horsing around, telling jokes, occasionally whacking each other on the ass, and generally acting as if they were a football team getting ready for the first quarter. One of the officers was pulling apart her report and dropping a copy into a wire basket marked *Watch Commander*.

There was a sudden chill when Katie walked in. Although she was well-liked, she'd spent over a year in Standards and Practices and had investigated officers. Despite the name change from Internal Affairs, the taint of the assignment remained. To many of the officers in the room, she was the enemy, a cop who preyed on other cops instead of the criminal world. During her tenure in S&P, some officers had been disciplined, one had been fired, and more than a few had been suspended. As Sean looked around the room, he realized that some of those officers were probably standing right there. Katie shrugged it off with her usual confidence and asked in a loud voice, "Anybody seen Chris Franklin?"

No one answered.

"He just came off," Katie continued. "Where is he?"

Someone muttered something, and Sean couldn't make out the words. But he got the tone just fine. It hadn't been pleasant.

"Wanna step forward and say that?" Katie demanded.

Silence.

"Bunch of pussies," Katie snapped, then turned on her heel and stalked out, Sean a few paces behind her. Sean heard more muttering once they were in the hallway.

"They'll hide behind each other and whisper shit," Katie fumed, "but won't step out like men." They headed farther down the hall, and she sighed. "That's the kind of shit you get when you work S&P." She dropped her voice a little and added, "That's why I'm glad I'm out of it. Too much shit."

◆

Sean followed Katie back to Matt's office and explained what had happened. Matt got up to go to the duty room himself, but Katie put up a hand. "He's gone by now, Matt."

"Yeah, but those guys need to hear a thing or two," Matt protested.

"I don't need you protecting lil' ol' me. I can stand up for myself."

"That's not the point."

"Sure it is. But thanks for being willing to do it." She smiled again and was gone.

"She's a good cop," Matt mused, still standing in his office doorway.

"I thought of something when I was in the duty room," Sean said. "If Records doesn't have any reports on the Resnic burglary, wouldn't Chris? I noticed those guys were making duplicates. I know one goes to Records, one to the watch commander, and don't cops keep their own copy, too?"

"Yeah, he should have one. If he visited several times, he should have a report for every time he went. But that's 'should have,' and we're dealing with a situation where the gap between 'should have' and reality is getting bigger by the minute."

"Speaking of which," Sean said as Matt moved back around his desk and sat down, "why *isn't* there a report on the burglary?"

"Right now, I've got to assume Chris didn't file one. He called it in as a 10-24, and you don't normally file reports on those—but then we've got him going back. That's not standard procedure in a normal case, let alone a 10-24. He should have turned it over to the watch commander; patrol cops don't investigate burglaries.

"Plus, we've got that rule that they have to finish up all reports before they leave the building, no matter how many calls they've been out on. That's why they usually sit in the duty room and work them up. On a call like this, the officer gets dispatched, does a preliminary look-over at the scene, and radios back. If it's an F&F, he'll have to write up a report when he comes off duty."

"F&F?" Sean asked.

"File and follow-up," Matt explained. "It means that further investigation is required. The officer will work up the report, forward it to Criminal Investigative Division, and they'll decide who it should get assigned to. With burglaries, it would go to Property Crimes, no question."

"And Property Crimes has no such record?"

"I just spoke with Art Swinson. There's no Resnic, no burglary in King's Way, not even a burglary call near that part of the county that day. I also checked the Dispatch records. There is a call for the Resnic house on the right day and time, but it's written up as a 10-24."

"But we know Chris Franklin went out there several times."

"We know *someone* went out there several times. We don't have a solid ID on Chris."

"Is he a friend of yours?" Sean asked.

Matt looked at him. "As a matter of fact, he is."

Sean didn't say anything.

"Some of us go hunting every year," Matt elaborated. "Chris. Jimmy

Bennett. Lee Church. Sometimes Steve Morningside."

"Is that going to be a problem for you?"

"What kind of question is that?" Matt's voice was low and dangerous.

"I'm just—"

"You need to button that up," Matt snapped. "I go where the case takes me."

Sean didn't reply.

"Chris will be home tonight. If I have to, I'll stop by his house. I'll fill you in tomorrow on what I get from him."

"Okay. Guess I'm heading back to the office, then. Here's my cell number and my home number." Sean pushed one of his business cards across the desk. Matt didn't pick it up.

"Goodnight, Matt."

"Goodnight, Counselor."

◆

When he returned to the office, Sean decided it was time to have a chat with his boss. Chief ADA Bill Shepherd was ex-military—but while he may have left the military, the military had never left him. He intimidated the hell out of Sean, especially since Sean knew full well that Shepherd didn't like him, so when Tom appeared out of nowhere and trailed after him as he headed for Shepherd's office, Sean didn't protest. It might be a good idea to have a witness for this particular encounter.

After introducing Tom, Sean sat across from Shepherd and dived into the Resnic case. When Sean got to the point about the missing police report, Shepherd suggested that Tom go check in with his law school advisor. "Find out from him when you can start trying cases. It was nice meeting you."

As Tom left, Shepherd closed the door behind him. "What the hell do you mean bringing a third-year in to hear this?" he snapped at Sean.

"What do you mean?"

"You know exactly what I mean."

"No, Chief, I don't."

Shepherd adjusted his thick black glasses and remained standing. "Who's the officer?"

"Chris Franklin. Am I missing something here, Bill?"

"You telling me you honestly don't know? Jesus," Shepherd said, sitting down and tapping his fingers, "you really are out of the loop, aren't you?"

"I guess so. What's going on?" Sean had a sinking feeling in his stomach that things were about to get even *more* complicated.

Shepherd sighed and took off his glasses to clean them with his tie. His eyes looked somehow naked without them.

"Chris got into trouble last month. He was getting a little too friendly with a family over in Snellville. They have a girl in the fourth grade. He let her play with his service weapon while he was over visiting. The girl told her teacher about it and, well, the shit hit the fan."

"I don't see the connection," Sean said.

"You are so right, you don't," Shepherd shot back, leaning away from his desk. "After you dicked around at HQ this afternoon, with you and Katie calling Chris out in front of the whole damn squad, I got a call. Somebody told me you were looking to hang more trumped-up charges on Chris."

Sean was dumbfounded. "Why—"

"The PD doesn't like it when some loose cannon tries to kick a man while he's down."

"Goddamn!" Sean exclaimed. "What the hell do they think I'm trying to do here?"

"I'm not sure they've thought it through that far. They just made sure they got me on the line and let me know I had a loose cannon in my office."

"I'm not a loose cannon," Sean protested.

"You just better watch your step, buck-o. Everything you ever heard about how cops look out for one another is true, in spades."

Sean digested this for a moment. "So, what do I do?"

"What would have been your next step, after coming to talk it over with me?" Shepherd wanted to know.

"I would have called Chris in to talk with him and find out what happened to the burglary report."

Shepherd resumed tapping his fingers. "Then do it. But I want someone from the PD with you. Matt's working this too, right? Take him along."

"About that, Bill. Why am I assigned to work with Matt, especially this early in the case? Normally—"

"Don't talk to me about 'normal.' We've got allegations against a cop, and there's nothing normal about that. Now we've got even more pressure, thanks to you, against the same cop. I need you and Matt to wrap this up and put it to bed. No press. No zoo. Just a straight-up investigation. Can you do that?"

Without waiting for an answer, Shepherd continued. "The two of you find a quiet place and ask him about this burglary screwup. Nothing official. Just a chat. You got it?"

Shepherd waited for Sean's nod before continuing. "But you be careful. That's why Matt is in on the deal. I want you working with him on everything you do on the Resnic case from here on out. I don't want some reporter jumping all over this and claiming that we're hiding evidence in a murder case or, worse, that we're too incompetent to keep track of police reports. You find anything else out of the ordinary, you come to me. I don't want anything going into the file until I've had a chance to look it over."

"Okay, Bill."

"And don't go wasting a couple of weeks on what's obviously a cut-and-dried murder case, got it? Last time I looked, you had a backlog of over fifty cases. This is a pissant, open-and-shut case with one little hinky detail. Iron it out, and move on."

Shepherd pulled a file out of the stack on his desk and opened it without looking up. Sean knew he was dismissed and walked quietly out of the room.

◆

It was after five o'clock when Sean made it back to his office. Just about everyone had left for the day, including Tom. Sean sat behind his desk and loosened his tie. Jesus, it had been a long day.

He pulled out his Officer Precinct Directory and looked up Matt's home number. He didn't get an answer but left a message. Next, he looked up Chris' home number. He dialed and got the answering machine. He left a quick message, asking Chris to call him as soon as possible.

Then he sat for a while, thinking. This whole thing was so messed up…

"Screw it," he said aloud. There was someone he knew could help. He got up, collected his belongings, and hurried down the hallway, hoping against hope she was still there.

He sighed with relief when he saw her light on. "Got a minute?" he asked from Debbie Blum's office doorway.

She leaned back and looked up at him. "Always," she replied, extending her arm to offer him a seat. She watched him appraisingly as he sat down. Debbie had been a trial attorney when Sean had started, but now she worked in the Appellate Division, handling appeals generated by convictions. He always got the impression that she could see more than most people. That plus the fact that she'd mentored him when he was first hired meant he often got advice from her. She was tough but fair, and he had a lot of respect for her.

"The student returns to the master," she joked.

"I was going to say that I'm not a student anymore, but that's not really true. I need some advice," Sean began.

"So you came to the woman who pulled you out of the gutter, cleaned you up, and turned you into the prosecutor you are today."

"Let's not get carried away here. I was green, but—"

"No, no," she said, holding up her hand. "'Green' doesn't cover it. Neon. You were visible from space."

"Anyway…"

"Diana Baker. Is that what this is about?"

That one caught him completely off guard.

"What? Huh? No!"

"If the advice you're seeking is, 'Should I ask Diana Baker out on a date?' then the answer is yes, you should."

For a moment, Sean couldn't think of anything to say. "How in the hell...?"

"I've got my ways," Debbie smiled.

"I just met her," he began.

"You know her father was a bad alcoholic," she cut across him.

"What? How do you... What does that have to do with anything?"

"She did track and field in college, and judo. That's my favorite part. Judo. Can you imagine? Hi-yah!" Debbie sliced the air with her hand.

"First of all, I don't think they do that in judo. And second, what are you, like, a human Google? Wait, *did* you Google her?" Sean raised his eyebrows.

Debbie feigned offense. "Please. Google is for weak minds. I have other methods."

"Well, as much as I hate to ruin your day, I'm not here to talk about my love life."

"The Resnic case, then?"

"Jesus, how do you do that?"

"I hear things."

"You hear a friggin' lot of things."

Sean sat back in his chair and felt a little stunned. He should have known, of course. That was part of the reason he was here. Debbie had a way about her. It wasn't just that she heard things, but she could put things together and always had good advice. Sean had few illusions about his brothers and sisters in the bar. Most were long on book smarts but came up short on basic human understanding. Long on arrogance, short on humility. But Debbie was another story.

"Do you remember the first things I taught you?" she asked.

"How to walk?"

"I'm not that old. The first things. Remember?"

"Stick to the truth. No matter what. Never sacrifice your good name for a case."

"And?"

"We're here to do justice, not get convictions."

She smiled. "Like the son I never had. Okay, so what do you need help with that those gems can't answer?"

Sean told her about the Resnic case and the problems he was having with the evidence, and then about Chris Franklin. That was where she stopped him.

"Shepherd said Chris was just spending too much *time* with a little girl?" she scoffed. "Sean, he wasn't just hanging out at her house. There are allegations of child abuse, sexual contact. He's in deep shit."

Sean sat back, aghast. "I didn't know that. Bill didn't say anything about that."

"Color me shocked. Okay, go on."

He explained about visiting the neighborhood and talking with Mrs. Jenkins, and how no report had been filed. Then he told her about the meeting he'd just had with Shepherd.

When he finished, Debbie sighed and leaned back. After a moment's thought, she announced, "It's a screw job."

"What?"

"Classic Bill Shepherd screw job. You know he hates your guts, right?"

"Well, I know he's not overly fond…wait a minute, 'screw job'?"

"Man, how do you get through the day with your eyes shut that tight?"

"I don't get it," Sean confessed.

Debbie leaned forward again, all trace of levity gone. "Sean, you've got to listen to me. You need to be careful. I can't see all of the pieces here, but I don't like the ones I can. It looks like Shepherd is setting up a fall guy in case this goes to hell. Any guesses who that guy might be?"

"*Me?*"

"And he sees the light." She thought for another moment. "Okay, let's get back to basics. All of this is *Brady*, and it should go into the file and be served on the defense counsel. Have you asked her out?"

Sean felt whiplash from the sudden change in topics. "Whoa, slow down. I know it's *Brady*. And I did ask, nosy parker, and she turned me down."

"You don't waste any time. Ask her out again. She'll say yes the second time."

Sean felt the room spinning. They were talking about too many things at once. He took a deep breath to steady himself. "She will?"

"She will. And hand-deliver this stuff to Resnic's attorney. Not you, obviously. Use one of our people, and have them certify the delivery. You'll get pressure from Shepherd to hold off. He'll probably use the old 'wait until it's ten days prior to trial before serving' crap, but serve it ASAP anyway."

"How do you know all of this? For instance, why do you say it's a screw job? Does Shepherd really hate me that much? What have I done to him?"

"Beats me," she said, throwing up her hands. "He just does. He thinks you want to be chief ADA one day, and that makes you competition."

"I would never want that job," Sean protested. "Not in a million—"

"Yes, yes, *I* know that. But he doesn't. So, first thing, *Brady*. Second thing, protect your ass. Shepherd sees a way of killing two birds with one stone, and he's going to throw that stone."

"What are the birds?"

"Getting rid of you and burying the rumors about police corruption."

"Police corruption? What the hell are you talking about? I thought this was about Chris Franklin."

Debbie sighed. "I was going to say, 'You must have heard the rumors,' but then I remembered who I was talking to. Of course you haven't heard the rumors. You never hear anything."

"There are rumors about police corruption?"

"Oh, trust me; they're a lot more substantial than rumors. That's why Katie Burnett got bumped out of S&P. She was too good at her job. Standards and Practices has been working overtime on several cases, and the word is that Chief Black doesn't like what they've found, so he's reassigned the officers who work there.

"Not just Katie, in fact, but Dave Cheek and Danny Rivers also got moved. They're calling it a 'lateral transfer' or some crap like that, but basically it's cleaning house."

"But that's everyone who worked there. The whole team."

"By this time next week, there'll be a whole new crew in there, handpicked by the chief, and I'm sure they'll have been given the right 'instructions' about what cases to focus on."

"Do you keep bourbon in your desk?" Sean asked.

"No, of course not. Nobody does. Why? Do you need a shot?"

"Maybe I need a new career. Why haven't I seen any of this?"

"Because you're a good prosecutor who does his job, doesn't have any ambitions, and tries to be a nice guy. That's going to cost you in the end, you know."

"Doing the right thing? I thought you said we're supposed to do the right thing."

"No, I said that your reputation is more important than winning a case. No, what's going to cost you is the 'good guy' thing. A lot of people see you as a pushover because you're nice. You may not be able to come through this Resnic business by being the nice guy. You may have to play it mean. Ethically, but mean."

"Jeez, I'm glad I stopped by. You really know how to brighten a guy's day." Sean thought for a moment. "But what has this got to do with the Resnic case?"

"I like you, Sean, but you're a little slow sometimes. Chris' involvement is part of the reason, but the real issue is that, on the night the Resnic woman was killed, someone saw a police car at the muffler shop."

"What?! Nobody has told me anything about that!"

"I didn't think so. Do you know the old line about going to a poker game, and if you can't figure out who the mark is, then you're the mark?"

"Yeah." He waited, then understood. "Oh."

"Now, I know you're working with Matt Burton on this, and he's always been a straight shooter. That means that either he doesn't know, or…"

"Or?"

"Or he's been told to keep it quiet. Maybe *he* decided to keep it quiet."

"Why would he do that?"

She looked at him. "You know they're friends, Chris and Matt."

"I've already gone over this with Matt. He said it wouldn't be a problem."

"Suppose you dig up something in this case that embarrasses the police department? They could handle it one of two ways: They could call a press conference, admit to everything, come clean with the public, and say they're really, really sorry and it will never happen again—even though the mayor is coming up for election this year and he pushed through the appointment of Rick Black—but what the hell, the voters will understand. Or they could go for what's behind door number two."

"Which is?"

"Blame an out-of-control, press-hungry prosecutor willing to crucify an honest police officer to further his career."

"Loose cannon," Sean muttered.

"What?"

"That's what Shepherd just called me. A 'loose cannon.'"

"There you go," Debbie concluded. "Classic, dyed-in-the-wool Bill Shepherd screw job."

"And all of this is because I'm trying to do the right thing."

"That," Debbie nodded, "is what makes you dangerous."

◆

Usually he left Debbie's office feeling better, or at least better informed, but not today. Now Sean felt like a hundred-pound weight had been hung around his neck. He wasn't sure what to do. He walked out to the employee parking lot, unlocked his car, and sat in it for a long time before he turned it on and drove home.

Monday, April 17, 7:15 p.m.

He crept up to the little cabin quietly. Everything was still; he had no reason for apprehension, but he stood in the shadows for a while anyway, smelling the breeze, listening, *feeling*. The early evening was quiet around him. The day had been pleasantly warm, not hot, and so the evening breeze that moved across him was cool. He saw her car parked just beyond the cabin, in almost the exact spot Gregor had parked a few nights prior.

He could feel a frisson of pleasure move through him. She would be waiting inside for him. *Hungry*. She was always hungry for him.

The thought of what was about to happen filled him with longing, a palpable ache, but he still didn't move. He thought of himself as a jungle cat, stalking the shadows. He would devour her tonight, the way he so often did. Her luscious body—big, full breasts, wonderful flat stomach, milky thighs. He would feast on her tonight.

As he walked up the same steps where he had killed Gregor, he toyed with a few other options. Putting the gun to her head, pulling the trigger?

No, not yet. Maybe not ever. He hoped not. But his hand had already found the butt of the automatic. He *could* do it. That was important. He could pull the trigger on his love, his little sex feast. For a moment, just a tantalizing moment, he wondered what her expression would be when he brought the barrel of the gun up and pressed it against her temple—no, her throat. Right under her chin. He would want to look into her eyes; he owed her that. Would she welcome the bullet? Strange thought. She had done everything he had ever asked of her. Would she also submit to his gun as a final act of obedience?

He had already circled the cabin once, sniffing the breeze, but he still waited before climbing the steps.

This is what Gregor should have done, he thought. *He should have stopped and smelled the trap.*

His sense of smell had always been extraordinary, but his other senses were sharpened now. The armored car robbery had flipped some switch in him, and killing the old lady had laid bare a whole new area of his soul he hadn't known existed. He was at a new edge of awareness. There was fear there, too, but the fear only sharpened everything, stripped away the bullshit. He felt afraid and powerful at the same time, and it was a heady combination.

It took another two minutes of absolute stillness before he knew, absolutely *knew*, he was clear. As soundless as a leopard, he took the steps to the front porch. She didn't even hear him open the screen door. He stepped into the room and watched her. She was sitting in a small chair near the big bed, wearing the slinky negligee she knew he liked. He could smell the tension in her, see the tautness of her muscles, feel her ache.

When she looked up and saw him standing there, framed in the doorway, she let out a low moan. He smiled. She moved to get up, but he motioned for her to stay still. He took off his belt and laid down his holster and cuffs. Watching her, he unbuttoned his shirt and pulled it off. She sat, mesmerized, as he ripped the Velcro straps from his bulletproof vest and let it fall. Next, he removed his T-shirt to let her see his muscles. She moaned and again tried to get out of the chair, to rush toward him, but he stopped her with a motion. He slipped out of his shoes and then unzipped his pants, stripping for her, flexing his muscles for her, watching the need grow in her eyes, feeling her desire and letting it feed his own.

She gasped when she saw his erection and squirmed in the seat as if she couldn't take it anymore.

Oh, yes, he thought. *Tonight, I am going to feast.*

CHAPTER SIX

Tuesday, April 18, 9:00 a.m.

Sean was standing, sipping some coffee, and looking out his office window at the front parking lot when someone knocked on his door. He turned to see Matt filling the doorframe.

"So, what's on tap for Butch Cassidy and the Sundance Kid today?"

"Probably covering somebody's ass," Sean replied. Jesus, Matt really was intimidating. The man was large, but that wasn't it. It was something in his manner, in his eyes.

Sean remembered the first time he'd run into the famous Matt Burton. He'd only been with the DA's office for a couple of weeks. As they did with most newbies, they'd put him to work in the grand jury, figuring he couldn't possibly screw that up since the grand jury's only function was to decide if there was enough evidence in a case for charges to be brought; they didn't vote on guilt or innocence. Sean's job at the time was to call police officers to the stand in the grand jury room, swear them in, and ask them some questions about the case to establish probable cause for the jurors. If they thought there was enough evidence, they would vote *true bill*; if they didn't, they would vote *no bill*. Sean had quickly realized the grand jurors voted true bill on almost everything. In fact, in the two weeks he'd been there, there hadn't been a single no bill vote.

Then one day Matt had been the police officer assigned to his case. He'd already heard about the legendary detective and had sidled up to Matt to ask some quick questions about the case before they began. Matt's response had stuck with him over the years.

"Did you read the police report?"

"Uh, yes," Sean had stuttered. "Yes, of course."

"Then you know everything you need to about the case. All you have to do is swear me in and let me do my job, okay?"

And that was exactly what Sean had done. Matt had taken over, given about five minutes' worth of testimony, and Sean had asked the assembled group if they had any questions. They didn't. Both he and Matt had left the room, because the grand jury always voted in secret, and they'd waited outside until the blue light above the door came on, signaling that the jurors were done.

True bill.

Sean hadn't had much contact with Matt since then, but he'd never forgotten that first meeting and the power and confidence Matt had exuded.

"I think we need to talk to your hunting buddy. He didn't return my call yesterday," Sean said, watching Matt closely for a reaction.

"Stop right there," Matt ordered. "We went through this yesterday. He may be my friend; he may be my biggest enemy. Doesn't matter. I go where the case takes me. The truth is that what we have so far doesn't necessarily add up to anything. He gets a call and for some reason decides to do a little detective work on his own. Maybe he's thinking that if he breaks a burglary case on his own it'll mean a promotion. Could be as simple as that."

Sean sighed. "And maybe not. Let's take a step back. Chris gets called out on a burglary. The perp is almost certainly the victim's own son. Chris does an unauthorized follow-up investigation in clear violation of established procedure. Then, a few nights later, somebody—again probably her son—blows the victim's brains out. A defense attorney looking into this is going to wonder about the burglary report and can poke a lot of holes in our case with that. I don't know if it would be enough to establish reasonable doubt and get a not-guilty verdict, but it's certainly something we have to consider.

"In any case, it's a loose end," Sean continued, "and something I'll have to hand over to the defense whether I like it or not. And, just in case anybody cares, I *don't* happen to like it. At best—*at best*—it looks like sloppy police work. At worst…well, you tell me."

"Tell you what?"

"You know where I'm going."

"No, I'm a bit slow. I don't have a law degree. Why don't you tell me where you're going?"

"Maybe you want to tell me about another investigation your friend Chris has hanging over his head? Something to do with a little girl in Snellville? Funny how you didn't mention that."

Matt's face was grim. "So, you've got the coffin built and the nails all ready to go."

"No, I don't. But you've got to admit that it calls some things into question."

Matt sat for a long moment, just staring at Sean.

Thousand-yard stare, Sean thought. *So that's what that looks like.* His throat felt dry, but somehow taking a sip of coffee felt like showing weakness in that moment.

"Well," Matt finally said. "You don't pull any punches, do you?" He eased back in the chair. "Let's give Chris a call right now and find out what happened."

The unwritten rule was that you always tried to reach a police officer through official channels first. You called his desk if he was a detective; you called his watch commander if he was a patrol officer. But after the chewing-out he'd received when he'd looked for Chris at the station, Sean felt that calling Chris on his cell this time was the better way to go. He dialed the number.

"Hello?" a voice answered, sounding a little wary.

"Is this Chris Franklin?"

"Yeah. Who's this?"

"Sean Turlow. I don't think we've met. I'm with the DA's office. Can you come in to talk with me today?"

"What about?"

Sean hesitated. "I'd rather not discuss it on the phone. Are you on duty this morning?"

"I'm out on patrol, but I get off at three."

"Why don't you stop by and see me then?"

"Okay," came the reluctant reply.

♦

By half past three, Sean and Matt realized Chris wasn't coming.

They'd been sitting in Sean's office since a quarter till, both of them drinking coffee and not saying much. Now, Matt stretched and threw away his Styrofoam cup.

Sean tried Chris' home number but got no answer. Matt pulled out his cell phone and punched buttons.

"Chris' cell," he explained. "Maybe he'll pick up when he's sees it's me." After a few moments, he hung up. "No answer."

"Hello, Mr. Prosecutor," a voice said from the doorway. Both Sean and Matt looked up to see Diana standing in the doorway, this time accompanied by Tracy. If anything, Diana was even lovelier than the last time Sean had seen her. He stood up immediately, and so did Matt.

"Uh, hello. Come in. Sit down." Remembering Matt, he added, "You know Matt Burton?"

"Everybody knows Matt Burton," Diana said, but Sean noticed she didn't extend her hand and Matt didn't offer his. They seemed to be sizing each other up. If Matt found her as intriguing as Sean did, he certainly didn't show it.

"I'll be heading along," Matt said. "Counselor," he nodded to Diana on his way out the door, engaging Tracy in conversation as they both walked away.

"Kind of freezes your blood a little," Diana commented when Matt was out of earshot.

"Well, once you get to know him, you realize he could probably kill you with his little finger."

"Not all warm and cuddly under the hard shell, then?"

"No, just more hard shell."

"This isn't a social call," she informed him, shifting the topic and settling into Matt's vacated chair.

"What can I do for you?" he asked.

"I represent Tommy Resnic," she announced.

Uh-oh. "Is Pat out of the picture now?"

"Mr. Resnic fired him. I was retained this morning."

"I see."

There was a pause.

"Can you give me some background on this case? Like, for instance, why my client's charged with murder?"

Sean sat back in his chair. "He's charged with murder because the evidence indicates that he committed the crime." Sean wasn't ready to point out any of the case's weaknesses until he had a better understanding himself of what was going on.

"Can I see the file?"

"Now, Ms. Baker, you know that we have a closed-file policy prior to arraignment. If you want to see what you are statutorily entitled to see, you'll have to file the appropriate motions." He almost added a *tsk, tsk,* but thought better of it.

"I thought we could handle this on a more informal basis," she explained, smiling.

"I could ask at this point just how *informal* you'd like to go, but I won't."

"No?"

"No."

"I heard you were easy to work with. That doesn't seem to be true."

Sean considered that. "Can I lay my cards on the table for a moment? Yesterday when you were in here, I asked you out. I'd still like to go out with you, but we'll leave that aside for the moment, since—as you pointed out—this isn't a social call. Right now, you're a defense attorney and I'm a prosecutor, no matter how attractive I think you are."

"Do you think I'm trying to charm you out of your file?"

"I don't know. Maybe you do it unconsciously. But I'm not about to change the rules just for a pretty face."

Diana straightened in her chair. "All right. I'll file the motions. You might also consider the fact that you're not being open about this case with me because you find me attractive and don't want to be thought of as being too soft. Maybe you're making up for it by being too tough?"

Sean didn't reply. Diana stood up, grabbing her briefcase. At the door, she turned. "And by the way, I *was* trying to charm you. I wanted to see how you'd react."

"Testing me, were you?"

"Yes. And you passed. Are you free for drinks tonight?"

Sean blinked. "Yes."

"Grogan's, at eight? Do you know where it is?"

"Uh-huh."

"I'll see you then." She latched onto a passing investigator to see her out the door and was gone.

◆

At five o'clock, Sean called Matt.

"No word from our guy?"

"Nothing on my end," Matt reported.

"What do we do next? We need to talk to him. Is it time to involve Chief Black, or at least Chris' watch commander?"

"Let's hold off. If I have to, I'll stop by his house tonight."

"Okay," Sean said. "But we can't sit on this much longer."

"Yeah," Matt responded, sounding tired. "I know."

Tuesday, April 18, 7:35 p.m.

They won't get me! Chris screamed inside his mind. *Not now. Not ever. I won't give those fuckers the satisfaction of seeing me in handcuffs, with them all laughing and pointing. They won't put me in a cage with those scumbags!*

It was important he do it right. He laid the plastic sheet across the floor first, and then pulled it tight to get rid of the wrinkles. Then he laid an old fabric sheet over the top of that. *Good,* he thought, *good. Nice and clean. Nothing for DeAnna to clean up.* The crime scene techs would do most of the ugly stuff.

The thought of DeAnna pulled him up short. Something caught in his throat.

He went into the den and pulled open the gun case. The pistol he wanted to use was in a mahogany box on the top shelf. It had belonged to his father.

After a few moments' thought, he got an extra sheet and tacked it to the wall. He pushed the tacks along the top in a nice, even row, each one about four inches apart. It seemed important somehow that they should be neat. Now the wall and most of the floor were covered. He surveyed his work.

Fucking maggots, he thought. *You won't be smiling long.*

He cleaned and oiled the pistol carefully. He removed each bullet and wiped them all clean. Pushing them back into the clip and then slamming the clip home gave him an almost visceral pleasure. He chambered a round.

Try this on for size, you fucking bastards.

He laid the gun on his desk and then seated himself behind his computer. He carefully adjusted his chair, pushing it back and forth several times until it was in the perfect position. He found a tissue and wiped off the keyboard before powering up. He tried not to think about anything, but that didn't work very well. In fact, he seemed to be thinking about *everything.* He thought about DeAnna. He thought about his life, all the events that had led up to this moment.

When his computer finished booting up, he began typing.

```
I want you all to know that none of you are
ever going to put me into a fucking cage.
```

He stopped and deleted the words. *No,* he thought, *I won't scream and yell like some animal. I'll do it with...dignity.* He began again.

```
I know some of you will think that this is
the chicken shit thing to do. You haven't
walked in my shoes. I can't go on. I can't go
to jail. I can't have my wife be disappointed
in me. I'm very sorry. When I got the call
today, that the ADA wanted to talk to me, I
knew it was all over. I'm not going to let
some little shit build his career on me, no
matter what I've done. If you see Sean Turlow,
tell him to go to hell.
```

He stopped typing and printed off what he had written. Not bothering to reread it because he knew he was already taking too much time, he left the printed sheet in the tray and stood up. After straightening a few items on his desk, he sat cross-legged in the middle of the sheet. The gun was heavy in his hand. He lifted it and pressed it to the side of his head. God, it was hard. There was something inside him that rebelled against the idea, some inner part of him that screamed in anguish and fear. But he knew what he had to do. He lowered the gun again and stared at it.

I won't cry, he thought. *I won't cry like a woman.*

Then he put the barrel into his mouth and squeezed the trigger. The sound was huge.

Tuesday, April 18, 8:30 p.m.

The conversation was delightful. Diana was quick-witted without being sarcastic, intelligent but not catty.

"So, why did you become a prosecutor?" she asked, brushing a strand of hair out of her face in a way he loved.

"I was trying to figure out some way I could violate Constitutional rights on a regular basis. Fast food didn't seem promising, so I decided on prosecution."

"Uh-huh."

"What about you? Why defense work?"

"I wanted to smash the male-dominated patriarchy while simultaneously getting killers off scot-free."

"Well, we seem to have both ended up in the perfect careers," he said, smiling.

"Haven't we, though?"

"Aren't you afraid your fellow defense attorneys will look down on you if they find out you're consorting with the enemy?" Sean wondered.

"They don't see you as the enemy."

"No?"

"No. Most of the attorneys I spoke with about you said you were a stand-up guy. *Integrity*, that's a word that cropped up a lot. *Honesty*. I heard that one a lot, too."

"All that money I've been sending out has finally paid off."

Diana laughed. "No, I'm serious. You have an excellent reputation among the defense bar."

"That's nice to hear. Just how many people did you talk to?"

"A few."

"May I ask why you were doing all this background work on me?"

"I was checking you out."

"Really? I'm flattered."

"I like to check out the competition," she added, and Sean's mood deflated a little.

"Oh, so you were just checking me out as trial competition."

Diana's eyes sparkled. "Not just for that."

His hopes soared again, but he tried to play it cool. He looked into her beautiful blue eyes and felt as though he were falling.

"That's nice," she said.

"What is?"

"The way you're looking at me. Into my eyes. Most men spend their time looking at my chest."

"Hmm."

Another strand of blonde hair had fallen into her face. Before she could reach up to push it back, he brushed it with his fingers.

Suddenly, it was very quiet. Her skin was unbelievably soft where his fingertips brushed along her face. He cupped his hand around her cheek. She reached up and placed her hand over his.

"This is a bad idea," she whispered.

"Yes. Very bad," he agreed.

When they kissed, he felt as though he'd never kissed any woman before. Ripples of pleasure passed over his entire body. When they stopped, their faces were very close; he could breathe in the wonderful aroma of her.

As if suddenly realizing where they were, she said, "Let's get out of here. Just about every attorney in Atlanta comes here."

They drove around for a while, but she kept sliding over on the seat, pressing her body close to him, kissing him softly and nibbling on his ear. He couldn't concentrate on driving; he couldn't think about anything but how wonderful she felt. She intertwined her fingers with his and began kissing his fingertips. He drove to his apartment complex and parked.

"I'm not trying to be ..." he said, motioning at the building.

She kissed him again, and he forgot everything but her. He led her upstairs to his apartment. Once inside, though, she seemed less certain of herself.

"Hey," he said, gripping her shoulders to look into her eyes, "we don't have to do anything. Okay? Would you like me to drive you back to Grogan's?"

She looked deep into his eyes, and Sean began to fall again. This time when they kissed, he ran his hands over her body and felt her own hands exploring his back. *My God*, he kept saying to himself, *my God*.

They started slowly, but then the heat began to build. Later, he couldn't remember if he'd led her into the bedroom or she'd led him. It really didn't matter.

◆

The phone rang three times before he heard it.

"Let it ring," Diana instructed.

"Okay," he agreed.

He heard the answering machine pick up.

"Turlow," a gruff voice barked, "if you're home, pick up the goddamn phone. This is Police Chief Black. I've got a dead cop, and you're involved."

Sean broke the embrace and picked up the phone. "This is Sean."

The answering machine continued to boom the conversation through the room.

"Do you know where 245 Altamont Heights is?" Black demanded.

"No."

"Well, load it into your GPS and get over here."

"It's ten o'clock at night. What's going on?"

"Oh, did I interrupt some fun? Too fucking bad. Put your pants back on and get over here. This is serious." Black growled the address again and hung up.

"What's going on?" Diana asked.

"I don't know. I don't know how I could be involved. I don't even know who lives at that address!" he protested, but even as he said it, he started to have the sinking feeling that maybe he did know after all.

"It was about time for me to get going anyway," Diana said. "You can drop me at Grogan's on the way."

Sean approached her, but the lazy, romantic mood had been shattered. How had life gotten so incredibly complicated so incredibly fast? "I'd like to see you again," he said.

"I don't know, Sean."

"I do. I know it's bad form for a man to say anything that even sounds like an emotion, but I'm crazy about you, Diana."

She looked into his eyes.

"You know, since I'm risking censure by the entire male populace, the least you could do is say, 'Sean, we'll do lunch tomorrow.'"

"I can't," she said, and a meat cleaver sliced his heart open. "I've got court. I am free for lunch on Thursday, though. One o'clock? Peaches Café?"

He beamed at her, cleaver forgotten. "Let me think, let me think. Thursday, you say? Thursday. Yes, I believe I'm free on Thursday. I would be happy to meet with you, Counselor."

The drive back to Grogan's was quiet. When they arrived, Diana pointed out her car, and Sean parked next to it. She kissed him on the cheek and slid out of the car before things could heat up again. Sean watched her get into her car and pull out of the lot before he drove away.

◆

It would have been impossible to miss it. As soon as Sean pulled onto the street, he could see the flashing lights. Every squad car in Atlanta seemed to be parked in front of the small white home. Sean parked four houses down and walked from there.

There was a cop standing outside the wooden barricade marked POLICE – DO NOT CROSS.

"Sean Turlow," Sean introduced himself. "Chief Black called me."

The cop glared at Sean for a moment, then moved aside so that Sean could squeeze between the barricades.

"I'm looking for the chief," Sean said to another cop at the front door.

"Second room on the left."

Sean passed by several people on his way down the hall. He recognized a couple of faces. Steve Morningside was standing in the living room, holding his camera. He didn't return Sean's wave. Lee Church was standing in the hallway. Sean had to squeeze by him when he acted like he didn't hear Sean say, "Excuse me."

When he got to the den, Sean wasn't prepared for what he saw. Chris had been sitting in the middle of the room, and a huge wad of his brain matter had splattered on the wall behind him and slid to the ground. There was blood everywhere. Chris' hands were still holding the gun, resting on his abdomen. He looked awkward and uncomfortable, with his head angled back so that his chin stuck straight up. He looked like a doll someone had thrown on the floor. Sean was grateful he couldn't see the dead man's face.

"Come on in, *Sean Turlow*," Chief Black called. "Don't let a little blood bother you."

All movement in the room suddenly stopped. Sean felt very self-conscious as he stepped in. He couldn't count the number of eyes staring at him.

"You recognize Chris, here, don't you?" Black asked.

"What's this all about, Chief?"

"Oh, come on now. You know what it's about."

"No, I don't."

The chief held up a typewritten note, encased in a plastic evidence bag. "Read it," he ordered, laying it on the desk. "Don't take it out of the bag. Just read it."

After Sean read it, he turned to stare at Black.

"Got any ideas why this poor motherfucker mentions your name in his suicide note?" Black demanded.

"I've got an idea."

"Care to share it with us?"

The room was very still, everyone staring at him. Sean didn't like the atmosphere.

"No," he replied, getting a little hot. "I don't particularly care to share it. If you want to question me, go through the DA."

Now everyone was looking at the chief.

"You're not going to help us with this investigation?"

"Look, what's going on here, Chief? You drag me down here and ask me loaded questions in front of a dead body. I called Chris today and asked him to meet with me. He never showed up. That's it. That's all I know."

Jimmy Bennett entered the room. He was holding a stack of what looked like photos. "Uh, Chief," he said, "I need to talk to you."

"Not now," Black growled, still staring at Sean.

"*Chief*," Jimmy insisted. "It has to be now."

Something in his tone made Black look up. Jimmy looked even more stricken than the other officers in the room.

"All right, Jimmy," Black agreed, and strode out of the room. Sean stood for another moment, trying to figure out what he should do. He looked around the room again, avoiding the thing in the middle of the floral-print sheet, and then walked out.

Matt was seated at the dining room table, absorbed in a small stack of photos he had pulled out of a large yellow envelope. Sean had had enough of cops and walked through the room without saying anything, heading for the front door.

"Just a minute," Matt called after him.

"What now?"

"Sit down."

"I don't feel like sitting down."

Matt pushed another yellow envelope toward him and asked the other cops in the room to give them some privacy.

"What's this?" Sean asked, still not sitting.

"Just look."

"I'm tired of getting jerked around," Sean snapped. "First your chief calls me and just about accuses me of—"

"The photos," Matt cut in. "Just look at the photos."

Sean pinched a corner of the yellow envelope and pulled it over to him. There were four or five photos on top that slid off. Sean looked down at them but couldn't really make any sense of the images. They looked like a jumble of arms and legs and eyes.

Then Sean realized what he was seeing.

"Jesus Christ," he whispered.

The little blonde girl was maybe five or six years old. Somebody had applied heavy makeup to her face; she looked like a hooker. The photographs were a series of her taking off her clothes. When Sean got to the pictures showing a man's hands on her tiny, naked body, he pushed the stack away.

"Jesus," he said again, louder this time. "Did these belong to Chris? He was a fucking pervert."

Matt had rested his elbows on the table and crossed his arms. His head was bent. "Yeah."

"None of these photos gives you a good shot of the man's face," Sean observed.

"It's Chris," Matt confirmed. He pushed another photograph across the table. Matt pointed at the spot where a tattoo on the man's upper left forearm was visible. "That's Chris' tattoo."

"Are you sure?"

Matt looked like he'd been hit with a hammer. "Yeah. I've seen it often enough. He might as well have signed his name to the photo."

"Did you see him tonight? I mean before, uh, *this*."

"What?"

"You mentioned that you were going to stop by."

"Oh. No. I just called a few more times. I didn't want to talk about all this in front of his wife. I thought it might upset her. Ain't that a bad joke? Instead, she gets to see her husband's brains painted on the wall."

Sean thought he might be sick.

A couple of cops had gathered in the doorway. Matt turned to them and ordered, "Get out!"

They vanished.

"Did you have any idea about this?" Sean asked.

Matt just shook his head.

They sat in silence for a while.

"When I first heard about this," Matt said, motioning toward the back of the house, "I was pissed off. I thought you'd done something to Chris to push him over the edge. Did you even speak to him after that first call this morning?"

"No. I called a few more times and left some messages, but I never got him on the line."

Matt sighed. "Cops don't like it when one of their own dies, especially when it looks like suicide. Chris' wife called the watch commander when she found him, but the chief got here first. He wants to cut your balls off."

"I didn't have anything—" Sean began, but Matt cut him off.

"I know. I know. But the chief read the letter and decided you pushed a good man to kill himself. He wasn't shy about sharing his conclusion. Then…" He paused. "Then this."

"That case with the little girl. It was a lot more than him letting her handle his service weapon, wasn't it?"

"Looks like it. To tell you the truth, I hadn't even looked into it. I knew Chris. Well, I thought I did. I just couldn't see it. Not him. Chris Franklin molesting little girls? Before this, I would have said you were out of your mind."

"It looks like he crossed the line a long time ago," Sean said, pushing the photos into the center of the table, away from him.

"Yeah. I'd like you to keep this to yourself for a while. I need to do some more digging. I gotta find out who this little girl is, for one thing."

"Sure," Sean agreed. "Do you need me anymore?"

"No. Come on. Let's get out of here."

They walked out together. Chief Black had suddenly been called away to another 'important matter,' but Sean couldn't think of anything that would trump a cop's suicide—especially at this time of night. He imagined that Black's disappearance was really about how drastically the optics had changed with the discovery of the photos. The chief wouldn't want to be anywhere near this now. Even so, a lot of cops continued to glare at Sean as Matt walked him out.

When they stopped just short of the wooden barricade, Matt extended his hand. Sean was confused but took it, and they shook.

"I'd like to talk with you some more about all of this," Matt said. "Your office, tomorrow, around lunchtime?"

"Sounds good."

"And, uh, thanks," Matt added. He held the handshake a few moments more than was customary. Sean noticed that just about every cop in the area was watching their exchange, and he realized what Matt was doing. The word would get out about the kiddie porn in no time, and that coupled with what Matt had just done would take Sean off the hook. With that handshake, Matt had wiped away any animosity toward Sean because of what Chris had written in his suicide note, bringing Sean back into the fold.

He's a pretty interesting guy, Sean thought as he headed for his car.

Wednesday, April 19, 1:50 a.m.

It was almost two o'clock in the morning before Matt returned to headquarters. He walked down the long hallway to the chief's office and pushed open the door.

Chief Black was leaning back in his chair, smoking a cigarette. The ashtray sat right next to the *No Smoking* sign on his desk. Rick Black had started out as a patrol cop and moved up through the department, eventually cultivating enough political contacts to get the chief's position. Matt didn't care for him very much, but, then, he couldn't remember liking any of the chiefs. Politics turned you into some other kind of person.

"Sit down," Black instructed.

Matt took a chair and let out a long sigh.

"Lay it out for me."

Matt spoke for five minutes. When he was finished, Black stubbed out his cigarette. "How many people know about the photos?"

"Jimmy Bennett, Sean Turlow, and me for sure. I don't know how many might suspect or have found out on their own. I'm sure the uniforms at the scene have already spread the word."

"Shit. Three for sure, and the whole fucking precinct by tomorrow. I think we can keep the lid on our own, but the lawyer is a wild card. What kind of man is he?"

Matt considered for a moment. "I think he's okay. He's not a glory hound, so he won't be calling any press conferences. He seems pretty laid back, but he's tougher than he looks. He won't be intimidated."

"I'll leave it to the DA to order him to keep his trap shut, then."

Matt leaned forward. "There's more."

"Oh, for Chrissake."

"Chris may also be linked to a murder case."

Black stood up, shoving himself away from the desk. "Goddammit! What the fuck is going on?!"

"Chris was called out on a burglary a while back. The call came from Imogene Resnic. Somebody stole about twenty grand from her house. Chris didn't file a report."

"The same Resnic who got murdered?"

"Yup."

"So?"

"Think about it, Chief. We can put Chris responding to the burglary call. Then we have a witness who says the same cop came back and did his own investigation. Then Mrs. Resnic turns up dead a few days later at a muffler shop, where another witness spotted a cop car. It doesn't look good."

"I don't give a shit how it looks," Black snapped, but Matt knew that wasn't true, not by a long shot. "You're not trying to tell me that Chris Franklin, in addition to be being a certified pervert, is also a murderer?"

"People around the neighborhood said that Mrs. Resnic kept a large amount of cash in her house. The stack that got taken was only *part* of it. She hid the money in multiple places. Twenty grand in that first pop, and at least as much more in the others."

"No. Uh-uh. It doesn't hold up. Why would she bring the rest of her money to some muffler shop?"

Matt shook his head. "I don't know. Maybe she got a call from someone who told her they'd found her first batch of money and had to check it against another stack. Like for serial numbers or fingerprints."

Black yanked open a drawer and fished around in it. "Jesus H. Christ. This is all I fucking need. Where are those goddamn cigarettes?" He lit one and jabbed it at Matt. "Okay, enough of this speculation. Do you have anything solid linking Chris with this killing?"

Matt shifted. "Not yet."

"Not yet," the chief mimicked. "Not now, not ever. This is the last time I hear any speculation about Chris Franklin killing people. Here's how it goes from now on: Chris was a good officer with some 'emotional problems.' Because of those emotional problems, he capped himself. It's a damn shame, but that's how it goes. There is no link between Chris and the Resnic case. End of story."

Matt stared at the chief, thinking how much of a bully and a blowhard he was. "It won't play that way, Chief."

"Why the fuck not?"

"Sean knows about the missing report. He's linked it to the Resnic killing. That's already enough *Brady* material that he'll have to turn it over to the defense."

"What? *What?*"

"The defense will have to hear about it."

"Bull-fucking-shit! This is the last time anybody talks about that. I won't have a dead officer's good name dragged through the mud. There's no evidence to suggest that Chris had anything to do with the

Resnic killing, is there?"

"I'll need to do some more digging to be sure."

"Fuck. All right, fine. Investigate Chris enough to satisfy yourself that he wasn't involved in the Resnic killing. That's it. I don't want to know about his life or his messy habits or the color of his fucking underwear. Resnic: yes or no. That's it."

Matt thought it over. "What if I find out Chris was involved?"

"You won't. I knew him. He wasn't a killer. Maybe he was a kiddie perv, but he wasn't a killer." Black looked at Matt. "If you find anything linking him to Resnic, you bring it to me first. I'll make the decision what to do with it. Okay?"

Matt shrugged. He didn't like it, but he couldn't see a better alternative at the moment. "Okay."

After a moment's pause, Black snapped, "Well, get on it."

As soon as Matt was gone, Black pulled over his Rolodex and thumbed through it. *That fucking shyster, Turlow,* he thought. *I'm gonna fix your little wagon, sonny boy.* He found the number he wanted and dialed it. While it rang, he looked at his watch. Nearly three in the morning. *Fuck it. Why should I be the only person awake at this hour?*

CHAPTER SEVEN

Wednesday, April 19, 8:30 a.m.

Sean had no sooner settled into his office than Tom Delaney appeared.

"Good morning," Tom chirped.

"Morning," Sean replied tiredly.

"Rough night last night?"

"You have no idea. Aren't you here kind of early for an unpaid volunteer?"

"I love it here. This is the only fun I've had since starting law school."

Sean smiled thinly. *Doesn't say much for his social life.*

"What's on the agenda for today? Deciding what charges to bring? Maybe attending an autopsy?"

"Paperwork," Sean said, crushing Tom's hopes. "This job is mostly paperwork. I'd like you to finish going through the arraignment bucket, pulling out *Brady* material."

After Tom left, Sean sat alone for a while, thinking. He liked mornings; his brain seemed to work better before lunch. He took out a legal pad and a pen and let his mind roam over the Resnic case, writing whatever popped into his head.

Burglary occurs five days before her murder

Chris Franklin is the responding officer

CF fails to file a report – VERY UNUSUAL

CF (or someone claiming to be CF?) does an unauthorized investigation

Large amount of money taken

She is murdered at an out-of-the-way location

Son is charged with murder

Is son the guilty party?

If son is not guilty party, then who is?

Who could lure her out to a closed muffler shop at ten o'clock at night? Her son, a friend, or...?

CF commits suicide after I call him. I don't mention Resnic case, but he does mention me in note. Why?

Sean put the pen down and stared at the legal pad. He didn't like the thought that had just popped into his head—about how a man desperate for money could very well have been driven to murder.

His phone rang. It was the DA's secretary.

"Can you come down here right now?" It was phrased like a question, but it wasn't one.

"I'm on my way," Sean replied.

The District Attorney's office was next to Shepherd's office, but unlike Shepherd's, the DA's office was a model of cleanliness and order. There were no stacks of files on the floor, no wadded-up pieces of paper that had missed the trash can. David Holloway had occupied the office for nearly twenty years, rarely facing any opposition in the local elections. He was a tall, thin, fastidious man who always wore very nice suits and seemed to be calm no matter what was happening. When Sean walked in, he was standing at his large picture window talking in low tones to Shepherd, who looked like he'd been up all night with his rumpled suit jacket and messy hair.

"Sean," Holloway said, turning from the window. "Nice of you to drop by."

"Mr. Holloway," Sean replied, nodding.

"Take a seat, Sean."

Unlike the other offices, Holloway's had space for a large sofa and several chairs arranged around a low coffee table. There were even magazines on the table, although Sean doubted anyone ever had the time or the chutzpah to actually read them. He noted that all of the chairs were already occupied, with a file on one and coffee cups in front of the others. That left the sofa, and Sean didn't want to sit on it. He felt like he would be on display. But he sat anyway, feeling uncomfortable. Maybe that was the point.

Sean had already felt a little uneasy. It was rare to receive a summons to visit with the DA. Although Holloway prided himself on staying in touch with his staff, almost all of his information was filtered through Shepherd. Knowing that Shepherd didn't like him and was setting him up as a fall guy also meant knowing those things had probably influenced the information Shepherd had relayed to Holloway.

"Coffee?" Holloway offered. He had his own machine in a corner, everything looking immaculate and orderly.

"No, thanks," Sean said. He didn't feel comfortable enough to sip coffee with the DA.

Holloway motioned for Shepherd to sit down, and they both took their chairs. Sean didn't want to fidget, but he couldn't think what to do with his hands, so he dropped them in his lap and tried to look calm.

"How are your folks, Sean?"

"Fine, sir. They're both retired and taking it easy."

"South Georgia, aren't they? St. Simon's Island?"

"Yes, sir, that's right." Sean wondered if Holloway had a phenomenal memory or if there was a private file on him somewhere in here that Holloway had recently reviewed.

"Mornin'," came a gruff voice from the door.

Sean looked up and saw Matt, with his shirt rumpled and stubble decorating his face. Suddenly, he felt a little better. Matt, at least, was on his side.

"Grab a seat, Matt," Holloway instructed.

Matt walked over to the third chair, lifted the file, and dropped it on the coffee table. Sean immediately wished he'd thought of that first.

"Need some coffee, Matt?" Holloway asked.

"No, thanks. I've been drinking it all night, and I've got heartburn."

Holloway picked a nonexistent piece of lint off his pants and said, "Why don't you fill us in on the Franklin case?"

Matt sketched out the details. When he came to the note, he pulled a folded piece of paper out of his pocket and handed it to Holloway.

Holloway didn't read it right away. He waited for Matt to finish talking, then unfolded the paper and took his time going through it. Sean had the feeling Holloway had already read the note and was just doing this for show.

"Sean, tell me about your phone call to Franklin," Holloway requested.

"I called him yesterday morning and asked if he'd stop by and talk with me."

"Did you tell him why?"

"No, not exactly. I said that something unusual had come up and I needed to talk it over with him."

"You didn't mention the Resnic case specifically?" Holloway studied Sean's face carefully as he spoke.

"No."

"Why not?"

"He didn't ask. He said that he'd come by after he got off his shift, around three."

"After his shift?" Holloway asked. "Wasn't that unusual?"

"Well, most officers come over during their shift to talk about a case. But I've had some who waited until they got off the road. It depends."

"But Chris wasn't on the road," Holloway explained. "He got reassigned to desk duty yesterday morning. He could've come at any time."

Sean hesitated, processing the new information. "I didn't know that. When I spoke with him, he told me he was on the road and asked if he could come at the end of his shift."

Sean noticed that Shepherd was still staring at him very intently. He decided to deflect the line of questions a little.

"I discussed all of this yesterday with Bill," he began.

But Holloway cut him off. "I know. Are you trying to suggest that Chris killed Mrs. Resnic for her money?"

Sean was stunned. That idea had only occurred to him a few minutes before. How long had Holloway—and by extension the others—been thinking it?

"I don't have a working theory. I was digging," he said, trying to give himself time to think. Sean noticed that Matt was staring intently, too—but not at him, at Holloway.

"It's a logical conclusion, isn't it?" Holloway demanded. "Chris answers the burglary call, sees the money, fails to file a report. He lures her out to the shop, kills her, and then takes her money."

"It does have a certain logic to it," Sean said slowly.

"No, it doesn't." Holloway's words were like a slap across the face. "It doesn't have any logic to it at all. It's the worst kind of speculation. It's scandalous and dangerous. And that's the problem. If the press gets hold of this, they'll scream it from the rooftops. They won't care about the truth. They only care about a good story, and fuck the human beings involved."

Holloway paused for a moment, letting his words sink in. Sean knew Holloway rarely swore. In fact, he'd never heard the man say anything stronger than 'damn.'

Holloway suddenly glanced at his watch and stood up, motioning for the others to stay put. "I have a meeting," he announced. "Bill can take it from here." He stalked out, nearly slamming the door behind him.

"Sean," Shepherd asked, "are you trying to screw this office?"

"*What?*"

"'Cause that's exactly what you'll do if you go around making these wild accusations. I've got enough crap in my life right now without going looking for more. My friend," Shepherd barked, pointing a finger at Sean, "you are on very thin fucking ice."

"Wait a minute," Sean protested.

"No, you wait a minute. You better start thinking about your career. The legal community in Atlanta is close. Word gets around. Don't say a fucking thing," Shepherd snapped when Sean drew another breath.

As he turned to address Matt, Shepherd's tone relaxed. "Matt, keep a muzzle on Perry Mason here. You guys will be on this for a while. And you," he snarled, turning back to Sean, "you remember that David Holloway gave you a job. He can always take it away again."

Sean sat in stunned silence. He'd never seen Shepherd this angry.

Shepherd turned to Matt again. "Put the whole thing to rest. No press. No newspaper exposés, no goddamn letters to the editor."

Matt rubbed his tired eyes. "I can't control what other people say. Maybe somebody's already talked to the press."

Shepherd spun on Sean. "You?"

Sean was confused. "No. I haven't—"

"Well, don't. Anything that goes to the press comes through this office first."

Sean was beginning to get angry. "I didn't invent this thing—"

"No, but I bet you wouldn't mind exploiting it to your own advantage."

"Bill, that's not true. I don't care about—"

"This meeting is over," Shepherd interrupted, practically pushing Sean out of the office.

Matt followed Sean out into the hall. "Let's go talk in your office," he suggested.

Sean didn't say a word.

◆

"Gave you kind of a working over, didn't they?" Matt began when they were in Sean's office with the door closed.

"Uh, yeah, you could say that." Sean was seething.

Matt dug a pack of gum out of his hip pocket. He put a tab in his mouth and started chewing. "Bad press makes them antsy," he shrugged.

"And that gives them the right to take it out on me? Just because Chris mentioned my name in his note? I don't think so."

"Hey, you know these guys are only worried about covering their asses. They probably started running scenarios on this case as soon as they heard about Chris offing himself. They knew about the missing report almost as soon as you did. Somebody—maybe somebody hoping to get hired over here—picked up the phone as soon as you left and let them know. And as soon as they heard there was no burglary report, they got worried. They've been at this game too long not to look for the worst-case scenario. And the worst case here is that Chris killed the old lady, took her money, and felt bad about it later, especially after you called and accused him of it."

"But I didn't accuse him of anything!" Sean protested, his frustration still growing.

"I know that. But that's how it'll play. He feels bad about it and blows his brains out. That's a messy story, in more ways than one. The minute Chief Black heard about you at HQ trying to talk with Chris, he started wondering what was going on. Black's no dummy. He put two and two together, made the connection with the Resnic case, and started sweating. A bad cop wouldn't look good for the DA's office, but it would be a nightmare for the PD—and Black would be the man on the spot. Who else could they go after? Chris is dead."

Sean digested this, calming a bit as he did. "So they decide to read *me* the riot act."

"Kill the messenger," Matt confirmed.

"Then this isn't over, is it? That's what that meeting was all about. We're going to be a team until this thing goes away, aren't we? The only problem is, I don't see how it's going to go away."

Matt sighed. "We're supposed to make it go away."

◆

An hour later, Sean was still trying to process the morning's events as Matt outlined two basic approaches for their joint investigation of Chris. "Number one," Matt explained, "we have to dig into Chris' life. Bank accounts, search warrant for the house, the whole shooting match. Number two, we take a look at the Resnic case, seeing what kind of evidence there is against the son."

"And what will that prove?"

"Could be that the son actually did kill his mother. That would get Chris, and by extension the PD, off the hook."

"Is this going to be a real investigation or just a cover-up of Chris' involvement?"

Matt didn't answer; he just chewed his gum loudly until Sean gave up.

"All right," Sean sighed. "Where do we start?"

"I always start with the basics and go from there. Let's get a search warrant for Chris' house and see what we can find. After that, we'll go through his bank accounts." Matt thought for a moment. "I wish I'd had a chance to question the Resnic boy longer. I wasn't with him long before he lawyered up."

"I met him. Well, I saw him at the preliminary hearing. He kept screaming that he was innocent. He looked me dead in the eyes and actually *screamed* it. They had to drag him out."

"Never seen anything like that at a prelim," Matt mused.

"Me either. I had a third-year with me. It made quite an impression on him. He'll probably expect it at every prelim from now on."

"Who's the Resnic boy's attorney?"

Sean shifted in his seat. "He had Pat Reardon, but he fired him."

"Smart move." Matt smiled a little.

"He hired, uh, Diana Baker."

"I don't know her. What's she like?"

Sean shifted again. "She's...nice."

"I'd like you at the scene when we execute the warrant."

"Why? It's not like I'm trained to handle evidence."

"I know, but we may need some legal advice. We have to keep the circle pretty close on this one. I've got a couple of guys I trust. We'll do the search ourselves, but if anything comes up that's out of the ordinary, I want you close by."

"Okay."

♦

By half past ten, Matt had obtained the search warrant. He picked Sean up in front of the courthouse and drove to Chris' house.

"Where are your guys?" Sean asked.

"They're already there, waiting."

"So, why the warrant? Couldn't you just ask for permission from Chris' wife?"

"Tried that. She told me to go fuck myself."

"That sounds pretty aggressive. I thought you and Chris were friends."

"This whole thing has thrown her for a loop. She's not cooperating with anybody who thinks her husband was a child molester. I guess I can't really blame her. The Chris she knew would never have done something like this. He hasn't been dead twenty-four hours, and now her husband's former friends want to search his house for child pornography. It's a messy job."

"So, your guys are just securing the scene?"

"Yup. They've been there since last night, doing shifts. I didn't want DeAnna to do something stupid like destroy evidence. They can't search yet, but my guys are making sure nothing gets lost in the meantime."

"And who are *your guys* exactly?"

"Jimmy Bennett. He found the first set of photos. Steve Morningside and Lee Church. Dave Cheek. He was just moved to Technology from S&P a week ago. Oh, and Rick Gartman from your office."

"That's not a lot of people."

"We have to keep this small. The fewer people who see what we might find, the better."

When they got to Chris' house, Sean waited in the car, window rolled down to let in the day's cool air. As soon as Matt knocked on the front door, it flew open to reveal a woman, presumably Chris' wife, rushing angrily toward Matt. She was screaming and tried to rake her nails across his face. Matt easily deflected her attempt and then spoke to her in quiet tones. At first she didn't want to listen, but gradually whatever he was saying started to sink in. Finally, the fight seemed to go out of her and she turned and shuffled back inside, followed closely by Matt.

Sean didn't have to wait long for his summons.

"What have we got?" he asked after Matt appeared at the door and motioned him inside.

"Trouble," was all Matt said as Sean followed him to the den.

Matt walked over to the computer where Chris had presumably typed up his suicide note. "I asked Dave to take a look at the computer. You'll never guess what he found."

"More child porn."

"No, that's just it. Nothing. No porn. No photos of anything. No files at all, in fact."

"Has it been wiped clean?"

"Not according to Dave. According to him, the only file on the computer was the suicide note from yesterday. But if you're into child porn, you get it electronically. I've seen these kinds of cases before. They encrypt it, but they almost always keep it on their home computers. Some of them get fancy and have programs that will automatically delete everything with a couple of keystrokes, but Dave says there's nothing like that here.

"DeAnna also told me that Chris always worked up his case files on this computer. I mean, he worked up his regular reports like everybody else and turned them in at the station, but he always wrote up his personal notes on his own computer. She says that he did it every time he came off duty; apparently it helped him remember the cases when he got called to testify later. Anyway, there isn't anything like that on this computer."

"Does he have another computer? Maybe a laptop instead of this dinosaur? Maybe a tablet?"

Matt was already shaking his head. "No. I asked."

Sean considered. "She could be lying."

"True, but I don't think so. Chris wasn't much of a geek. I never saw him with a laptop, and he never mentioned owning a tablet or anything. He just liked to type up his personal notes when he got home to help him remember important details about his cases."

Sean moved to where the desktop sat. He nudged the mouse with his finger and then looked at Matt.

"Yeah," Matt confirmed. "It's been dusted. You can use it."

Sean sat down and pulled out the small flat drawer that housed the keyboard. You just didn't see many desktops anymore, at least not for personal use. The text of the suicide note was still up on the screen. It chilled him a little to see the text and think that typing it had been Chris' last act before killing himself.

On a whim, he clicked the Save button to see if Chris had set up a hidden file somewhere where he might have stored things, but a "Drive Not Available" dialog box appeared. Sean thought about that for a moment, then started digging around the tower, which was on the floor. He found a USB cable plugged into the back of the tower, but the other end wasn't connected to anything. *Chris must have had an external hard drive,* Sean thought. *That could be where he kept both his police reports and his kiddie porn.* He continued looking around but couldn't find a drive anywhere.

Sean pushed the keyboard drawer closed and took a closer look at the tower. The light cover of fingerprint dust on top of the unit had left the suggestion of an outline. Something rectangular had definitely sat there.

"Hey," he called out. "Anybody find an external drive yet?"

"Why?" Matt wondered.

"Chris must have had one. It was plugged into the USB port, but I don't see it here. Did one of your guys log it into evidence already?"

Matt conferred with Jimmy, and together they looked at a list.

"No," Matt said. "There's nothing like that here."

"Maybe you should talk to his wife again," Sean suggested. "I think she may have taken it."

Matt came back a few minutes later, looking even more haggard. "Just spoke to her," he told Sean. "She says she didn't stay here last night, that she stayed with friends and didn't take anything with her. Jimmy drove her, and he confirms that part. My guys were here before she got back, and they've kept the scene secured. They say she never came anywhere near this room."

Sean sat and thought for a moment. "What about last night? There were a lot of cops here."

"Yeah?" Matt said, a warning in his voice.

"Somebody *could* have taken it. I'm not pointing any fingers."

"Hmm."

Sean decided to let it go for the moment. "Okay. Whatever. There may have been an external hard drive, and somebody may have taken it. The important point is that it isn't here now. It would be nice to have it, just to see if he had more child porn on it, but he's dead and he can't be prosecuted anyway. So—"

He was interrupted when Steve walked into the room and whispered to Matt. Ignoring Sean, they walked out together.

"So," Sean called after them, "I'll just sit here, then?"

There was no answer, and Sean decided he didn't want to stay in that room one minute longer. He wandered around the house and found himself in an alcove just off the dining room. There were framed photos here, mostly featuring Chris and DeAnna. The Franklins apparently didn't have any children, and Sean was grateful for that. He also saw several pictures of a group of men wearing camouflage, kneeling over deer carcasses or just posing with rifles for the camera. He spotted several familiar faces: Chris, Jimmy, Lee, and Matt. There were other photos including additional people, but the core group seemed to be those four.

Wandering again, Sean decided to check the trash cans outside the house. Chances were the cops had already done that, but he was here and knew that his presence at the scene last night had already made him a witness. He could never be involved in the prosecution of any case that might come out of this.

Outside, he was surprised to discover that it had become a clear, sunny day. That felt wrong somehow. What was inside the house seemed to demand weather that was gloomy and overcast.

As he stood in Chris' driveway, Sean remembered another driveway he'd been standing in recently: Mrs. Resnic's. And it came to him again. A glimmer. Something Mrs. Jenkins had said that hadn't fit quite right. He thought for a few minutes but couldn't remember what it was that had seemed off. Shrugging, he went looking for Matt.

In the master bedroom, he found Jimmy kneeling at the foot of the bed, where he had apparently pulled off part of the frame's wood veneer.

"What have you got?" Sean asked, but he was brought up short when Jimmy turned to him, face sheet white.

"What is it?" Sean whispered.

Jimmy's gloved hands were full of photos. "These are just fucking kids," he said, his voice breaking. "I mean, they're children for Chrissake."

Sean didn't want to look at the images. He'd seen enough the night before. "How did you think to look there?"

"I've got the same kind of bed. You order it online and put it together yourself. I noticed it was the same right away when I walked in. I remember seeing this false front thing when I was putting mine together and thinking it would make a great hiding place. I wondered if Chris had thought the same thing. I guess he did."

"I guess so. I'd better go tell Matt."

◆

Sean found Matt in the garage, searching through a large freezer.

"Find anything in there?" Sean asked.

"Worth a look," Matt responded. "You'd be surprised how many people hide things in freezers."

As Sean told Matt about Jimmy's discovery, Matt lifted the lid on a toolbox and began to search through it. He bent down lower and picked something up, straightening with a small, rectangular piece of plastic between his pinched fingers.

"What's that?" Sean asked.

Matt wasn't saying anything, so Sean moved in closer for a look. It appeared to be a driver's license.

"Gregor Itz, uh, Itzvan—"

"Gregor Mikel Itzvanov."

"What's it doing here? You pronounced that name pretty easily. Do you know him?"

"Yeah. I met him the other day when he was rolled into the morgue."

Sean wanted to ask more questions, but something in Matt's body language told him that wouldn't be a good idea. This case and these last few days had raised more questions than he'd had to consider in years. Maybe he was better off not knowing.

Matt putt the driver's license in an evidence bag and turned back to Sean. "More child porn?" He shook his head. "You think you know someone.

"I went hunting with Chris more times than I can count. You should've heard him go on about child molesters, how they should be shot or electrocuted, not just put in jail to hang out with other criminals." Matt shook his head again.

Something else seemed to catch his eye, and he knelt next to the toolbox again.

"Turn on the lights, will you?"

"Have you found something else?"

"The lights," Matt repeated.

Sean complied. Matt fished a pair of tweezers out of his coat pocket and gingerly worked a small piece of paper out from the lining of the box. He held it up to get a better look, then frowned.

"What is it?"

Matt turned to look at him. "These are directions to Mick's Muffler."

"Wait a minute. *What?*"

Matt didn't reply as he carefully put the page into an evidence bag. Holding it up again, he said, "Looks like blood spatter here. Little drops." Matt dropped the two evidence bags into a larger bag. "I need to get these logged into evidence."

"Why would Chris have directions from the Resnic home to where Mrs. Resnic was killed?"

"Something the crime scene tech told me about the scene at the muffler shop," Matt began, avoiding Sean's question. "She said there was blood spatter in the car from the victim's head wound." He paused. "Come sit in this chair."

"Why?"

"I'm going to show you something."

"What? More dead bodies? Children being raped? Mass graves?"

"Just sit."

Once Sean sat, Matt moved to Sean's left side. "Okay," he said. "You're sitting in your car. Your window is rolled down. I'm outside the car. Okay?"

"Okay."

Matt cocked his finger like a gun. "I shoot you in the head. *Pow.* The force of the bullet knocks your head over, and then your body. The bullet, which is propelled by exploding gases, cuts through the side of your skull, and that damage kills you. But those same gases cause some issues."

"Like the star pattern from a muzzle close to the head."

"Right. But when the bullet goes in, some blood comes back out. The blood could be in a spurt, but some will also be in droplets in the air. Some gets vaporized, and some of those vaporized droplets are going to land on my wrist. If my hand is so close to your skull that we get contact starring, then I'm going to get some blood blown back on my sleeve. And there's also going to be some blood droplets in the car."

"Yeah," Sean said, waiting for the point.

"Well, the crime scene tech said that, when she examined the seats, there was an area that was empty. Like something had been lying on the seat when the Resnic woman was shot and whatever it was had been removed after the blood droplets had settled."

Matt deliberately acted out walking around the imaginary car from the driver's side where he had just 'shot' Sean. "I open the passenger door and take the money, which had to have been in her purse, and I also take something else. Something like a note that was lying on the seat."

"Something like a note with directions to the muffler shop that the victim wrote down when her killer called her and told her where to go," Sean added, understanding dawning.

"Give the man a cigar. The killer certainly took the note that gave the directions. Maybe he thought there was something on it that tied him to the murder. Who knows?"

"And here it is, in Chris Franklin's garage," Sean finished.

"Hmm."

"What's the problem? This certainly makes it look like Chris is the killer."

"Yeah, I know. But I don't like it."

"Why? Doesn't it solve all your problems? Chris is a child-molesting murderer. He got the initial call about the break-in, realized the old lady kept even more money in her house, went through the motions of doing an investigation while the whole time sizing her up to kill her and take the money. Bad cop got cornered and killed himself. I can already see the headlines."

Matt was silent.

Sean got out of the chair. "If it's any consolation, I don't buy it, either."

"You don't?"

"No, there are some problems."

"More holes?"

"Yes, starting with one great big one: Chris is smart enough to get rid of the gun, but he keeps the note? I don't think so. If you and I can see the blood drops on the note, then so could he. I assume he wasn't stupid or blind, so there's no way he would have disposed of a gun and kept a bloody piece of paper. We haven't found a gun anywhere, right?"

"Nope, and we're just about finished searching the house," Matt confirmed.

"Right. So he dumps the gun but keeps the note? That doesn't add up."

Suddenly, Sean's brain tossed him an idea.

"Can I borrow your car?" Sean asked. "I want to go check a detail with Mrs. Jenkins."

"Mrs. Jenkins? Now?"

"It's not that far. I can be there and back in about an hour."

"Okay, I guess. We've still got to wrap up here, and it will take at least that long."

♦

Sean drove to King's Way, parked, and knocked on Mrs. Jenkins' door.

"Hi," he greeted her when she answered. "I'm Sean Turlow from the DA's office. We met the other day, remember?"

"I remember," Mrs. Jenkins said. "I'm not senile."

"Okay, uh, sorry. Can I ask you a few more questions?"

She didn't say anything, just walked away from the door and into her living room. Sean followed her.

"So, you couldn't call first?" she asked. "Nobody calls first. They just stop by. A call is a simple courtesy."

"To be honest, Mrs. Jenkins," Sean replied, sitting down in the same seat as before, "this is a bit of an emergency."

Mrs. Jenkins wasn't impressed. Sean noted there was no offer of lemonade this time, either.

"The other day, when I was here with the detective," he began, "you mentioned something that's been rolling around my head, and I wanted to see if I could clear it up."

"Head puzzle, huh?"

"Excuse me?"

"That's what Earl used to call them. Those things that rattle around in your head; you can't quite remember, and it eats away at you. Head puzzles."

"That's a good name for them, Mrs. Jenkins. I like that. My particular 'head puzzle' is that you said something about Imogene calling you 'that night.' Do you remember that?"

"Do I remember saying it, or do I remember that night?"

"Uh, either one."

"Well, yes. I remember saying it, and I remember that night."

"Can you tell me what you meant?"

"I simply meant that I didn't believe her, that's all. And I think she knew it."

"You didn't believe what?"

"That Tommy wasn't the burglar. I have children, too, you know. You want to think the best of them, but sometimes they can be little devils. Of course Tommy was the burglar. Who else would it have been? But she said they had proof, so who was I to say different?"

"What proof?"

Mrs. Jenkins fixed him with a look. "You know, I really don't understand you. I know that TV isn't like the real world, but I have to say that you don't seem to do your homework. Why come and ask me about it when it's surely all in the police report?"

"If you could just indulge me for a moment, I'd appreciate it."

"Okay, okay. They said they had the real thief. That's what she was all up in arms about. You'd have thought it was Christmas. It probably did take a load off her mind, that's all."

"What did?"

"The phone call. That's something I never understood, either. I mean, why didn't they just arrest Tommy right there?"

"I'm sorry, Mrs. Jenkins, but I'm not understanding. Why didn't who arrest Tommy when?"

"Are you sure you're cut out for this type of work, Mr. Turlow?"

Sean smiled a little. "There are times when I wonder that, too."

"What I mean is, if the detective was right there, why not arrest Tommy? He must have been close by. I can't imagine why the detective would leave and let Tommy kill her."

"Right where, Mrs. Jenkins?"

"The muffler shop. Why didn't the detective get him right then?"

"The muffler shop? You mean where Mrs. Resnic was killed?"

"Yes."

"There wasn't a police officer there, I'm afraid."

"Oh yes, there was. He told Imogene to meet him there."

"What?"

"Imogene called me. She called me that night, right before she drove over."

Sean sat forward. "She called you the night she was killed?"

"Yes. See, I never liked that boy. I think she knew that, which was probably why she called to tell me I was wrong about him stealing the money. He was a wild boy. He always had long hair and tattoos. I despise tattoos." She shuddered. "Needles. Can't stand them."

"I'm sorry, Mrs. Jenkins, but this is really important. Mrs. Resnic called you the night she died. Do you remember when she called?"

"Right before she met with the detective."

"What detective? What did he say?"

"The one who'd been working the case and, I'm sorry to say, had a lot better handle on this whole affair than you do. He told her to meet him at the muffler shop. See, that's what I don't understand. If he was there, why didn't he stop it? Tommy was bad, like I said, but—"

"I'm sorry," Sean interrupted. "What did the detective say to her?"

"He told her to come to the muffler shop. He said he'd recovered the other money," and here she leaned in conspiratorially, "and we know from *who*. He said that he needed to compare the serial numbers or some such thing. I don't recall the specifics. Well, it stands to reason that, if he'd recovered the money, he got it from Tommy. So, Tommy must have been there. Then, what? He leaves her all alone and lets Tommy kill her? That just doesn't make sense."

Sean's head was beginning to ache.

"Of course," Mrs. Jenkins continued, leaning back, "maybe Tommy followed her. Maybe the detective never saw Tommy. I don't know. The whole thing is just confusing and sad."

Sean was beginning to feel the same way. "Mrs. Jenkins, do you happen to remember the name of the detective?"

She thought for a moment. "Matt something."

"*Matt?*"

"Yes, I remember it made me think of Matt Dillon. That was before your time, but it was a show on TV forever. *Gunsmoke*. Matt Dillon. But that wasn't his last name, just his first."

Sean hesitated. "Matt *Burton?*" he asked in a small voice.

"Yes! That's it. You know, I heard that name again just recently…"

◆

When he got back to the car, Sean was still reeling from the shock of having his whole world turned upside down. He tugged at the neck of his jacket, feeling vaguely trapped.

Jesus. Matt?!

Giving up, he yanked off his jacket and threw it in the back seat.

What the hell am I going to do now?

◆ Chapter Eight ◆

Sean drove to the DA's office, his mind racing. Of course, it was possible that Mrs. Jenkins had gotten the name wrong. She hadn't acted like she recognized Matt when they'd stopped by the other day, but it was also possible at her age that her memory was starting to go and they'd caught her on a bad day—or a good one.

Was Mrs. Jenkins wrong? Could she be wrong about not only Matt but also the phone call? Sean ran it through his mind. His gut told him that, no, Mrs. Jenkins wasn't misremembering or lying.

Did that mean Matt was involved? It would actually explain a few things. He'd kept back pieces of the story and waited a whole week before telling Sean they'd been assigned to work together. Had he used that time to cover his tracks or put things in place to frame Chris?

There was no parking in the shaded section of the employee lot, so Sean parked on top of the structure. He'd have to get Matt his car back, and soon, but right now he needed to talk to Debbie again. He got out, opened the back door to retrieve his jacket—and that's when he saw it.

There was an external hard drive sitting on the back seat of Matt's car.

For a moment Sean wasn't sure what to do, but then he realized he already had his jacket in his hands, and that solved the problem for him. He wrapped the drive in his jacket and carried it inside. There wasn't any problem with the metal detectors. The deputies routinely waived ADAs through, beeping or not.

Once he was inside the office, he stopped to think for a moment. Who could he go to? It would have to be an investigator. Making up his mind, he marched down the hall. Fortunately, Eddie was behind his desk, sipping some coffee and reading a report.

"Hey, Eddie."

"Hey, Sean. What's up?"

"I need you to help me log something into evidence."

"Since when do you guys get your hands dirty transporting evidence?"

"Eddie, can we just do it? Now, please."

Eddie looked surprised at Sean's tone, but he got up and fished his keys out of his pocket. They walked without speaking toward the evidence room.

The DA's office occupied the third floor of the courthouse. The interior was really just one open space, with partitions creating two long hallways that ran from one end to the other, separating the offices along the exterior and in the center, like a long island. The only room with real walls was the DA evidence room, located at the far end of the floor. While the DA evidence room wasn't as large as the one at police headquarters, it didn't have to be. The evidence held in it was for upcoming trials or cases that had gone up on appeal. When a case was nearing trial, the ADA assigned to it would file a request to have all evidence transferred from the police evidence room to the DA evidence room. From there, DA investigators would bring the evidence to the courtroom when it was needed. If any defense attorneys requested a review of the evidence prior to trial, they would come here to see it.

On a nail just inside the door, there hung a clipboard where things were supposed to be logged in and out, but the list was seldom reviewed. Evidence was kept in the drawers of dozens of large filing cabinets that took up almost the entire space. For oversized objects, there were storage bins. Little tags hung from the rifles, machetes, and bags of marijuana Sean could see in the clear tubs.

The only safeguard on the room was that there were two keys required to open the door. ADAs had one key and DA investigators had the other, the idea being that if an ADA needed to review evidence in a case, he or she would need to go to an investigator and they would enter together. In practice, of course, that safeguard wasn't a particularly strong one, since ADAs and DA investigators were generally happy to loan their keys to one another.

In fact, Sean probably could have borrowed a key from an investigator and logged the drive into the evidence room by himself, but he wanted a witness. Despite Eddie's overemphasis on the female form, Sean trusted him and had no doubts he was honest. He had also never worked for the Gannett Police Department, so he didn't have strong ties there. That seemed particularly important at the moment.

"What is that?" Eddie asked as he glanced at what was inside Sean's coat.

"Give me one of those plastic bags, will ya?"

Eddie handed him an evidence bag, and Sean wrote a few notes on the outside with a permanent marker.

"What is it?" Eddie asked again.

Sean used the edges of his coat to push the drive into the bag. "It's an external hard drive. Looks like it could be a terabyte, or maybe even larger. You could store a lot of files on that thing. Or photos."

"Uh-huh. Not gonna tell me what case it's for, huh? That's okay. We about done here?"

Sean made an entry on the evidence log and then found an empty file drawer to store the hard drive. "Yes, we're all done."

As they locked the door, Sean asked, "How long have you known Matt Burton?"

"God." Eddie thought for a moment. "It's got to be at least twenty years. I met him, let's see...oh, how could I forget? I got called out to this house in the country. Guy got three bullet holes in the chest. We figured the brother-in-law was good for it, and that he'd probably used a rifle. The exit wounds were huge. So, we had a warrant to search the brother-in-law's house, and we came up empty. Matt looks around and finds this tree, right off the back deck, maybe thirty or forty yards away. I don't know how the hell he found it. Anyway, this tree looks like it's got bullet holes in it, but the bullets are, like, ten feet off the ground. Matt figures the brother-in-law used the tree for practice. The range was almost the same. Well, everyone's hemming and hawing about what the hell they're gonna do. That was back when Rick worked for the police department, and he thinks we should get a ladder and dig them out. Somebody else suggests a metal detector, but how you gonna get a metal detector that high up on a tree?

"Anyway, we're all standing on the deck talking, and all of a sudden we hear this racket. We run over to the side of the deck and look down. Matt's got a chainsaw, probably from the perp's shed, and just cuts the fucker down, right there. You should have seen it. He cuts out the part with the bullets in it and picks the log up and puts it on his shoulder. His fucking *shoulder*. He carries it over and dumps it into the bed of the crime scene tech's truck. He was always as strong as a bull. That was a long time ago, but I still wouldn't want to tangle with him. He looks like he's got some whoop-ass left." Eddie laughed at the memory.

"Has he ever done anything…iffy?" Sean wondered.

"What are you asking me?"

"You know. Cut some corners, maybe…I don't know, anything not necessarily straight up."

Eddie's demeanor changed immediately. "You put a sock in that shit right now. Matt's straight as a damn arrow. He put away the Shadow Creek rapist. He's a fucking legend around here."

"I know. I know."

"You shouldn't have to ask a question like that."

"Well, in this case, I do."

"You best watch your ass, then. You don't want to go around asking questions like that in Gannett County."

Sean held up his hands. "Okay, I get it."

"Yeah. Well." Eddie walked away.

Sean went back to his office, pulled out a legal pad, and started making notes. He wound up with the same old stuff, only with Matt's name right in the middle of it and Sean not knowing what that meant.

Arthur Deacon, ADA, knocked and stuck his head in the door.

"How are you doing?" Arthur asked.

Sean smiled. Arthur was invariably a bit formal, but for some reason Sean had always liked him.

"What brings you to my neck of the woods?"

"As much as I hate to say it, I am drumming up support for the softball team. Signing people up. That sort of thing."

"*You?* Do you play softball?"

"Lord, no." Arthur edged into the office a little more. "I can't think of anything I would like less than putting on shorts and trying to hit a ball someone threw at my face. But," he looked down at the clipboard in his hands, "I was given the job by Shepherd. I think it is some kind of punishment."

"Softball can be fun, though."

"Were you a jock in high school?" Arthur asked.

"Lord, no. I avoided it like the plague, but then a few years ago I started playing racquetball with a couple of defense attorneys and discovered I wasn't as bad at sports as I always thought."

Arthur mulled it over. "Well, I *am* as bad at sports as I always thought." Motioning with his chin, he asked, "What is the diagram about?"

Sean immediately kicked himself for not covering the pad and tried to look nonchalant as he flipped the page over to a blank one. "It's how I figure things out. I diagram them. It makes it easier to think things through."

"Hmm. You know I used to be a middle school teacher before I went to law school?"

"No," Sean replied, genuinely surprised. "I didn't know that."

"One of the great parts of teaching was using those huge whiteboards to write things out. I do the same thing when I am working on a problem. I like to find a huge surface and put down all the relevant information and see if any patterns emerge. You know they have a whiteboard in the grand jury room?"

"Now that you mention it, I do remember that. Maybe I'll try it out sometime. Thanks for the tip."

After Arthur was gone, Sean flipped the page back over and looked at it. He wrote "external hard drive" below Matt's name and realized that, if he were going to get anywhere, there was someone he had to talk to.

◆

"You look like you've got the whole world sitting on your shoulders," Debbie said when Sean appeared at her door. She was playing with a rubber band, stretching it between her fingers.

"Maybe I do. Can I have another chat?"

"I assume we'll be talking about the same stuff as before?"

"Only more so."

"That sounds both scary and interesting." She put down her rubber band.

Sean closed the door before sitting down. "Debbie, I'm in real trouble." He explained what had happened since he'd met with her on Monday.

"So, you're helping Matt execute a search warrant at Chris' house. That makes you a witness."

Sean nodded. "I know, but I was there the night before when the chief called me out. Besides, Chris is dead. There won't be a prosecution anyway."

"Okay. Real nice on the part of the chief, by the way. Asshole.

"So, Chris was a pervert and child rapist. Good riddance. But that's not the whole thing, is it?"

Sean hesitated. "Chris' computer was still on, and I clicked the mouse. I thought if I could see where his computer automatically saved documents, I could find other information."

"And…"

"And it asked for an external hard drive. I looked everywhere, and it wasn't there. I checked with Matt, and nobody had found anything like that. It was just…gone. But the weird thing was that it had to have disappeared after they dusted for prints."

"Why?"

"You know how that dust gets everywhere. There was an outline on top of Chris' tower that matched the shape of an external hard drive. So, somebody comes along, dusts for prints, and the dust gets on top of the drive. When it gets moved, the clean rectangle underneath shows where it was."

"Well, the wife could have taken it," Debbie suggested.

"No, she couldn't. There were cops there all night, and she slept at a friend's house. She didn't come back until the cops were back the next day."

Debbie was watching Sean's face. "What are you not telling me?"

"I had to borrow Matt's car to go talk with Mrs. Jenkins again, because I'd remembered something. I did speak with her, and she said that she remembered the name of the officer who came out and investigated the burglary after the first call. You know, the unauthorized investigation that we've all been assuming was carried out by Chris?

"She said the detective's name was Matt Burton."

Debbie started to protest, but Sean held up his hand. "I know, I know; there could be a dozen reasons why she'd remember his name. We'd been there a few days before, and she could have just confused the two. But remember I told you I'd borrowed Matt's car to go there? I threw my coat in the back seat, and when I went to get it, I found a drive. An external hard drive. It looked like it would be a perfect fit for the one missing from Chris' house."

Debbie turned away and looked out the window for a few moments. "No," she said, turning back. "It doesn't add up."

"Before you get started, I've already thought it through, and if you're going to say that Matt is too smart to hide incriminating evidence in his car, then I agree with you. If Matt *were* going to commit a crime, he wouldn't tell Mrs. Jenkins his real name. If Matt *were* going to take evidence from a crime scene, he wouldn't hide it in his car. Even if Matt had gone insane, he still wouldn't be *that* crazy."

"Oh, I see where you're going. And you're right, you're screwed."

Sean smiled at her. She was always so quick.

"This is a frame," she continued. "Someone is deliberately pointing you toward Matt."

"And they've either overplayed their hand or Matt is doing a double bluff—and, as you so eloquently put it, I'm screwed either way."

"Yup. Either Matt really is the killer and is deliberately doing these things to make you think exactly what you are thinking, or someone else is involved and trying to frame Matt, in which case you're going to get caught up in the fallout."

Debbie stood up suddenly. "We need to go to your office."

"Why?"

"Trust me," she replied.

Sean followed her down the hall. She stepped through his office door and then closed it behind him. "Play your messages," she demanded.

"You mean on my answering machine?" he asked, bewildered. "Why?"

"Just a hunch. Go on."

He put the phone on speaker and punched in his code. The first message was a woman's voice that he didn't recognize. It sounded as though she was speaking through a voice changer.

"Mr. Turlow, you want to know who killed that Resnic woman? Take a look in the back of Matt Burton's car. You'll get a real surprise."

Sean played the message again, listening even more closely, but he couldn't hear any background noise. It was just the voice. After the second replay, he sat back in his chair and looked at Debbie.

"How the hell…?"

Debbie looked very pleased with herself and sat down in one of his chairs, stretching her legs out so that her heels rested on the top of his desk. She blew on her fingernails and rubbed them on her blouse in a caricature of self-pride. "God, I hate being right all the time."

"How the hell…?" Sean repeated.

"If someone was trying to frame Matt, they'd have to make sure you found the drive in his back seat. It wouldn't work if someone else found it. They couldn't use an email or text because that would leave a trail, but a message on your answering machine? That would do the job just right.

"You said it yourself," she continued, lowering her feet. "Mr. X—or Mrs. X, given the message—has overplayed his hand. He's trying to throw you two different suspects or just gum up the works as much as he can. It's like he's too smart for his own good. If he'd just stuck with Chris, this whole thing would have gone away, but now he's pushed it."

Sean was impressed. "I've got another question for you."

Debbie smiled. "Hit me, baby. I'm on fire today."

"What the hell do I do now?"

"Well, I assume you've logged the drive into evidence." She waited for his nod. "Then the next thing is going to be the hard part: You have to decide if you trust Matt."

"I don't know. Before today I would have said absolutely, no hesitation."

"But now?"

"Now I don't know."

"Well, meet with him. Figure it out."

"You mean you want me to confront him? 'Hey, Matt, you didn't happen to kill a little old lady, did you? Oh, and what's up with the hard drive? You didn't happen to just leave that in your car for me to find, did you?'"

"No, idiot." Debbie sighed. "I mean feel him out. See what he tells you. Compare that with what you know to be true. Direct and cross-examination. You *have* been trained on that, haven't you?"

Sean sat back and thought. "I guess I don't really have any other choice, do I?"

"Watch yourself, though. This thing is getting pretty serious."

◆

Sean sat alone in his office, going over what he and Debbie had discussed. He felt guilty for leaving out what could be considered a material fact: He was sleeping with Tommy Resnic's defense attorney. He'd left it out partly because he knew it was stupid and partly because he knew what she'd say.

You idiot.

And she would have been right. He *was* an idiot.

He picked up his phone and called Matt. Regardless of everything going on, he still needed to return the man's car.

"You still at Chris' house?" he asked in reply to Matt's gruff greeting.

"No. And what the hell happened with you and my car? 'One hour,' you said. I had to catch a ride with a patrol officer back to HQ. I sure hope you have something good to share."

"I've got something; not sure I'd call it good. I'm on my way."

◆

"I looked through Chris' finances," Matt announced when Sean appeared and handed over the car keys. "And I found a whole lot of nothing. Zilch. Like a lot of cops, he had a second job doing security at a local school, but that's it."

Sean's ears pricked up. "School?"

"Yes." Matt sighed. "Elementary school. He did security either in the mornings during arrival or the afternoons during dismissal, depending on when he was on duty for the PD."

"I thought schools already had safety officers."

"Public ones, yeah. But this was a private school. Looks like they paid pretty good, too. But that's it. No thousands of dollars deposited in the last few weeks. No offshore Cayman Island accounts."

"Well," Sean began, studying Matt. "It's not like he'd be stupid enough to just take Mrs. Resnic's money and put it in his checking account."

"You'd be surprised," Matt said, tucking pages into a file, "just how stupid some people can be."

Sean let that one slide. "What about the external drive?"

"I checked with Kathy Whisnant—she's our best crime scene tech, and she dusted the place for fingerprints. She said she remembered seeing a black box on the tower, but she didn't dust it for prints because it had ridges all over it. But she also says she didn't pick it up or put it into evidence."

Sean mulled that over. "Do you think the drive will turn up?"

"I don't know. But I do know something for sure."

"What's that?"

"Somebody is messing with us."

Sean let that hang in the air for a while. "Is there more to that statement?"

"The note. I think somebody planted it. I think somebody is framing Chris for the Resnic murder. I've asked Kathy to run prints on it, by the way. We should hear from her tomorrow. I've also asked her to get some of the blood, and we'll run DNA on it. I'd put good money on it coming back belonging to Mrs. Resnic."

"So would I. Anything else I should know about?"

Matt thought. "Close the door. I should've told you this before, but the chief and Shepherd were having kittens about it and wanted to keep it to themselves..." He paused.

"Yes?" Sean prompted.

"I've got at least one witness who says there was a police car at the muffler shop the night the Resnic woman was killed. Maybe even there at the time she was killed."

"How long were you going to hang onto that?"

Matt glanced at Sean, and his expression changed. "You already knew, didn't you? Okay. Fair enough. I should've told you earlier. I hate this political stuff." Matt continued studying Sean. "Where'd you hear it?"

"A little birdie."

"You play it close to the vest, don't you?"

"That makes two of us. Care to let me in on what the deal is with the driver's license? I was watching your face when you found it. You went white, just for a moment. I didn't think anything could surprise the great Matt Burton."

Matt rapped his fingers on his desk. "There's a couple other things before we go there. I had another talk with DeAnna, Chris' wife. I showed her the pictures."

"Jesus!"

"I know, but I had to. It's going to come out. Better that she hear it from us than from some reporter. The thing is, though, she already knew."

"*What?*"

"She knew. Oh, she tried to cover it. Acted all weirded out and shocked, but I've been doing this for a long time. And she was lying."

"She knew this whole time?"

"She knew, or at least suspected. She also confirmed that Chris kept detailed notes for all of his cases on his computer. Once she got through her Oscar-winning performance, she broke down and told me that Chris did have that external drive you were asking about. I asked her if she got rid of it, but she said she hadn't thought about it until this morning and we were already there when she came back. She said she was planning on getting rid of it but never got the chance."

"Did she say that she knew there was child porn on it?" Sean asked.

"Of course not. But she was planning on getting rid of it. She wouldn't say why, but we can fill in the missing pieces."

"So, we've got Chris keeping his own set of notes on his arrests on the drive and, perhaps, a whole lot of child porn on it, too."

"Yup. Which starts to make that drive look pretty important."

Sean considered for a moment and then made up his mind. He fished a digital recorder out of his pocket and set it on Matt's desk.

"What's that?" Matt asked.

"It's the updated version of what you carry around. This one doesn't require tapes. Anyway, I got a message on my answering machine this afternoon that you might find interesting."

Sean pressed PLAY, and they both heard the distorted voice of the woman telling Sean to look in Matt's back seat for evidence.

Sean stared at Matt for a reaction, but Matt didn't move a muscle. He simply gazed at the recorder for a while. Sean finally decided to break the silence.

"Anything to say to that?"

Matt sat back in his seat and looked at Sean. He held a coffee cup in his big hand that said, "Grand Canyon – One Big Ass Hole."

"I can hear the wheels turning from here," Matt said, finally.

"That's not an answer, Matt."

"Have you got me tried and convicted on this one, Counselor?"

"No. I'd like to hear what you have to say."

"Let's go take a look in my back seat." Matt started to get up.

"I found it there already. In fact, I found it there before I even got this message. I logged it into the DA evidence room."

Matt sat down heavily. "Well, screw you, too," he said, but without conviction. "That's why you asked about it just now, right? Trying to pin me down?"

"Matt, I need a straight answer. We need to get this straight between us."

"Tell you what, hotshot," Matt replied, more heat in his voice now, "if you think you've got enough on me for a murder charge, then you get someone to arrest me. Until then, I don't wanna hear about it."

"There's more."

Matt didn't reply.

"Remember how I borrowed your car because I wanted to talk with Mrs. Jenkins? Well, she told me today that she remembered the name of the police officer who did that investigation of the burglary: Matt Burton."

Matt still didn't say anything.

"Mrs. Jenkins also told me that Mrs. Resnic called her the night she was killed. Mrs. Resnic told Mrs. Jenkins that the police officer who was investigating the break-in had just called her and asked her to drive to the muffler shop. He asked her to bring the other money she had in her house so they could compare serial numbers or something like that. Mrs. Resnic thought her son had been cleared. That's why she called Mrs. Jenkins. You remember how Mrs. Jenkins kept going on and on about how she knew Tommy had done the burglary? Well, Mrs. Resnic called her to tell her she'd been wrong."

Sean stopped, but Matt remained stubbornly silent.

"You see how it looks," Sean began again, tentatively. "I want you to know that I don't believe it. I think someone's trying to frame you and isn't doing a great job of it."

"Well, aren't you just a great guy? What do you want me to do? Give you a medal?"

"Look, we've got to work together on this. Someone out there knows all about this case, and they're working real hard to frame you or Chris or both. If he'd just stuck with Chris, it might have worked. But he had to push it. We're not dealing with a genius here."

"Street-smart, though," Matt added.

"How's that?"

"Street-smart, but not good with forensics. Somebody who knows enough about police procedure to get parts right, but not enough to stage everything perfectly."

Sean sighed. "I guess that means you're not going to shoot me now?"

Matt sighed, too. "Nah. Not today. I can see how it looks from your side. I would've thought the same thing."

"Okay. Since we're talking, who's the woman? Could it be Chris' wife? Is there a woman involved in this case that I don't know about?"

"There's Neeka. And there's the unknown blonde. With Chris' wife, that makes three possibly involved women."

"You know, I'm getting a little tired of not knowing about my own case. Who's Neeka? What blonde? What are you talking about?"

"There wasn't any reason you should know about them. At least until now."

"Why not? You said yourself that they figure in this case. How come no one's told me about them?" Now there was anger in Sean's voice.

"I said, 'might be involved.' We'll have to find out for sure. But before we can do anything, I need to know where we stand. You sure you don't buy this whole story about me killing Resnic and hiding the external drive in my car so that you could find it?"

"I'd like to hear it. I'd like to hear the words."

"Okay. I did not kill Imogene Resnic. I did not take her money. I did not take the drive from Chris' house and then have an attack of stupidity and leave it in the back seat of my car. That good enough for you?"

"Yeah, that's good enough for me," Sean agreed.

"This guy has also made a major mistake."

"What's that?"

"He's let me know that he's out there, that he's trying to screw with the investigation. Now I know it. Now I'm going to hunt him until I have him in cuffs and sitting in a cell."

"So what do we do next?"

"First thing, we get Dave to look at the drive you found and see what he can come up with. You can have one of your investigators sit in while he does it, if that makes you feel better."

Sean sighed. "Matt, there hasn't been a single thing about this case that has made me feel better. I trust Dave. Let's see what he can come up with."

Thursday, April 20, 9:15 a.m.

Dave Cheek was one of the newer breed of cops—tech savvy and not afraid to show it. To a certain extent, he looked exactly like what Sean pictured as the stereotypical geek: a little on the heavy side with a crew cut and thick horn-rimmed glasses. He would launch into an extended conversation about exobytes and teraflops and metadata with only the slightest provocation.

Sean had accompanied Eddie when Eddie had taken the external drive out of the evidence room and driven it over to police headquarters, but Sean didn't stick around to watch Dave do his thing, and he didn't bother asking Eddie to supervise, either. Eddie wouldn't know what Dave was doing any more than Sean did, and they might get in the way or distract Dave as he worked.

By the time Eddie was heading back to his car, Sean's curiosity was eating him alive. He got to Matt's office, closed the door, and began without preamble, "You mentioned three women. Who are they?"

"Good morning to you, too." But then Matt hesitated. "This is going to take us some places you might not want to go."

"Like I've only done things in this case that I was in love with so far."

"All right." Matt stood up. "It's time for a field trip."

◆

"There's the bank." Matt was standing on the edge of Sandhill Road, oblivious to the traffic surrounding him. He had that kind of presence. None of the motorists honked at him; they just made a wide circle around him. Sean opted for caution and stood on the sidewalk.

"You've got an armored car coming down the street from that direction." Matt pointed over his shoulder. "It makes pickups and deliveries every day to the bank.

"You see how Sandhill cuts into the main road here, Haywood Street?"

Sean looked. "It's a pretty sharp angle."

"Yup. That was probably part of the plan. Sandhill practically merges with Haywood, and it makes it a tough turn, especially if you're in an armored car. You actually have to turn onto Haywood and then make another sharp right onto a little side street called Vermont before hanging a left into the bank parking lot."

Sean nodded, but he still had no idea what any of this had to do with his case.

Matt stepped back onto the sidewalk. "Then we come to this." He pointed at the brick wall immediately behind Sean. That retaining wall was the other reason Sean had opted to stand on the sidewalk: It was practically on the street, with only the thin concrete sidewalk—not more than two feet across—between it and the cars shooting past. Sean mused that the whole setup couldn't possibly be up to code. Everything was too close. Too tight.

"There's barely any room for someone walking on the sidewalk," Sean observed.

"Bingo. That's what makes this the perfect setup for an armored car robbery."

"Is that what we're here about? And how does that relate—"

"Just listen. Suppose you've got three vehicles. You follow the armored car, and then when it comes to this street, you have one vehicle pull out in front of the armored car, you slide another alongside, and the last one blocks the rear. There's no place for the armored car to go."

Sean looked around, picturing it. "Okay. I get it. Only, you've got it blocked, but those things are built like tanks. They aren't just going to open up if you ask nicely."

"True. So that's when you open up with your .50 cal."

"Your fifty what?"

"Rifle. Your .50-caliber rifle. Probably mounted on a stand. You'd have to be pretty strong to hold and aim that thing with just your arms. It's a miracle they didn't kill the driver, the idiots."

"So this actually happened?" Sean asked, a little incredulous. "I didn't hear about it."

"Well, it kind of happened," Matt explained. "They attacked the car, but they picked the wrong day or got the wrong intel or something because the armored car was empty. The armored car company routinely changes the schedules and the routes. Our guys didn't know that. They thought the company was getting ready to drop off money, but instead it was a pickup day. So, our guys went storming in with ski masks and guns and discovered there was no money inside. That had to sting."

"Really?"

"Really. They got pissed off, but what were they going to do? They backed out in a hurry and took off, but not before both the driver and a guard heard one of the guys talk. They both said he had a strange accent, like he was from another country. It wasn't a Mexican accent, and one of them thought it was Russian, but who knows? There were two other guys, but all we've got on them is that they were bulky, had on ski masks, and were white. No age. They skedaddled when they didn't find the money, and that's the end of our story."

Sean waited a moment. "Okay. Interesting story. I still don't see where it ties into anything we're working on, though."

Matt smiled thinly. "You asked earlier about any women involved in this mess of a case. Both the driver and the front guard are certain that the person who pulled out in front of the armored car and blocked them was a woman. A blonde woman. She actually rammed them, although they were already stopping. Still, it was a gutsy move. The witnesses say the car was a two-door, maybe Honda, maybe Toyota, but not something you'd normally put up against an armored car."

"How does all of this tie in—"

"In a minute. We got three guys and a blonde woman," Matt repeated. "No fingerprints at the scene. A big, spent hunk of metal that used to be a bullet. No ID on the robbers. No ID on the woman. We find two vans later, torched, that must have been the other vehicles used. Would have been the perfect crime except for the not-getting-any-money part. There's not much to go on, except for the rifle. You don't just find those lying around. The ballistics guy at the state crime lab says the bullet was probably fired from a Russian model, given the type of ammo. Maybe an…" and here he pulled a note out of his front pocket and glanced at it, "an *OSV-96*. That's a little odd for a regular ol' crime here in Atlanta. We've got a guy with a weird accent that one witness says is Russian. Then we find that both vans were stolen from the vicinity of Copper Street."

Sean decided not to interrupt. Matt was going somewhere, and Sean would just have to wait it out until he got there.

"I think the Russian in the armored car was Gregor Itzvanov," Matt concluded.

The name rang a bell. "Wait. Didn't you find his driver's license at Chris' house?"

"Yup, found it in Chris' garage."

Sean waited.

"Gregor is with, well, *was* with a girl named Neeka Tatum who lives on Copper Street." Matt looked around. "Let's head back to the car."

Once inside, Matt continued. "Here's where we get into flat-out speculation, 'cause at this point I can't prove a damn thing. But if Gregor was the guy with the weird accent who was part of the robbery, I think he also provided the weapon. I spoke to a friend of his who said Gregor might have known somebody in the Russian mafia, and that's the kind of connection that could get you that kind of rifle. These guys work up the plan, and Gregor provides the firepower. Then, *bam!* The whole thing goes south. No money. And for whatever reason, Gregor's partners decided to kill him. They kidnapped him from the trailer or lured him somewhere and then smothered him to death by wrapping his head with duct tape."

"Jesus."

"I know. Not the way I'd pick to go. Anyway, after they killed Gregor, they dumped his body behind a defunct strip mall, and that's where we found it last Saturday."

"Okay. But I still don't see how this connects to Chris, except that you found Gregor's license in Chris' house."

"Remember, I spoke with Gregor's roommate," Matt reminded him. "He didn't want to tell me anything at first, but then he finally said Gregor had been working with a bad cop. He said this cop and Gregor were doing jobs together."

"And you think Chris was the bad cop?"

"It would explain what Gregor's license was doing in Chris' house."

Sean thought it over. "Chris was a big guy. He obviously worked out, but then so does just about every patrol cop in Gannett. Lee even owns a gym, right? But you said there were three guys at the robbery. Who was the third? Another cop?"

Matt shrugged. "I don't know."

"And another thing. Who was the woman? Could it have been Gregor's girlfriend? Neeka, wasn't it?"

"No." Matt shook his head. "The driver and guard were quite sure the woman was white and blonde. Neeka is black."

"Hmm." Sean thought for another minute. "Well, I still think we should talk with her."

"I already did, but it might be a good time to drop by and talk to her again. She wouldn't give me anything solid, but she hinted that Gregor was working with a cop. Let's go on over."

"To Copper Street? Rather than bringing her into HQ?" Sean couldn't completely remove the apprehension from his voice.

"Sure." Matt slid a glance toward him. "What's the matter? Copper Street bother you?"

"No. Copper Street scares the shit out of me. Do you know how many of the drug cases I've prosecuted happened there?"

"They give you guys service weapons, don't they?"

"Yeah, they issued me a gun, but it's sitting in my sock drawer at home. I never carry it."

"Why not?" Matt wanted to know.

"Because I'm not that crazy about guns. Also, I'm a lousy shot. About two months after they gave me the gun and the badge, I began to wonder what the hell I needed either one for. If I get in a shootout, I'm screwed. I'm a lawyer, for Chrissake. I don't draw down on anyone. I do trials. I question people."

"So, you don't carry the badge either?"

"Oh, I still carry that. It impresses girls and gets me out of speeding tickets."

"Our tax dollars hard at work."

◆

They drove to Copper Street, and Sean was glad he was inside Matt's car. The Crown Vic stuck out like a sore thumb and seemed to shout "police" at the men and women moving around outside. He noticed that most of them disappeared as soon as the car rolled up to the trailer Matt identified as Neeka's. They both got out, and while Sean looked around nervously, Matt went to the front door and knocked. There was no answer. Matt wandered around to the back, and Sean trailed after him. There was no car, and the place just felt empty.

"I don't think she's here," Sean ventured.

"No kidding." Matt was standing with his hands on his hips, looking at the back door. Someone had just about pried it off its hinges. Matt took a few more steps and then slowly craned his neck to look inside. Sean noted that Matt's right hand had gone to the butt of his gun. When Matt suddenly drew his weapon, Sean regretted leaving his own at home. Having a gun in his hand, no matter how little experience he had with it, would have felt pretty good just then.

Matt went slowly up the back steps and stopped at the threshold, most of his body leaning against the doorjamb. He quickly glanced inside before pulling his head back. Then he looked again and seemed to relax a little. After a moment, he crossed the threshold, calling Neeka's name. Sean was left in the backyard, staring at the garbage strewn everywhere.

After a minute, Matt came back out of the trailer and holstered his weapon. He was already talking on his phone.

"Yeah, send the techs. I've got blood on the carpet and more on the doors. No body, but one hell of a struggle." He listened for a moment. "Okay," he replied and hung up.

He turned to Sean. "Neeka's gone. Looks like someone took her and used a lot of force to do it. Broke the door, smashed a few things. Her purse is still in there. So are her phone and a head of lettuce."

"Lettuce?"

"Yup." Matt sighed. "When I met Neeka the other day, she was just getting home from buying groceries. There are still some things on the table that haven't been put away. Stuff you wouldn't leave out: milk, butter, lettuce."

"You think she got snatched right after you spoke with her?"

"It sure looks that way."

♦ CHAPTER NINE ♦

Thursday, April 20, 10:30 a.m.

Once the crime scene techs descended, Sean relaxed. Copper Street had turned into a ghost town with the arrival of multiple cop cars, and Sean no longer felt like he had a target painted on his back. He stayed at the scene for a while, but when it became obvious that there weren't going to be any immediate answers as to what had happened to Neeka, Matt suggested they head back to the precinct.

When they got back, Sean walked to his own car and sat behind the wheel for a while without turning the key. He wanted to talk to someone. A specific someone, in fact, but he knew it was a bad idea.

He dialed her cell anyway, and waited.

"Hello," Diana answered.

"Hey. It's been a long and terrible day. Could you say something nice to me?"

"How about, 'you're good in bed'?" Diana purred, and he could hear the smile in her voice.

"That's not bad," he replied, smiling too. "If you could throw in something about my enormous size, that would round it off nicely."

"Let's not get carried away. Hey, it's not even noon yet. Why has it been such a long and terrible day?"

"Jesus." He let out a long sigh. "Are we still on for lunch? Please say yes."

"Yes."

"Okay, I'll tell you about it then. Some of it may blow your mind."

"This sounds serious."

"Very."

"Peaches Café at one o'clock still okay?"

"Still works for me. See you then."

♦

Sean drove back to his office and took care of the paperwork that had been piling up on his desk. Beth, his secretary, pointed out several items that needed immediate attention. She liked to stay on top of things, and although Sean wasn't the typical procrastinator attorney, all of this extra work with Matt had put him behind. By the time he'd signed his name to over a dozen discovery packets and reviewed some work submitted by Tom, it was getting close to lunch.

He couldn't wait to see Diana.

She was five minutes late, and each minute felt like an eternity to Sean, who couldn't help glancing at the door every few seconds.

God, you've got it bad. You'd better play this cool, or you'll turn her off.

But when she walked in, everything in his world settled back into a comfortable rhythm. She saw him, waved, and sauntered over. He loved the way she moved. He stood and pulled out a chair for her.

"Thanks. Not many men do that anymore."

"I'm old-fashioned," he told her.

They ordered lunch and settled back into their seats. He liked looking at her.

"Do you mind if we dispense with some business first?" she asked.

"Okay."

"You know I'm representing Tommy Resnic in that murder charge. You may remember him from prelims last week."

Sean nodded. Had that only been last week?

"He wants to talk to you."

"What?"

"That's what he told me this morning. He wants to talk to you, personally."

"Why?"

"He wants to tell you that he didn't kill his mother."

"I assume you told him—"

She was already nodding her head. "Yes, I told him. Defendants never talk to prosecutors. I advised him not to talk with you, or anyone in law enforcement, but he stuck to his guns."

"What does he think he'll gain by talking with me?"

"Apparently, you made quite an impression on him. He's also been asking around at the jail. You seem to have a good reputation there, too. He thinks he can get you to dismiss this case if you'll just hear him out."

Sean shifted uncomfortably. "Great. The guys at the jail think I'm a solid guy. Somehow, that just makes my day. This meeting with your client: I don't think that would be wise."

"Oh, I agree. But he asked me to relay the request, and so I'm doing it." Diana sat back and studied him. "So, what's going on?"

"I'm not sure where to begin." Sean drummed his fingers for a moment, considering. "I've got a problem."

"I'm all ears."

"I've been asked to do something I don't think is right. If I don't do it, my career may be in jeopardy. If I do it, then my ethics are in jeopardy."

"I see." She tapped the glass she was holding.

They waited while the waiter served their food, and then Sean looked at her again.

"I think the whole story about the Resnic case hasn't come out yet."

She froze, hand halfway to her fork.

"I don't think that your client killed his mother. I haven't thought so for a while now."

"Are you telling me this as his prosecutor or as a…friend?"

"I'm not telling you this because I'm gaga over you, if that's what you're asking."

"I wasn't trying to—"

"I think there may have been a police officer involved in the killing," Sean told her.

"My God! Are you sure?"

"No. I'm not sure. But you need to know."

"I see."

"And there's something else. This whole case just feels wrong. I've got my boss on my ass kinda sorta suggesting that I bury any evidence that would make the police department or the DA's office look bad."

"They actually said that?"

"Kinda sorta. No one is going to come out and tell me to my face, 'Hey, Sean, make this whole problem disappear,' but the vibe is certainly there. And there's another problem…

"I'm incredibly attracted to you, but this…whatever this is…it could take a major toll on both of our careers."

She sat very still. "You mean, if you're seen consorting with the enemy."

"No. Well, yes. I've told you these things because I think you have the right to know, as Resnic's defense attorney. I'll be serving them on you later, to make it official, but…"

"But?" Diana was obviously getting angry.

"I'm not entirely sure of my own motives. I really like you, but we're already crossing a line here and, Christ, I don't know what I'm doing."

"Okay." Diana stood up. "I think we're done here." She reached for her briefcase, movements jerky with anger. "When you get your shit together and figure it out, you let me know."

Sean just sat there as she stalked out the door, wondering how everything had gone so wrong so quickly.

♦

"Who died?" Matt greeted Sean when Sean appeared in his doorway after lunch.

"Me." After a pause, Sean continued, "Can I sit down?"

"Free country," Matt observed.

"You know the other day, when we were talking with Mrs. Jenkins?" Sean shut the door and took the visitor's chair. "She said that maybe I wasn't cut out for this line of work. I'm starting to think she was right."

"You didn't look so grim this morning. What's happened?"

"Nothing you could possibly want to know."

"Try me."

"Woman trouble."

"Ohhhh." There was grim understanding in Matt's voice.

"I just got in a fight with a woman I really care about."

"Uh-huh."

"Like I said, you don't want to know."

"Do you love this woman?"

Sean looked up. He hadn't expected that question. "I, uh," he began— and was suddenly at a loss for something to say.

"Okay, that means 'yes.' So, why'd you fight?"

"It's complicated."

"Well, this reaffirms my faith in my fellow man."

"How does it possibly do that?"

"Here I was thinking you were Mr. Straight Arrow. Mr. Clean."

Sean sighed. "So, it makes you feel better to know that I'm just as much of a screwup as anyone else?"

"Actually, it does." Matt looked at him for a while. "I was married before Angela, you know."

"I didn't know."

"I fooled around. I lost the love of a good woman. It was the lowest point of my life. Then, a few years later, I met Angela. We didn't exactly hit it off, not at first." He smiled at the memory. "But we eventually got it together. Turns out, it was the best thing that ever happened to me."

Sean didn't say anything.

"I also learned that all that passion and intensity you get when you first start with a woman, well, it doesn't last. You've got to build your life together on something a bit more solid than a good lay."

"Relationship advice? From Matt Burton?"

"Once you get a good woman, a woman who'll stand by you, you don't ever screw that up. You hear?"

"I hear."

"Okay," Matt said, shrugging off the whole conversation. "Let's talk about our own problem. Oh, and open up the damn door. I need some air."

Sean got up and opened the door. For a moment he stood there, looking at all of the cubicles and the various officers, some in uniform, most in street clothes. They were working on dozens, maybe hundreds, of cases.

And one of them might be a murderer.

"I went ahead and pulled Tommy Resnic's bank records. I figured if we checked Chris, the least we could do was the same for Tommy. Same result. Nothing. No large deposits. Just little things here and there. Looks like maybe his mother was depositing money into his account every few weeks. Here." Matt handed over a stack of paper. "Take a look."

"You've got her financials here, too."

"By the book. We go through everything. I had warrants worked up and sent an officer out to pick everything up this morning."

Sean went through the different pages.

"Take a look at March for both Mrs. Resnic and her son. You'll see what I'm talking about," Matt advised.

Sean saw it immediately, setting the two bank statements next to each other on his side of the desk. "You're right. For every check she makes out to him, there's a corresponding deposit into his account. I don't know if this helps or hurts our case, though."

"How do you mean?"

"Well, on the one hand, a defense attorney might say, 'Why did Tommy need to kill his mother for money when she was already paying his bills?' Of course, I could argue that maybe he got tired of that arrangement, maybe even resentful, and decided to take out the middleman. Quite literally. But—"

He was interrupted when the phone on Matt's desk rang.

Thursday, April 20, 2:05 p.m.

"Pick up the phone, bitch."

Neeka cowered in a corner. Her face was already puffy from the repeated blows. Her lips felt huge. One of her eyes was swollen shut.

"I said, pick up the phone, you fucking bitch."

Neeka's trembling hand reached out. Her vision was so blurred that she couldn't quite make out the phone being handed to her. Her mouth was filled with the coppery wetness of her own blood.

"What do you want?" Neeka cried out shakily. "Why are you doing this?"

"Dial this number!"

Neeka's head reeled. She was going to black out. A hand sliced through the air again, hitting her in the same swollen eye. She screamed.

"Do you want to die, bitch?"

No, Neeka thought, but had a hard time forming the word. "N-no. Please."

She dialed the number. She got it wrong the first time and was rewarded with a kick in the stomach. Neeka pitched over and retched. There wasn't anything in her stomach; they hadn't fed in her days. She'd had to piss in the corner of this little room like some kind of animal.

"You do this right, and we'll let you go."

Neeka wanted to believe that. Oh, Lord, she wanted to be let go. She had a picture of herself walking through a mall, smelling the food. People would smile at her. *Hey, Neeka. Looking good, girl.*

The kick in the ribs brought her back. Neeka couldn't even scream, it hurt so bad. Something had given way inside her; she could feel it. Terror ran through her. *If they let me go now, maybe I'll still look okay. My face will get better.* She gagged on her own blood. There seemed to be a lot of it. She drifted for a moment. *Looking good, Neeka.* Ever since she was a girl, they'd said that. She remembered choir practice, a long, long time ago. They'd even said it then, as she took the microphone, singing a solo before the packed church. *Such a pretty girl.* They would say that as they looked up at her. *Such a pretty girl.*

Looking good, Neeka.

"Are you listening, you fucking bitch?"

"I, uh…" She was desperate to avoid another blow. "Yes. I was—"

The next slap made her head bang into the cinder block wall behind her. Not the face. God, how did she look? If they let her go now, even with that last slap, she might be all right. She'd heal up fine. Something felt sheared and broken in her side. Broken ribs. They would heal, though. No scars.

"I won't tell!" she suddenly screamed. "Just let me go. I won't tell. Don't hit my face, that's all. I won't tell, just don't hit my face."

The words came out distorted by her swollen lips. *They'll be all right,* she told herself again. *Nothing permanent.*

Looking good, Neeka.

Such a pretty girl.

The phone was pressed against her ear.

"What do you want me to say?" Neeka stammered.

She heard a man answer. "Hello?"

Neeka cried softly, feeling the tears working out over her balloon-sized cheeks. "Help me…"

"Tell him your name," her tormentor ordered.

"This is Neeka," she sobbed, ready to do anything to avoid another blow.

Then the gun came out. She could see it through one bleary eye. She could make out the face behind it, and she knew, *she knew*.

"Oh my Lord!"

The gun exploded. *Not my face*, she thought as her head snapped back against the wall.

Looking good, girl.

She felt the blood pouring out of her. Neeka turned toward a light and began to fall. *Such a pretty girl*, she thought as she died.

Thursday, April 20, 2:15 p.m.

Sean watched Matt gently place the phone back on its cradle.

"Damn," he said quietly.

Sean didn't speak. He didn't need to be told that something bad had happened on the other end of the line.

"That was Neeka, Gregor's girl. I think someone just killed her." Matt stood up. "I need a few minutes," he tossed over his shoulder as he walked out the door.

Sean was still wondering what the hell was going on and decided to wait for more information. After a moment or two, he bent back over the financial records.

"Where's Matt?" asked a voice from the doorway.

Sean glanced up and saw Lee standing behind him, holding some reports.

"He just left. He'll be back in a few minutes."

"I was going to ask him something, but since you're here, maybe you could give me some legal advice?"

Lee laid a report down on Matt's desk and explained the facts. "I pull a guy over for a DUI. He's a real fucking 10-73, talking about Jesus and the Second Coming. Fucker smells like a beer factory. Fails the field sobriety tests, no problem. Now he's under arrest. I can't leave his car by the side of the road, so I ask him if he has a particular towing company he'd like to use. He says, 'No, just leave it. I'll call my wife from the station.' I say, 'No, uh-uh, it's got to be towed.' He says, 'What if I make sure you get something nice next week for leaving it there?' I say, 'What do you mean?' He clams up. Have I got enough for a bribery case?"

Sean thought for a moment. "Technically, maybe. But I wouldn't want to prosecute it. I don't think any jury would convict on those facts."

Lee rolled back on his toes. "Yeah, that's what I was afraid of. Oh, well. Thanks." He paused for a moment. "You look like you've got something heavy on your mind."

"Just trying to figure something out. I've had something right here," Sean touched his temple, "but I can't get it."

"Head puzzle, huh?"

"Uh, yeah."

"Anyway," Lee said on his way out the door, "tell that old fart that I stopped by."

Sean stared after Lee for a moment, feeling more than ever like he was on the verge of discovering additional pieces of the puzzle, then saw Matt walking back toward the office, weariness clear in his every movement.

"So you think she's dead?" Sean asked once Matt was back inside.

"Yup."

"This is the same Neeka you were telling me about? The Russian's girlfriend? Why would someone want to kill her?"

"I don't know."

"Still, it's pretty cold. I mean, that sounds like something only a psychopath would do."

Matt sat in silence. Then he seemed to make up his mind. "I'm going home."

"What about...? You know, the case and..." Sean's voice trailed off.

"It'll wait."

◆

After Matt left, Sean decided to head back to the DA's office. He certainly had plenty of work to do. He settled in and started reviewing case files, figuring that work would keep his mind off his own troubles.

He spent the rest of the afternoon alternating between looking out the window and working. Somehow, in the span of just a few days, his whole life had been thrown upside down. He didn't even want to ask Debbie for advice this time. He'd made his mistakes, and now he'd have to live with them.

◆

Sean got home at six o'clock, took off his coat, and draped it over the arm of his sofa. God, he was tired. He started when the phone rang.

Then he saw who was calling.

"Hello," he answered, almost gingerly.

"Hi," Diana replied. "I'm in the neighborhood. Mind if I drop by?"

"No! Uh, not at all. Please do." He grabbed his coat and rushed around the room, picking up dirty clothes and unwashed dishes.

"Look out your window. I'm in the car on your far left."

Sean stood at his balcony and stared down into the parking lot.

"That's a lot of clothes you have in your hands."

He shrugged. "Well, I thought it would be a good time to straighten up. I normally clean my apartment on Thursday evenings, whether it needs it or not."

Diana got out of her car, still holding her cell phone. She stared up at him. He dropped the bundle of clothes by the dining room table and gazed down at her.

"Why don't you hang up and let me in?" she suggested.

He ran to the door.

He loved watching her come up the stairs. She moved like a cat, surefooted, easily, with an athletic grace. When she turned at the landing, she was facing him, and her eyes never left his as she climbed the final steps. He was entranced.

When she reached the top, she kept moving directly into his arms and kissed him. He'd never felt anything so wonderful in his life. He couldn't remember what he'd been thinking about before she called; he couldn't remember anything at all. The only thing in his universe was her body pressed against his and the soft warmth of her lips. She gently pushed away and walked past him into his apartment. He swallowed and followed her.

"Would you like something to drink?" he offered.

"No."

"Okay."

She looked around his apartment as though inspecting it. She'd been there once before, of course, but she seemed to be seeing it with new eyes tonight. She took off her coat and draped it over a dining room chair. Her restless gaze finally locked on him.

"We have some things we need to discuss."

"Yes." Sean shifted. "I know. Look, I—"

"Don't say, 'I'm sorry' again."

"Okay. It's just that, after lunch today…I didn't think you'd want to speak with me again."

"Oh, I was pretty angry. But then I started thinking about it from a different perspective. I decided to give you the benefit of the doubt. Maybe, just maybe, you are telling the truth. Maybe you are a good guy. Then again, history has shown that I have incredibly bad taste in men. Maybe you're just a womanizing jerk."

Sean didn't say anything.

"This is the point where you jump up and defend yourself."

"I don't have a defense. I'm crazy about you, but what we're doing could hurt us both. Somehow, though, I don't care. Ever since I met you, I've been…"

"Swept off your feet? That's supposed to be my line."

"I don't have any lines, not anymore."

"You could've avoided the whole problem by not telling me anything."

"I know."

"Why *did* you tell me, then? Was it because you like me? Or because you felt an ethical obligation?" Diana's face was serious.

"I don't know. I'd like to think I would have told you if you'd been sixty years old, overweight, and a man, as long as you were still Resnic's attorney."

"Maybe it's important to you how I feel about you, though?"

He didn't say anything.

She nodded to herself and continued to move around the room. "You are an unusual man."

There still didn't seem to be anything for him to say.

"Aren't you going to say something?"

"Every time I look at you I seem to be at a loss for words."

She smiled and stepped past him into the bedroom.

♦

Diana was up and dressed early the next morning. She kissed Sean awake, and he reached for her.

"I have to go," she said as he tried to unbutton her blouse.

"But Counselor," he protested, "I'm in dire need of legal advice."

She gently pushed his hands away. "You've gotten all the legal advice you're going to get for a while. I've got court at nine. Stop that, now."

She kissed him again, and then she was gone.

He lay there for a long, luxurious moment, drinking in the peace and the memories of the prior night. After a while, he got up and made himself some coffee. He couldn't seem to stop smiling. He put on his bathrobe and sat at the dining room table, sipping and smiling.

God, he thought. *God, what a woman.*

♦

Sean grabbed another cup of coffee from the break room before heading into his office. The pile of work that had been there the day before seemed to have doubled in size, but his mood was considerably better. He resolved to at least start chipping away it.

After ten minutes, Tom stopped by. "Hey."

"Hey, Tom."

"What's on the agenda for today? More thrilling paperwork?"

"Actually…" Sean considered as an idea started to form. "I could use your help."

"Okay." Tom sat down, looking eager.

Sean wasn't sure where to start. "Tom, why don't you close the door?" When Tom had done that, Sean began. "Just how sure are you that you want to be a prosecutor?"

"Very. Just being here has been great! I've learned so much from you, the other guys; it's been amazing."

"Okay. Well, I can't think of any other way to get into this than just to jump in. Can I have your word that anything we talk about right now won't go any further? I'm serious. No talking it over with other third-years, nobody."

Tom hesitated a moment. "Okay. Yeah."

"I have a dead Russian. He was murdered. He may or may not have had contacts with the police department—and by 'contacts,' I mean that he may have been working with a police officer to commit crimes. You getting the picture?"

Tom's eyes grew large, but he didn't say anything.

"It occurred to me last night, when I was doing…something else, that, if our Russian had a record, then maybe he met this cop when the cop arrested him. Okay so far?"

"Okay."

"I want to turn you loose in our case database and see if you can find any cases we had against this Russian. Then I want you to pull up those cases and see who the arresting officer was. Do you think you can do that?"

"Sounds really interesting. Do you want me to use your computer?"

"No, I need mine to work through this mountain of paperwork. But there's a free terminal in an empty office down the hall. I can set you up in there."

"Okay, what's the Russian guy's name?"

Sean had to write it out for him. Once he'd logged Tom onto the computer in the spare office, he went back to his own. He started working up his *Brady* notice to Diana, including the material about the witness who may have seen the police car at the murder scene, a copy of Resnic's short statement to Matt, and a copy of the handwritten directions from Imogene's house to Mick's Muffler. After that, he called Eddie.

"What's up?" Eddie said, walking in.

"How would you like to hand-deliver some discovery stuff to Diana Baker? She'll need to sign for it herself."

Eddie's grin was lascivious. Sean felt a pang of guilt for subjecting Diana to Eddie's behavior, but if there was anyone in the office who would make sure the material got to her, it would be Eddie.

Sean handed him the package and gave him Diana's office address. Eddie marched off with an apparent song in his heart and an added bounce in his step. Sean just shook his head.

♦

Sean's cell phone rang, and without checking the name, he answered. "Sean Turlow."

"My, you sound like a man who had a relaxing evening," Diana said.

He smiled. "Well, I have had some wonderful nights lately. I was in a great mood when I got up this morning."

"Me, too. It's been hard to focus. But I was thinking, we never did get around to talking last night. You said yesterday at lunch that you had some things to tell me."

"I do, but they're official. We need to talk about this whole mess, and I just sent Eddie over to serve you with a bunch of *Brady* material."

"I see. I don't suppose you could tell me why you've been working so closely with Matt on my case?"

"Yes, I can. But I'd prefer not to talk about it on the phone."

"How about we meet for lunch somewhere out of the way?"

"Someplace dark, with cozy seats, where we can sit close together?"

"Sure," she agreed, a sly smile in her voice. "I'll call you in a couple of hours. I've got to get into court now. Bye, lover."

"Bye-bye." He hung up the phone, trying not to count the minutes until lunch.

Sighing, he pulled a legal pad toward him and started to write but realized there was just too much. Then he got an idea. He gathered up some notes and left his office.

The grand jury room was on the same end of the DA's office as the evidence room. The grand jury met every Tuesday to hear cases, but it was vacant the rest of the time. Arthur had reminded him about the huge whiteboard in there, and when he unlocked the door and flicked on the lights, Sean realized that it was perfect.

He picked up a marker and started writing on the big, white space.

Facts:

Imogene Resnic was burglarized

A few days later, a police officer calls and tells her to meet him (only have Mrs. Jenkins' word for this)

Imogene is killed

No gun is found

Son is charged with her murder

Son had motive (money) and opportunity

Per Mrs. Jenkins, a police officer came out after the burglary call and did an investigation. This was not authorized.

Who did the investigation? Chris Franklin? Someone else? If someone else, then how did they know anything about the call?

Here, he stopped and thought for a moment.

Break room at police HQ. Officers finishing up their notes from arrests during that shift.

Did someone see the burglary report? Did they take it so it wouldn't go into the system?

Possible suspects: other officers who worked that same shift or were just going onto a new shift. Pool of suspects? 20 or 30 officers.

He almost added some profanity but decided against it. Then, after a pause, he continued.

Is Matt involved?

No money found in Chris' accounts or Resnic's accounts. Where did money go?

Who was in police car at muffler shop the night before? Any way to pin this down?

He thought, but didn't write, *How much of this do I tell Diana Baker?* Sean froze when someone opened the door and walked in. It was

Angela Burton, Matt's wife.

"What are you doing in here?" she asked.

"Working. I needed someplace to write out a bunch of notes, work out some ideas." He'd already picked up the eraser and started removing his scribbles, focusing on the part with Matt's name. "What are *you* doing back here?" He tried to sound nonchalant while wondering frantically if she'd seen her husband's name on the board.

"The bathroom is better back here."

"It is?"

"You've never seen it? It's twice the size of the ladies' room on my end. They even have magazines in there."

"To tell you the truth, I've never been to the bathroom in this area."

"Well, don't spread it around. I don't want everyone coming back here. It's our little secret, okay?" She smiled at him.

He couldn't help but smile back. "You got it."

Angela stopped again before she was entirely through the doorway to the bathroom area. "Did you get your idea worked out?"

"Not really."

"Maybe you should lay your cards on the table with Matt. All of them." She stepped through the door, and he heard her call out, "See ya, Sean."

He stopped erasing and wondered what she'd meant. There had been a message there, and it seemed that at the very least she'd seen her husband's name in the mess he'd put up on the board. For some reason, he didn't want to still be there when Angela came out, so he hurriedly finished erasing everything and returned to his office.

◆

Tom knocked on Sean's open office door, and Sean motioned him in. He got up and closed the door before taking his seat again.

"What did you find?"

Tom was pleased with himself. "This Gregor guy was into a lot of stuff. There were three separate cases for armed robbery. I could pull up the two most recent, but the third once said 'AC' and nothing else."

Sean thought for a moment. "'AC' means 'archive.' Those were cases that were made before we had gone completely to the scanned system. They didn't scan all the old files; they just picked an arbitrary date and started scanning everything from that point forward."

"So, where would I find this old case?"

"The basement. There's a huge archive down there stretching back…well, I don't know how far it goes, but there are a lot of boxes. I've only been there once." Sean paused. "Before you go, who were the arresting officers on the two cases you did find?"

"There was an A. Hernandez and a J. Felson."

"Okay." Sean pulled out a piece of his letterhead. "Take this with you to the basement and show it to the custodian. That will get you in the door. After that, you'll have to figure out how they've got it organized and then find the right case. You may be down there a while, and it may even be a wild goose chase. But I need to know who the arresting officer on that last case was."

Once Tom was gone, Sean worked steadily until he got a text from Diana with an address and time for lunch. They met at a Mexican restaurant on the other side of town. It was dark, and the booths were secluded and built for quiet conversation. His face lit up when he saw her, and a slow throb of pleasure moved through him. They kissed lightly before sitting down. She took his hand, and they stared into each other's eyes.

Sean's brain whirled, torn between pleasure in her company and dread of the work-related talk he knew had to happen. He didn't really want to discuss any of it, but he had to tell her. He rolled it around in his head. How much should he tell her? Would it get him in hot water with Shepherd? Would it get him fired? And what about Resnic? They had him all lined up to be the fall guy, but Sean still wasn't convinced Tommy had anything to do with his mother's murder.

"Hey." Diana pinched Sean's arm lightly. "Pretty girl at the table."

"Sorry," he apologized. "I've got a lot on my mind."

"Why don't you tell me about it?"

"I'd like to, but…"

"But what?"

"Our professions kind of get in the way."

"Oh, legal stuff. I thought it was something more…personal. You did say you were crazy about me."

Sean actually blushed. "Too much? Too soon? Lately everything seems out of focus, and…"

She put a finger across his lips. "You don't have to walk on eggshells around me. So, what's the legal problem on your mind?"

He thought for a moment. Should he lay his cards on the table? "I'm in an ethical dilemma."

"What about?"

"Let me lay out a hypothetical problem for you, and then you can tell me, in your legal opinion, what you think I should do."

"Okay."

"Let's say there's a prosecutor. He's got a murder case that seems a little thin to him. He starts looking into it, and the more he digs, the less he likes what he finds. Say, for example, he discovers that a police officer may be involved, in some way, with the death of the victim.

"Say there was a burglary at the victim's house several days before the victim was killed. A certain police officer who was called out to the scene radios back that there's nothing to report. But then this officer, or someone, does their own unofficial investigation of the burglary. There's no record of this investigation because, as far as Property Crimes knows, there's no case. Then let's say that, on the night of her murder, the victim receives a telephone call…from a police officer. The officer asks her to come to a muffler shop."

Diana looked stricken. "Please tell me you're joking."

Sean shook his head. "There's a witness who says she got a call from the victim shortly before the victim left for the meeting. See, the witness never liked the victim's son and had basically accused him of committing the burglary. The victim gets a call from a police officer saying that someone else took the money; the victim picks up the phone and calls the witness. 'N'yah, n'yah, it wasn't my boy after all.' That sort of thing. The victim tells the witness that the officer has asked her to bring the rest of her money with her, so they can match serial numbers or something like that; she goes to the meeting and gets killed. Got the picture?"

"I think so." Diana's voice was quiet.

"Now the ethical dilemma part. Our young, idealistic prosecutor wants to get at the truth, which is pretty stupid of him, but he does anyway."

Diana gripped Sean's hand a little more tightly.

Sean continued. "He calls up the officer who failed to file the burglary report, and what do you suppose happens?

"He kills himself."

"Oh, my God," Diana whispered. "Chris Franklin."

"Hypothetical, remember?" Sean corrected.

Diana nodded, her face white.

"Our young prosecutor gets hauled in front of the DA and the chief ADA and is basically read the riot act. They tell him to put the whole thing 'to rest.' They pair him with a veteran detective to investigate the dead officer to see if his suicide has anything to do with the murder. Of course, they strongly suggest, even before the investigation starts, that the answer will be no. The detective who's working with the young prosecutor is hard to get a handle on. The prosecutor begins to suspect that a massive cover-up is in the works. Our prosecutor doesn't want to be part of any cover-up. So, now you see the prosecutor's ethical dilemma."

"I do see," she agreed.

"Oh, and I forgot something. The prosecutor is romantically involved with the defense attorney assigned to the original murder case. That's kind of an important point in our ethical analysis."

"And our prosecutor chooses to unburden himself to the very same romantically involved defense attorney," Diana added.

Sean sat back in his seat. "Jesus, how did things get so complicated?"

Diana stared at her iced tea for a while, considering. The waiter had brought their lunch, but they hadn't touched any of it.

"What about Matt?" she asked suddenly. "I've always heard what a straight arrow he is. Would he really be involved in a cover-up?"

"I don't know. But you haven't heard the worst of it."

"There's more?"

"Yeah. Remember the officer who called and asked the victim to come out to the muffler shop?"

"Yeah?"

"Well, she told the witness the name of the officer."

"And?"

"The witness remembers the name because she used to be a big fan of *Gunsmoke*. It was Matt. Matt Burton."

Diana sat back in her chair, too stunned to speak.

"So, you can see my problem," Sean said. "The guy I'm working with is either trying to cover up things that might make the police department look bad..."

"Or is covering up for himself. Jesus Christ." She thought for a moment. "But I can't believe Matt would kill anyone. He's been a cop forever."

"Is it easier to believe that Chris did it?"

Diana sipped her drink. "You also know that by telling me all of this..."

Sean nodded. "Yeah, I'm putting my career as a prosecutor on the chopping block. If Holloway finds out, I'll be canned."

"So, why are you doing it?"

"Because it's right. I took an oath when I became a prosecutor. It wasn't to rack up convictions or to only try the easy cases and plead out the tough ones to keep my stats pretty. It was to do justice. That's what you say. 'I promise to seek justice.' I'm proud of what I do. At least, I've been proud up until recently."

"I'm impressed."

"I'm not doing this to impress you!" Sean felt agitated now. "My old man was a drunk and a wife-beater. I wanted to make my life stand for something more than how many bar fights I'd been in. Being a prosecutor has been the greatest thing in my life. I do make a difference; I help people." He wound down a little. "At least I did until now."

Diana looked surprised by his passion. "Hey, I'm not putting you down." She put both her hands over his. "It's just the opposite. I really am impressed. I'm in awe. I didn't know you felt like this."

He shrugged.

"What are you going to do, though?"

"I don't know. I keep going over it in my head, trying to find some way out of this total mess. Preferably with a job and my license still intact."

"You could go to the papers," she suggested.

"Yeah, I could do that. But I'm not sure what good it would ultimately do. I can't stand Carl Rogers, and he's the guy I'd have to talk to. Gannett is his beat. He'd puff up the story, grandstand for a few weeks, all to his greater glory, but in the end would anything actually have been accomplished? Except that I get fired."

"What about this?" Diana leaned closer. "What if you and I form a team? We'll investigate this case together. If you can't trust Matt, at least until you know more, then we'll investigate it ourselves. If it turns out that Chris is the killer, the case could quietly disappear."

"How?"

"Don't you see? If we prove that Chris killed Mrs. Resnic and Chris is now dead, they'll have to drop the charges against my client, and the only threat to the police department is already gone. Everybody would come out okay. Especially you."

Sean thought it over. "I don't know."

"Sean." She kissed him lightly on the cheek. "I'm not sure you have any other choice."

CHAPTER TEN

Friday, April 21, 2:45 p.m.

"Hey, Sean," Matt said when he saw Sean in his doorway.

"How goes it on the Franklin investigation?"

Matt put down the file he'd been reading and closed it. "Not much left to go on. Like I said before, his finances don't show anything. He had some money in savings, about five grand. Nothing to sneeze at, especially for a cop. Of course, a lot of that money came from his part-time job at the private school, and that does tend to make you wonder, but nothing I can put my finger on. We don't have a gun for the Resnic murder. We don't show that the money went into either Chris' or Resnic's account, but that doesn't mean anything. Either one of them could have just buried it in the backyard."

Sean sat down across from Matt. "Anything else?"

"Not really. Got any ideas?"

"Yeah, as a matter of fact, I do. Let's go back through all the paperwork. Maybe there's something there we missed."

Matt shrugged. "I doubt it. There wasn't much stuff in his den. He had a small file cabinet, but it just had copies of bills in it."

"Well, I'll take a look. Maybe a fresh pair of eyes would help."

Matt shrugged again. "I guess it couldn't hurt. Why don't we go into one of the conference rooms, where we can spread out?"

Once they were settled, Matt handed over the file he'd been reading. It contained a brief report entitled "Suspicious Death." The name of the victim was Gregor Itzvanov. Sean quickly leafed through the pages, trying to glean the essential facts: numerous bruises—probably defensive wounds, death by suffocation, lividity indicating the victim was killed somewhere else and then dumped at the scene, later identified by Jimmy Bennett.

Jimmy Bennett. Hmm.

"Anything in particular I should be looking for in here?" Sean wondered.

"His wrists."

Sean read and then looked up again, shrugging. "Bruising consistent with restraints?"

"If you read a bit more, you'll see that the coroner says there were two types of lesions: one caused by rope, which you'd expect since it was on his wrists when we found him, but there was also evidence of other restraints used before he died. Solid, metallic restraints."

"Handcuffs?"

"That's what it looks like."

"So… He was handcuffed first, but then the cuffs were taken off and the rope put on. Why bother?" Sean thought for another moment before answering himself. "Oh, Jesus. Handcuffs, but the killer didn't want him found cuffed or even for anyone to know he'd been cuffed. So, after he's dead, they take the cuffs off and then tie his hands with rope, trying to avoid any suggestion that a cop might be involved."

"Remember what I said before?" Matt reminded him. "Street-smart, but light on forensics. He probably figured that if we found Gregor's wrists bound with rope, we wouldn't bother looking any further. He doesn't know Doc Henderson very well."

"I guess not. You know this makes a case for a bad cop even stronger."

"That's why I showed it to you."

Sean turned more pages. There was another report in the file, this one regarding the attempted robbery of the armored car. Matt's account had been pretty accurate. Sean looked at the photo of the door.

"Man, that's a lot of damage from one bullet."

"Those rifles are pretty powerful."

"You know," Sean began again. "You're missing someone in all of this."

"How do you mean?"

"The armored car robbery—well, the *attempted* armored car robbery.

Those witnesses say there were three men, not two. And looking at this autopsy report on Gregor, he was in pretty good shape. I can't imagine just one guy holding him and being able to wrap his head with duct tape. But..."

"But two men could do it pretty easy," Matt finished.

"So who's the third man?"

They were both silent for a moment.

"You think it's another cop, don't you?" Sean finally asked.

Matt glanced at him and was about to say something, then seemed to change his mind. "Yes. I think it's another cop. That brings the grand total of likely dirty cops to two, and I don't think we're done yet."

◆

They went through Chris' financial records again and reviewed the photos. They also had some hard copies of directories and some photos Dave had pulled off Chris' external drive. It was depressing to see the sheer number of images he had of children being sexually abused. Sean didn't even want to look at the small thumbnails Dave had printed off.

"Here are his private supplemental reports." Matt tapped a stack of papers that had been stapled together. "He was meticulous, I'll give him that. It looks like he wrote up his own notes on just about every arrest he made, at least as far as I can tell. Here's his follow-up on the Resnic call. There just isn't much here. He mentions being called out, finding nothing, and that he'll pass it along to Property Crimes, but he doesn't sound too enthusiastic about it."

"Well, it's not like he'd write down, 'Next time I see this woman I'm going to kill her and take the rest of her money,'" Sean argued.

"No, I guess not," Matt conceded.

"You know, he really shouldn't have private files on arrests. When defense attorneys file their discovery motions, I'm supposed to hand over everything. If we've got cops making their own files about cases, that could leave us wide open to all kinds of claims."

Matt just stared at him. "I think," he began slowly, "given what else

Chris was into, that wasn't very high on his list of things to worry about."

"Good point. What about his recent mail?"

"No letters from bill collectors, if that's what you're looking for. And no bank statements from the Cayman Islands."

Sean drummed his fingers on the tabletop. "Could he have kept some of his records elsewhere?"

"Like where?"

"I don't know. Do cops keep files in their lockers?"

Matt snapped his fingers. "I didn't look. It's probably been cleaned out."

"Can we go see?"

"Can't hurt."

They made their way to the locker rooms and found Chris' locker, which still had a combination lock on it.

"Great. Does your search warrant cover this?"

Matt was fingering the lock. "Beats me. He's not going to complain about his Constitutional rights being violated, though." He spun the dial.

"Don't tell me you can crack combination locks," Sean half-joked.

Matt continued working the dial back and forth. "It can be done." He popped open the lock and removed it.

"How did you do that? I thought you had to listen for tumblers falling or something like that."

"That's not the best way to crack a lock."

"What is?"

"Know the combination." Matt flashed a sly smile.

"Oh. Was it written in his file or something?"

"No. But his birth date is. I bet you could open half the lockers in this room if you knew the people's birth dates."

Matt pulled out a spare uniform and a yellow rain slicker. He laid them on a bench nearby and then returned for a systematic search of the locker. A thick file was lying on the top shelf.

"What have we here?" Matt laid the file on top of the clothes and opened it.

"Is his copy of the Resnic report in there?"

"Hold your horses. There's a lot of stuff in here."

Along with the canary-colored officer copies of filed reports were white sheets of paper. Sean guessed they were memos.

Matt pulled one such memo out and straightened while he read it. Since he seemed absorbed in it, Sean picked up where Matt had left off and leafed through the other pages.

"No," he announced a minute later. "It isn't here."

"Hmm. What?"

"The Resnic copy isn't here," Sean repeated.

"Oh, you didn't really think it would be, did you?" Matt said over the paper in his hands.

"I was hoping." He watched Matt reading. "What's that?"

Matt handed it to him.

It was headed NOTICE and read, "Be advised. Bronson Armored Car reports that beginning on March 25 of this year, it will change its pattern of deliveries and pickups at local banks. Instead of picking up deposits in the afternoon, it will now deliver currency between 1 p.m. and 5 p.m. Deposits will be collected in the mornings, between 8 a.m. and 11 a.m. Please note any suspicious activity in or around these or any other armored cars."

Sean handed it back. "That armored car case you told me about. That was Bronson Armored Cars, wasn't it?"

Matt didn't say anything for a while. "Yup. Let's bag up all this stuff and put it in the evidence room."

♦

Sean was putting his things together to leave for the day when Tom appeared in his doorway looking distinctly worse for the wear, with dust covering his hair and suit and sweat trickling down his face. For a moment, Sean wondered why. Then it hit him. The basement archive! He'd completely forgotten about Tom's project.

"Man, you weren't kidding about the basement," Tom began.

"Grab a seat. You look like you could use it."

Tom sat down and pulled out a yellow legal pad. "It took me hours of going through those old boxes, but I finally found it." He gave a big smile.

Sean didn't have the heart to tell him that he already knew about the connection between Jimmy and the Russian. "It was Jimmy Bennett, wasn't it?"

Tom looked confused. "No. That's not what it says here."

"Really? What does it say?"

"Richard Gartman."

Sean stopped dead. "Richard Gartman? You mean Rick was one of Gregor's arresting officers?"

Tom looked at his notes. "That's what it says."

Sean thought. "I'd forgotten that Rick used to work for the police department. He's been here so long…" He let the thought trail off.

"You know him?"

"He works for us. He's one of our investigators. He was there the day that Resnic…"

Sean shook off the thought. "Excellent work. Go on home now, and remember what we said. Not a word to anyone."

Tom beamed, and for a moment Sean thought he was going to give a salute, but he just stood, dusted off some smudges on his coat, and left.

Sean sat for another moment. *Rick?* That didn't make any sense.

◆

Diana had already gotten a table by the time Sean arrived at the restaurant for dinner. Typical for Atlanta, every restaurant in the city was booked on a Friday night, and Sean wondered how on earth she'd managed to be seated.

"How did you get a table in this madhouse?" Sean asked, sitting down.

"Connections, sweetie." Diana winked.

"Got here early?"

"That, and I tipped the guy up front."

"Uh-huh." They ordered drinks and an appetizer, and then Sean filled her in on the afternoon's developments.

"Handcuffs. They handcuffed the poor guy and then wrapped his head with duct tape." She actually shivered. "God, what a terrible way to die."

"Are there any good ways?"

"I did hear something about a body being found the other week," she continued, ignoring his question, "but none of the specifics."

"Yeah, I know. They kept those particular details out of the press."

He told her about the attempted armored car robbery and Matt's theory that Gregor had been one of the thieves.

"Okay. Let me wrap my head around this. This Gregor guy fell in with some crooked cop, and they decided to rob an armored car. Odds are stacking up that Chris was that crooked cop. I mean, the Russian's driver's license was found at his home and all." She thought for a moment. "Does that strike you as odd?"

"Everything, absolutely everything about this case has struck me as odd."

"No, the license. Why keep his license? I mean, serial killers sometimes take trophies, and this *was* a particularly brutal way to kill someone, but are we now saying that, in addition to being a pedophile and a bad cop, Chris was a serial killer? I mean, when did he find time to sleep?"

"I hadn't thought about the driver's license that way. It could be another indication of a clumsy attempt to get someone to make a connection between Gregor and Chris when there really wasn't one."

"And Mrs. Resnic's note?" Diana just shook her head. "I mean, there's reasonable doubt if you ever wanted it."

"Okay. One thing at a time. We have a long way to go before we're at the trial stage."

Diana mulled things over. "I just can't believe that Matt is involved in anything underhanded. I mean, he's a legend around here. He's been involved in just about every big case in this part of Atlanta for the last twenty years."

"I know, I know. I don't like it either. But I'm not making up these facts."

Diana swirled her straw around in her glass. The waiter arrived with their dinners, and they settled down to eat in silence for a few minutes. Sean hadn't realized just how hungry he was.

"You know what we need?" Diana asked, pointing at him with her fork.

"A vacation?"

"More information."

"Well sure, but how do we get it?"

Diana smiled at him; it was a beautiful smile. "See, this is why you need me. You're so used to having the vast machinery of the State at your disposal. You don't know how to use guerrilla tactics."

"My 'vast machinery of the State' usually consists of a police report and a criminal history."

"Still, it's time you learned how to think like a scrappy defense attorney. We're used to getting things done with no money, no time, and no resources."

"Okay, Scrappy. Where do we start?"

"I'll pick you up tomorrow, and we'll hit my favorite place for digging up dirt."

Sean thought for a moment. "The jail?"

"No." She laughed. "The library."

"Oh." Then he made a sad face. "You'll pick me up?"

"Is that look on your face supposed to guilt me into going to bed with you?"

"Only if it's working."

"Maybe." She smiled and went back to eating.

♦

The next morning, they drove to the local library.

"You know, there's this thing called the Internet," Sean said as they walked in. "You can access it from home. You can access it from *my* home, in *my* bed, on *my* laptop, actually."

"I know," Diana said, poking Sean's arm playfully. "But they don't always put all of the articles online. Sometimes you still have to do a bit of old-style digging."

The index for the *Atlanta Journal-Constitution* had only one entry for "Itzvanov, Gregor, murder victim."

"Bingo."

Sean looked around. "Do you really come here a lot?"

"Sure, this is a great place to find things out."

"Like what?"

"Like the name of a Russian émigré who was murdered a few weeks ago. Hardly anybody comes to libraries anymore, so it's a great place to do some thinking. I prep a lot of my trials here. No cell phones, and only the occasional weirdo."

She found the newspaper article, and they both sat down to read it. When she pushed a strand of hair out of her eyes, Sean realized he was more interested in her wonderful aroma than in the article.

The article had appeared the day after the body was found behind the strip mall. Sean noted the salient features: body tentatively identified as Gregor Itzvanov, a Russian emigrant who'd been in the United States for almost nine years; Itzvanov had an extensive criminal record; Matt Burton assigned to the case.

"Not much information here, really."

"No. What was the name of that armored car company in the memo you and Matt found yesterday?"

Sean thought. "Bronson, I think."

"Let's see what we can find out about that."

Diana found thirteen entries for Bronson Armored Cars and sighed heavily. "These people have been hit all over the place."

Sean looked down the entries. "This one." He pointed. "The report said 'attempted' armed robbery."

In what police have called a "daring effort," a Bronson armored car was the victim of an aborted robbery attempt yesterday morning at the corner of Sandhill Road and Haywood Street. The crooks had apparently planned their heist forgetting one important detail: make sure the money is there. When the robbers stormed into the armored car around nine o'clock yesterday morning, they found that the inside was empty. In a strange twist of fate, the armored car had recently changed its delivery schedule.

"If they'd hit us last week," said driver Ruben Schaul, "they'd have got a lot more than what they got today."

Schaul told police that he and guard Toby Hanks were stopped on Sandhill Road yesterday when a woman driving a late-model sedan blocked their path.

"We hit the brakes to keep from hitting her," Hanks explained. "I thought she was just a bad driver. Then I heard something like an explosion, and I knew we were in trouble."

In fact, police say that as soon as the armored car was brought to a halt, the thieves pinned the car from the side and back with vans and then shot out the side door with a large-caliber rifle. The door was blown open, and two men in ski masks entered the car. According to the guards, the men were shocked when they saw that it was empty.

"They kept yelling at us, 'Where is the money?' I told them we hadn't picked up any money yet. One of the men, the one with the weird accent, looked like he was going to kill us. They looked around for a minute, then took off. They took our guns and then ran back to their cars and drove away."

Other than a vague description of three Caucasian men approximately six feet tall, one with a heavy build and one with a foreign accent, police have little to go on. The Gannett County Police Department is asking anyone who was in the vicinity of the attempted armed robbery yesterday to contact them.

Sean and Diana sat in silence for a while after reading the article.

"Do you think the foreigner was Gregor?" Sean asked her.

"Not much of a description: 'foreign accent.' My mom is from New Hampshire. Every time she comes down here people think *she's* got a foreign accent."

Sean looked around the library. "Let's go somewhere we can talk a little more freely."

They sat in Sean's car. "Okay, try this on for size," Sean started. "Gregor and some unknown men and a woman decide to rob an armored car. They work out a plan but miss the most obvious thing: The armored car didn't have any money. They walk away from the robbery with bupkes. Then, for some reason, the other three decide to kill Gregor."

"Okay. I mean, sorry for Gregor, but what does this have to do with anything?"

"Think about it," Sean prodded. "Who could the other men have been? If Gregor was working with a dirty cop, couldn't one of them have been that cop?"

"So, you're thinking Chris was another man in the robbery? God, this Chris was quite a character. We've got him killing a little old lady and committing armed robbery in broad daylight."

"But don't you see how it hangs together? Chris and Gregor and the other two hatch this plan; they're going to knock off the armored car. Chris needs the money, or maybe he just wants the thrill, who knows? They blow the back door and—holy shit—there's no money in there. Now they've committed armed robbery and are facing a minimum twenty-five years in prison, and they don't have a dime to show for their efforts. Maybe Gregor said something after it was over that made Chris think Gregor was going to turn him in. Maybe they were always planning on killing Gregor; who knows? Either way, Chris and the other two kill Gregor. But Chris still doesn't have any money. Then, *presto*, he gets this burglary call and thousands of dollars practically drop into his lap. He lures the old lady out to a quiet place, shoots her, and takes her money. He probably figures, what the hell, I'm already in serious trouble."

Diana thought it over. "But I thought you said Chris' finances were in good shape. You said he had a lot of money in his savings account."

Sean nodded. "I know. That part doesn't quite fit. He didn't seem to be hurting for money. So maybe he did it for the thrill. Or maybe he had money problems we don't know about."

"Did you ever meet Chris?"

"No. I mean, I saw him around. I called him the day…well, you know."

"But you didn't know him personally?"

"No. Is that important?"

"It could be. See, I did know him. I don't mean that I knew him well. But I had a case where he was the lead officer. DUI. I thought he was a very fair person. He didn't strike me as the kind of person who would do something like this."

"According to Matt, you never know what a murderer looks like. Maybe he had a split personality."

"I don't know. It just doesn't seem to fit."

"Give me an alternate theory, then" Sean prodded.

"I don't have one. At the very least, though, this information seems to put my client out of the picture. Maybe it's time to start thinking about a bond reduction and letting him out. I mean, it's looking more and more like he's not guilty of anything."

"Well, there's something else to consider."

"Other than getting my client out of jail for a crime he didn't commit?"

"Don't go getting all defense attorney on me. I think we both know that someone else out there is trying to pull strings. This Mr. X, he's already killed Gregor and Gregor's girlfriend."

Diana held up a finger. "Supposedly killed. Has anybody come up with a body? Maybe she isn't dead."

"Okay. What I was trying to say is that, suppose Mr. X gets it into his mind that killing Tommy Resnic would help sew the case up nice and tight for him? It could be that jail is the safest place for Tommy right now."

Diana thought for a bit. She clearly didn't like it, but she didn't argue.

Sean drummed the steering wheel. "How about this? Let's suppose we're going about this the wrong way. Maybe Chris has nothing to do with it. Where does that leave us?"

"No Chris," Diana mused. "Then he wasn't involved in the armored car robbery, he didn't need money, and his suicide didn't have anything to do with Mrs. Resnic's death."

"Damn, that really leaves us with nothing."

"Maybe. But if Chris wasn't involved in any of that, then someone else was."

Sean thought for a moment. "I don't want to put you in an ethical dilemma, but is there anything your client could tell us that might help?"

Diana frowned. "I'm not comfortable with that. You know anything he's told me is confidential."

"You said he wanted to meet with me. I agree that it's normally a bad idea, but maybe bad ideas are all we have left.

"Besides, isn't it in the best interests of your client to get him exonerated? You already have enough information to raise a huge stink with the press. But what if we produce the real killer? Your guy is off the hook."

"Yeah, all right. I'll go by and talk with him this afternoon, but I can't guarantee that I'll tell you what he tells me."

"Okay, that's fair enough."

She patted his hand. "You know, most prosecutors wouldn't have stuck their necks out like this. Thanks."

"You're welcome. But you may be wrong. There are a lot of ethical prosecutors, and ethical police officers too for that matter."

"You really believe that?"

"I do." He looked at her face. "Hopelessly naïve?"

She nodded her head. "Very cute, though."

"How about we go get some lunch?"

"Sounds good."

As they pulled out of the library parking lot, Sean caught a glimpse of a gray car pulling out after them.

◆

Over lunch, they rehashed everything but didn't get any further. Sean was beginning to have serious misgivings about the course of action he'd taken. Working with a defense attorney to prove that a cop, and not her client, had killed the victim was…unconventional at best. He mulled over what his bosses would say about it: *Crazy. Criminally negligent. Thinking with your dick.* He wondered if they'd be right.

His eyes played over the restaurant. They'd decided to eat early, and it was only now getting crowded. He'd deliberately sat so that he could see the parking lot—and sure enough, the gray car had appeared, slowly trolling among the cars.

He watched their waiter approaching from across the restaurant with the bill in his hands. He was thinking about his career, Diana, and just how complicated life had become when something else flashed in his mind.

"Diana! We forgot something!"

"What?"

"The memo! The memo that Matt found in Chris' locker. You know, the one that mentioned the changed scheduled for Bronson Armored Cars? Remember, I said that Matt was paying a lot of attention to it; it was the only thing he kept from Chris' locker."

"Yeah?"

"Well, that means Chris couldn't have been involved in the robbery."

"Why?"

"Because he had a memo that told him about the schedule change! He would have known the armored car would be empty in the morning, not full the way it used to be. He wouldn't have hit the car then; he would've hit it in the afternoon."

"Maybe he didn't read the memo."

"But it was right on top! Besides, if you're thinking about knocking over an armored car, wouldn't you pay close attention to any little snippets of information about it, especially schedule changes?"

"I suppose so."

"That must be what Matt was thinking when he read it. He realized that Chris couldn't be involved. If there is a connection between the robbery and the murder, then Chris is out."

"Okay, I'll go along. But where does that leave us?"

"Back at the paperwork." He sighed. "We should forget about the armored car and concentrate on the murder."

"But we've already gone over everything."

"No." Sean was getting excited again. "We've missed the most obvious detail. If the person who lured Mrs. Resnic out of her house that night really was a cop, he may actually have been on duty. We could cross-check the cops on duty the night she was killed with the day that Chris filed—or didn't file—his report on her break-in. There can only be so many cops who were on duty both days."

"How would this mystery cop even know about the break-in?"

"I've been there on shift change. It's a madhouse. The cops coming off duty are all writing up their reports and turning them in. The cops going on duty are all cutting up and laughing. When the cops finish their reports, they put them in a little wire basket on the watch commander's desk. Nobody pays the slightest attention to them. Any one of them could have fished Chris' report out and thrown it away."

Diana thought. "But how would they even know to do that?"

"Here's my idea: Chris mentioned the burglary to someone at the precinct. It would have had to be someone at the precinct; anybody else couldn't have moved fast enough.

"Picture it. Chris comes in, probably at the end of his shift, and he meets Mr. X. He happens to mention to X that he just answered a burglary call at this lady's house and she has stacks of bills, thousands of dollars. X hears this and immediately hatches his plan. He knows the procedures at the precinct, so when Chris turns in his report, he sidles over there and just picks it out of the pile. *Voilà*, no report. If anything weird happens at that house, Chris will be a suspect. For good measure, he opens Chris' locker and takes the officer's copy, too."

"How does he know the combination?" Diana asked.

"The same way Matt does; he guesses that it's the same combination that most of the officers use: their birthdays. Or," Sean snapped his fingers, "he's been close enough to actually see Chris put the combination in."

"Another patrol officer, then?"

"Yes. Someone who could stand right next to Chris and watch him dial it in. Someone who knows the procedures, where copies of police reports are filed. Someone who wouldn't look strange or out of place standing near the files or hanging around in the locker room."

"So, you still haven't ruled out Matt."

"But I think we can. If Matt was going to do this, he wouldn't have been stupid enough to tell anyone his real name. Also, if Matt wanted to conceal his knowledge about Chris, he wouldn't have opened Chris' locker in front of me. He would've done it first thing after

Chris' suicide. There wouldn't have been anything for us to find when I got the idea to check his locker. But he didn't do that. He opened it in front of me and even let me see the Bronson memo. A guilty man wouldn't do any of that." He paused. "I think."

Diana was slowly nodding. "So, you're saying not only that it couldn't have been Matt but also that it had to be another patrol officer. Someone based in that precinct, someone who could come and go without being especially noticed—because he worked there. And we know something else about Mr. X."

"What?"

"It has to be a *Mr.* X, not a Mrs. X."

"Huh?"

"All along you've been assuming the killer was a man. Not me. But now we can rule a woman out."

"Because they have a different locker room," Sean said, getting the point.

"Yes. And if our other theories are right, we're talking about a patrol officer who is also in financial trouble."

Sean pulled out a napkin and began making notes. "Okay, here's what we have: an officer based in the same precinct who has financial troubles and worked some shifts in common with Chris."

"Why do I have the impression that you have a suspect in mind?"

"Wow, am I that obvious?"

"You are to me. Who?"

"I don't know." Sean smiled, taunting her. "I don't know if I should tell you…"

"Come *on*," she insisted. "Tell me. Tell me!" She began pinching him all over.

"All right, all right." He glanced around and lowered his voice. "Jimmy Bennett."

♦

As they drove back to his apartment, Sean outlined his reasons for suspecting Jimmy.

"I've been wondering about him for a while. Apparently, there's been a persistent rumor for the past couple of months about an officer taking bribes on Copper Street. I heard about it from Debbie Blum."

"You mean the Copper Street over in Buford?"

"Yeah, you've been there?"

"Once. I was looking for an alibi witness." Diana shivered. "God, what a place."

"I agree with you. Fifteen or twenty minutes from the courthouse, and you'd think you were in another country. But it's where a lot of people go to buy meth, heroin—whatever they need. Consequently, there are a lot of arrests made out there. That means there are a lot of police officers there, and a lot of money rolling around. If a cop was inclined to take some money as a bribe for looking the other way, that'd be a good spot for it."

"And Jimmy works out there?"

"Yes. I actually saw him there once when I was investigating a case for trial. I was riding with Lee Church, trying to find a witness. Since it's such a problem area, they make it an overlapping beat."

"Overlapping beat?"

"Yeah, each patrol officer is assigned to a specific area of the county, but Copper Street is one of those areas that falls inside the regular patrol zone of a couple different cops. Jimmy is one of them."

"Okay, Sherlock. So far you haven't convinced me very much," Diana informed him.

"Just listen…Watson."

"I'm Watson? I don't think so."

"If I'm Sherlock, you must be Watson."

"Then you're not Sherlock."

"You think you're Sherlock?"

"Let's just stick to the point."

"I think I'd make a pretty good Sherlock," Sean muttered.

"Solve the case first, then we'll talk."

"Okay, where was I?"

"Jimmy Bennett."

"Okay, yeah. Here are some interesting facts about Officer Bennett. First, I saw him at Chris' house the night Chief Black called me out there. He didn't seem too happy to see me, but that doesn't really mean very much. They all must have known what was in the note and were probably blaming me for Chris' suicide. But there's more: I happen to know that Jimmy works out of the same precinct as Chris. I've seen him over there plenty of times."

"Circumstantial, and pretty weak circumstantial at that."

"I'm not finished. It was Jimmy who identified Gregor's body. I saw it in the report."

"We're back at the Russian again?"

"Yeah. I still think that ties in." Sean patted his pockets. "What else did we say about Mr. X?" He searched while he drove. "Look around for that napkin, will you?"

"I can't find it," she said after a minute.

"Damn, I must have dropped it somewhere. Well, we said that our Mr. X would have to work at the precinct, have access to the locker room, know the procedures for filing reports…and what else?"

"Would have to be in financial trouble or at least need some money fast."

"Okay. I don't know anything about Jimmy's finances," Sean admitted.

"Can we find out if he was on duty the night Mrs. Resnic was killed?"

"It wouldn't be hard to verify, but doing that will draw a lot of attention. The last time I went looking for a cop, every other cop in the county knew about it before I left the building. So did Shepherd. That's what got me in hot water in the first place. If I go over there today, on a Saturday, and ask to look through the duty rolls…well, let's just say the shit will hit the fan."

"But we're so close. We could maybe solve this thing today. You'd be off the hook, and so would my client. Maybe you could get Matt to do it."

"Yeah, I may have to. But Jimmy's his friend, too." He shrugged. "Anyway, we'll burn that bridge when we get to it."

"Do you really think Jimmy was on duty when he killed her?"

"He'd need an alibi, wouldn't he? Being on duty would be a great alibi. Besides, Mrs. Resnic would've been calmed by the presence of a police car at the muffler shop.

"We're talking about a lady who's so paranoid she doesn't trust banks. She drives to some secluded spot and sees a regular car sitting there, maybe she'd get scared; maybe she'd go home and call the PD to check the facts. The killer couldn't risk that. It's just a hunch, but I think if she saw a patrol car sitting there, she wouldn't hesitate to pull in next to it."

"You may be right."

Sean glanced in his rearview mirror. Saturday afternoon in Atlanta—it was impossible to see if anyone was following them. He decided not to mention the possibility to Diana. "I'll give Matt a call and see if he'll do it. I may have to spill the beans about my suspicions, though."

"If he's as straight as everybody claims he is," Diana assured him, "then no problem."

"But, if he and Jimmy are in this together…" Sean let the sentence hang there.

"They might decide to kill you."

"I don't think it would come to that."

"I'll bet the Russian didn't think so either."

♦

They parked back at Sean's apartment.

"Why are we stopping here?" Diana asked. "Let's go see Matt."

"I think I should see him alone."

"Why?"

"He doesn't know you and I are working together, for one thing."

"And you want to make sure no one knows about our arrangement. Is that it?"

"No, that's not it. I just think Matt would be a lot less forthcoming if a defense attorney was standing there. He'll play his cards close to the vest around you, and that's exactly what we don't need right now. I need to be frank with him and hope that he'll be frank with me."

"Are you going to tell him you've been working with me?"

Sean frowned. "I don't know. If the DA finds out I told you everything about this case, in direct violation of his orders, he'll fire me."

"He won't. You'll be a hero. I'll make sure everyone knows—"

"No, you won't. I don't want anyone to know, especially the gossipy defense bar. They'll be falling all over themselves to tell as many people as they can. Word will spread. Maybe Holloway won't fire me using that as a reason, but he'll know I can't be trusted. He'll turn Shepherd loose on me. They'll make my life a living hell and find some other reason to fire me or, more likely, make me so miserable I'll just quit. I like being a prosecutor, Diana. I think we both know I'd make a shitty defense attorney."

"I disagree. I think you'd make a great one. You have a passion for the truth."

"Well, let's put it this way. It may sound a bit conceited, but the DA's office needs someone like me. Someone who can work with the defense, someone who doesn't view the job as a crusade or a career stepping-stone. Help me stay there. Please?"

"Okay, okay. Go see Matt by yourself. You probably want to scratch your balls and smoke cigars and talk about babes anyway. I'd find the whole thing pretty obnoxious."

"Not all men sit around scratching their balls and talking about women, you know. Sometimes we sit around scratching our balls and talking about sports."

"Wise guy." She smiled. "Are you going to see him today?"

"Yeah." He wasn't looking forward to it.

"Call me when you get through?"

"Sure."

CHAPTER ELEVEN

Saturday, April 22, 2:30 p.m.

If A equals B and B equals C, he thought, *then A equals C.* He didn't remember exactly what it meant, but it was one of the few things he'd learned in high school that had stayed with him. *A equals C.*

He banged the steering wheel. He hadn't missed anything, damn it! So why did he have this feeling that things were spiraling out of control? The shyster and the bitch seemed to be moving closer to him, and he couldn't see how. But the notes he'd read on the napkin they'd dropped in the parking lot made it very clear.

They suspected "Mr. X." He actually liked the sound of that name, even if he didn't like how much they'd figured out.

As he drove along, he let some of the other cars pass him. Normally he drove fast, but not today. Today he was content to hide among the sheep, concealed in the flock. He liked that. A wolf in sheep's clothing. It seemed appropriate. He studied the flow of traffic around him, sensitive to anyone who might be watching him and, through it all, watching the car of the bitch defense attorney cruise along.

Moving surveillance was the worst kind. He remembered an instructor saying that once. On TV, private detectives were always trailing people in cars, but that was bullshit. It was very hard to follow another car without being noticed. You needed a minimum of three cars, constantly changing positions, to do it right. He didn't have three cars. It was just him. He might have gotten his woman to help, but he'd dismissed the idea as soon as it had popped into his head. She wasn't good at this kind of thing. He had one advantage, though, and the thought of it gave him a glow of pleasure.

This bitch doesn't even suspect that anyone might be following her. He checked his position among the other cars and slowed a little more, letting an old truck get between him and the brand-new Honda she was driving. *Fucking cunt.* He touched the gun on the seat beside him and felt its power.

The Honda pulled into an apartment complex, and he drove past, pulled into the entrance of another apartment complex about a quarter of a mile up the road, and made a quick U-turn. He pulled his car into her entrance, hoping she hadn't turned off on one of the side streets in this hodgepodge of apartments stacked one on top of another. She hadn't. She'd stopped at the mailboxes by the management office and climbed out. He parked in front of another building and watched her in his rearview mirror.

Uh-huh. Nice legs; hefty rack. He wondered if she would fight when he came at her. He wanted her to fight. It would be so much more fun breaking her if she thought she was tough.

He watched her climb into her car and drive up the street. She got out, lifting her purse and briefcase out of the back seat, and then climbed a set of stairs in the back of the building.

Apartment 3. Building L. L-3. Lick me at three. He smiled to himself. He pulled out the napkin he'd recovered from the restaurant parking lot and wrote her license plate and apartment numbers down on it.

See ya, Counselor. See ya real soon.

Saturday, April 22, 3:00 p.m.

When Sean called Matt, he learned that Matt was actually at home for once. Matt invited him out, and after a moment's hesitation, Sean agreed. Matt's directions were clear and easy to follow. He'd said over the phone that he lived a "good ways out," which turned out to be true. Sean was almost at the county line when he turned down the long driveway. He hadn't even known this part of the county existed.

The Burton residence was off a country lane and at the end of a two-hundred-yard grass-and-gravel driveway. After the drive in, Sean had been expecting some kind of hillbilly retreat, but when he came around the last bend in the driveway, he saw a pretty house with flower gardens surrounding it.

He got out and looked around, impressed despite himself. The warm afternoon had brought out the aroma of the flowers. Sean noticed that a lot of the plants seemed to be roses. There were dozens of them, maybe hundreds, scattered in little islands all over the property.

Matt came out on the front porch. The house was built into the side of a hill, and the front door was at the top of a staircase with at least ten steps.

"Sorry to bother you at home," Sean began, feeling uncomfortable.

"Come on up. You want a beer?"

"That would be nice."

Sean followed Matt through the front door and into a house that was as clean on the inside as it was on the outside.

"This is very nice," Sean said, meaning it.

Matt opened the refrigerator and pulled out two bottles of beer. "Let's go out on the back porch."

The porch was about twenty feet off the ground due to the sweep of the hill. At the bottom of the hill, almost a quarter of a mile away, there was a small creek winding in and around rocks and trees. It was very beautiful, and Sean stood for a moment, taking it all in.

"Wow," he finally said.

"Grab a chair," Matt offered, settling into a rocking chair himself and sipping his beer.

Sean tore his eyes away and came back to reality. He remembered why he'd come and wondered how he'd go about telling Matt his suspicions. Looking at Matt's frank expression and remembering that he'd insisted on this meeting on a Saturday and in Matt's home, he decided to get straight to the point.

"I've been thinking about what we found in Chris' locker."

"I see."

"I don't think Chris was involved in the attempted robbery. I don't think you do, either."

"Could be." Matt sipped his beer.

"You wanna cut me a little slack here? I've been caught up in this thing for a while now, and every time we get together it's like pulling teeth to get you to tell me anything."

Matt just gazed steadily at him.

"Look, I'm here because I'm in deep shit and, frankly, so are you. I'm thinking the DA and Chief Black would like to cover this whole thing up, and if that means throwing me—and you—to the wolves to do it, well then, what the hell, why not?"

"Sean, there's not gonna be any cover-up."

"Oh, really? So how come you and I are working together? Aren't you reporting back to your chief about what we're doing? I know my boss is sure as hell staying on *my* ass."

"You need to make up your mind, sonny. Which is it? Am I a killer or part of some cover-up?" Matt's face was inscrutable.

"I just want to know where I stand. Until last week, I would have said that our two offices work pretty much on the up and up. Now I'm not so sure."

"You aren't sure about very much, are you?"

Sean glared at Matt for a moment. "I won't bury this thing. I won't stick my head in the sand. I'm not going to stand by and let Tommy Resnic get tried for this murder just because it's the most politically convenient way to handle the situation."

"Have you told your bosses that?"

"No. I didn't think they'd want to hear it."

"But you stayed on the case anyway. Don't you think they're assuming you'll hold to the party line?"

Sean shrugged. "They probably are."

"It's time for you to look at this thing from my side." Matt rocked back in his chair. "For all I know, the DA's office wants to sweep the whole thing under the rug. My chief's not as bad as he looks. True, he's a bully and a moron, but whose boss isn't? The thing is, he does care about the department. He could have reassigned the case to some ass-kisser who would do whatever he was told. He knows me well enough to know that I won't pull anything underhanded. This thing is going to come out, one way or another."

Matt took another sip of beer and studied Sean. "But I wasn't sure about your end of things. Don't get me wrong. I like the DA's office; God knows I've worked with them often enough. But lawyers are all politicians, and a politician will smile at you while he's lifting your wallet. I figured I'd be paired off with someone since this thing is pretty hot. I was dreading working with one of the senior ADAs, all bucking for judgeships or cushy jobs with private firms, or anything that'll put their names in the paper. But instead I got you. And you I think I can trust."

Sean leaned forward. "What are you saying?"

"I keep tabs on the ADAs. You're a career prosecutor, and you don't seem to have any political ambitions. Everybody who's ever spoken about you has said that you're a straight arrow. I liked that. So, imagine my surprise when they put us together." Matt took a sip from his beer. "Us working together. It's either a very good thing or a very bad thing."

He got up. "Come on," he said, motioning for Sean to follow.

◆

"Step into my office," Matt invited, walking into a den off the living room. It was a mess. It reminded Sean of Matt's office at headquarters.

"I suppose you're going to tell me you know exactly where everything is in here."

"Oh, no. I'm a slob; I admit it. Step over those files and come here."

There was a large table in the center of the office. After a moment, Sean realized that, underneath all the files and stacks of paper, the desk was actually a picnic table. He seated himself awkwardly on the fixed bench across from Matt and looked around.

"What is all of this?"

"This is a lot of work on our problem."

"Which problem?"

"Let's call it the Bad Cop Scenario." Matt placed his hand on the stack of papers nearest him. "Here are all of the reports on the Resnic killing. Next to that, a duty roster for all Gannett precincts for the night in question. Next to that, over on the edge there, are all of the reports about the armored car robbery. Beside that is the duty roster for that day. There, in front of you, is everything we have on the Russian's murder. Duty roster there, too. Finally, some miscellaneous reports about some things that have been happening over in Buford and Copper Street."

Sean looked around. "And here we thought we'd have a tough time getting you to pull the duty rosters."

"We?"

"Me," Sean corrected himself. "So, what does it all boil down to?"

"Unfortunately, it doesn't point to one person. I have been able, though, to narrow it down to three officers, aside from Chris."

"And they are?"

Matt ticked them off on his fingers. "Jimmy Bennett, Lee Church, and Steve Morningside."

"Okay." Sean took that in. "Is there anyone we can take off the list?"

"Not really."

Sean hesitated. "Don't you know Lee?"

"I know all of these guys."

"Yeah, but don't you know Lee better than most?"

"I've gone hunting with him a lot. I used to go hunting with Chris, too."

"Point taken. Are you sure one of them is the killer?"

"No, I'm not sure. But I had to start somewhere, and the more I dug, the more it looked like a cop had been involved."

"It could be a cop from another department."

"You're just playing devil's advocate. Nope. I'm afraid that it's a Gannett County cop. Only a Gannett cop would have the means and the opportunity."

"And the motive?" Sean wondered.

"That's what we'll have to find out."

"How are we going to do that exactly?"

"Good old-fashioned police work. Starting tomorrow morning, we execute search warrants for all three officers' lockers and patrol cars. We also get subpoenas for their checking and savings accounts."

"Do you really think the killer would be stupid enough to leave anything incriminating in his police locker?"

"You gotta work the basics first. Besides, our killer may be clever, but we've already seen that he doesn't have a good knowledge of forensics. Street-smart, but not good with the science. You wouldn't believe what they can find on clothing these days."

"Are you talking about DNA? Assuming our guy was actually wearing his uniform when he killed the Resnic lady, wouldn't he have gotten rid of any blood-stained clothing?"

"If he knew it was stained." Matt saw the look on Sean's face and fished around on the table. He found a page of handwritten notes and pulled them forward. He reached into his breast pocket, put on his glasses, and started reading.

"You ever hear of high-velocity blood spatter?"

"I remember us talking about it in Chris' house right after you found the driver's license and the note."

"Well, then you might remember that some of the blood from a close-range gun wound gets vaporized. It's like little bubbles of blood, floating in the air. Some of this blood is so small that, when it lands on a surface, a person can't even see it with the naked eye. But it's there. I'm betting that whoever pulled the trigger didn't know that."

"And that's why you're looking at their uniforms."

"Right. We find blood on the uniform, we find the man."

"Are you going to be able to get a search warrant to execute on a Sunday morning?"

"Sure. It may be the best time to go. Shouldn't be too many cops over there."

"I guess there'll be some cops who won't take too kindly to you investigating your own men."

"Cops see things in black and white. There aren't any gray areas for them. You're either on this side, or you're on that side. A few of them might say that I've turned against my own, but I don't care. This guy is the one who put us all in this position, not me. He's the one who's crossed over, and he's the one who's going to have to pay."

Saturday, April 22, 3:20 p.m.

The Gannett County Jail was only two years old and had all of the modern incarceration features. There was a double line of chain-link fencing surrounding the entire facility, with razor wire at the top and the bottom. There were a couple of discreet guard towers, but this facility relied more on video cameras than on exterior guards. The lobby was one huge room, with a thirty-foot ceiling and a guard's booth at the far end. The metal detectors led down a long incline that actually went underground. There were doors at either end that could only be opened by the guard on the far side, and anybody wishing to pass through them needed to wait—trapped like a rotting rat—until someone in the guard cage decided to buzz them through the second set of doors. Once through the doors and the underground tunnel, visitors had the choice of stairs or an elevator to take them back to the surface, to the offices, administrative facilities, and visitor rooms on the edge of the prison cells.

Diana had never liked coming to the Gannett jail. She'd been to other jails, of course, but they looked more like the one in Mayberry than the futuristic monstrosity that surrounded her here. For some reason, she liked the old ones better. She supposed she preferred her steel bars out in the open.

Diana chose to climb the stairs to the third floor. That was where all the preliminary hearings took place, where the Magistrate judges could be found, and where the inmate conference rooms were. Since she was an attorney, she requested that Tommy be brought to meet her in one of those rooms. Attorneys had an unqualified right to speak with their clients face to face, with no telephones or other barriers in the way and no chance to be overheard.

She had to wait twenty minutes before they brought Tommy in.

"Hi, Tommy," Diana greeted him.

He was even more subdued than the last time she'd seen him. He already had that prison pallor and seemed to be folding in on himself.

"Hello, Ms. Baker."

"Tommy, I've been doing a lot of investigation into your case, and I think I've got some good news."

Tommy just looked at her. *Not good*, she thought. There should be more of a reaction to that statement.

"I don't want to get your hopes up too much at this stage." She chose her words carefully. "But I think we've got a good chance of getting you out of here."

"Uh-huh."

"Tommy, do you understand what I'm saying to you?"

"Yeah. You might could get me out. But I can't afford bail, Ms. Baker, you know that."

"I'm not talking about bail, Tommy. I'm talking about getting the charges against you dropped." That brightened him up a little, Diana was pleased to see. "I need to know some more information, though. I need to know if there's anything you can tell me about where your mother got all that money, where she kept it in the house, anything like that."

"Why?"

"Because I'm working with the DA on this." She'd told Sean she wouldn't tell anyone about his involvement, but Tommy was her client and she was on shaky ethical ground already. She didn't want to make matters worse by withholding information from him. "He's a fair man, and I think if I can bring him some more information, he might drop the case."

"Okay."

What's wrong with him? Diana wondered. Most people would be doing handstands right about now. Why wasn't Tommy?

"Do you know why she kept that much money in her house?"

The question seemed to cause Tommy physical pain, and Diana began to wonder if he was sick.

"She hated banks. Ever since she was a little girl. Something about the Depression and her mom and dad losing everything. I don't know. She took her retirement from the company in a lump sum and changed it all over to cash. She kept part of it..." Tommy faltered. "Part of it in the safe. The rest...the rest she hid somewhere else."

"Are you feeling okay, Tommy?"

"Yeah, sure."

"You don't look like you do. Are you in pain? Is your stomach upset?"

"No." Tommy slowly shook his head. "It ain't my stomach. It's my soul."

"It's your *what*?"

"It's my soul. My soul is heavy."

Diana wasn't sure how she should respond to that. She decided to skip over it and focus on some details. She didn't want to hear Tommy's confession, whatever it might be. If he should confess some crime to her, then deny it later, it would put her in an ethical bind she would just as soon avoid.

"When did your mother retire?"

"About four years ago."

"How much money did she get in the lump sum?"

"Close to $80,000."

Diana gasped. She'd had no idea; she'd thought it was $40,000 at most.

Tommy nodded his head. "I know. Crazy. That's what Daddy used to say. Crazy. It took First Union two days to pull it all together and give it to her. I went with her. The bank manager looked like we was taking the money out of his own pocket. I thought he was going to get sick all over us. They wanted to have the security guard walk us out to the car, but Momma said no."

"Do you know how much she kept in the wall safe?" Diana asked, jotting some notes on a legal pad.

There was a long pause. "No."

Something in his tone made her look up. He was even paler than before.

"Tommy, if you're not feeling well, we can stop. Would you like me to come back some other time?"

Tommy shook his head. "It's 'cause of me that Momma's dead," he blurted.

Uh-oh. Well, it was out, and now she would have to deal with it.

"What do you mean, Tommy?"

"I shouldn't-a took the money from the safe." He stared down at the table, utterly defeated.

"You knew the combination?"

Tommy nodded.

Her natural curiosity screamed for her to ask the next question, but she didn't say it out loud: *Did you kill her?* She knew it was more trouble than it was worth to ask that.

"Tommy," Diana said instead, rapping the table to get his full attention. "I'm not here to listen to your confession. You don't have to tell me anything about it, and in fact I'd rather not hear it. But if you know something that will help me defend you, tell me."

Tommy looked up at her, nearly crying. "I robbed Momma. I needed the money, and I knew she had it. She wouldn't give me any, though. She said I was loose with money, that I'd just spend it. She was right, too. Momma was always right."

Oh, God, Diana thought. *Here it comes.*

"She must-a known something, or suspected something, 'cause she divided it up. I hate to think that she was afraid of me. But when I opened the safe, I thought there'd be something like $60,000 in there. But there was only twenty. I took it." Tears began flowing down his cheeks. He didn't try to wipe them away. "I took it. I took it. I took it all." He began to shudder softly with his sobs.

Diana reached across the table and patted his hand. "What did you do with it?"

"Spent it. Most of it, anyway. I still had some at the trailer. I can't remember how much. It was in that envelope that I was bringing back to her that day."

"You said earlier," Diana began slowly, as though wading through a verbal minefield, "that you were *responsible* for your mother's death?"

Tommy nodded and savagely wiped his face, as though the tears offended him. "If I hadn't-a broken in, word wouldn't-a got around about Momma's money. Somebody must've heard and decided to take the rest. They killed her for it." He buried his face in his hands and began sobbing in earnest.

Diana studied him, her mind racing. Tommy's statement was what she'd been hoping to hear because it vindicated her view of the case and validated what she'd believed. But now, in a moment of what should have been minor triumph, she was unsure. She'd been conned before. Clients never told you the truth. They always selectively remembered things and doled out facts to you like precious gems. Now that she'd heard from Tommy what she'd wanted to hear, she was suspicious.

She watched him for a few more moments, then reached across and patted his shoulder.

"It's going to be okay. Tommy, look at me."

He lifted his face.

"It's going to be okay."

Tommy nodded like a little boy.

"I need to go now. Do you need anything before I leave?"

He shook his head.

"I'm going to do some more digging, okay? As soon as I find out something, I'll come back and tell you about it. You understand?"

"Yeah." Tommy wiped his face and glanced around. Apparently, he didn't want the guards to see him crying.

"Okay." Diana gave his shoulder a squeeze before motioning for the guard. After Tommy had gone, she sat for a long time alone in the small conference room, thinking.

Saturday, April 22, 6:00 p.m.

After Sean helped Matt with the wording on the warrant application, he got ready to head home.

"There isn't much else we can do until Monday," Matt told him. "I'll handle the police lockers myself tomorrow. On Monday, though, we'll need to hit the banks."

"You mean the police officers' banks?"

"Well, them, too. But I'm going to let you in on a little secret. It's possible to track every hundred-dollar bill in this country. If we can find out which bills Mrs. Resnic got, we can see if any of them have surfaced lately."

"I didn't know you could do that."

"A lot of people don't. The banks don't like to advertise it; you can see how it would create a lot of extra work for them."

"Is there anything you want me to do tomorrow?"

"Nah. Enjoy the day. I'll be at the PD, going through lockers. I'm going to have one of the crime scene techs with me—Kathy probably, since she's the best. We'll look over the uniforms for blood traces, and if we find any probables, we'll send them on to the state crime lab."

"You think you'll know who our guy is tomorrow?"

Matt shook his head. "Just the fact that there's some blood on a uniform won't tell us enough. There are a lot of reasons for a patrol officer to get stained with blood. We'll have to do DNA testing on any drops we find."

"Okay, so you test all three officers' uniforms—"

"Four," Matt corrected.

"Four? Who's the fourth?"

"Chris Franklin."

"I thought we'd ruled him out."

"I'm not ruling out anyone at this stage. We test his uniforms just like everybody else's."

"Of course, if our guy wasn't wearing his uniform at the time…?" Sean let the question hang in the air.

"Then we'll try something else. Police work teaches you to be resourceful."

"I've been hearing a lot about resourcefulness lately."

◆

It was dark by the time Sean got home. He fished around in his freezer, found "Salmon Surprise," and popped it in the microwave. There was a message on his answering machine from Diana.

"I spoke with Tommy this afternoon," she told him once he'd gotten her on the phone. "He didn't really tell me anything helpful."

"I see. You don't happen to know why Mrs. Resnic had all that money in her house, do you?"

"Yes, as a matter of fact I do. She took her retirement in a lump sum and decided to keep it all in her house."

"Kind of odd."

"Well, she strikes me as an odd lady."

"Where did she retire from?"

"Brooks Sheet Metal. She'd worked there forever."

Sean wrote the information down. "Matt might find that useful."

"How?"

Sean explained about being able to trace hundred-dollar bills. "Knowing where she retired from might help us track the money."

"I see."

"Maybe we can get together tomorrow?"

"Okay."

"I'll call you in the morning. I'm looking forward to it," Sean said.

"Me, too."

When he hung up, he had a warm glow inside him. He unhooked his bicycle from the ceiling in the second bedroom, put on his bike clothes, and decided to try a few miles. Exercise always cleared his head, and he certainly had a lot to think about.

Sunday, April 23, 8:30 a.m.

Matt had gotten to headquarters at eight o'clock that morning and hung a sign on the men's locker room that read, "Closed. No admittance until further notice."

He had planned his search well, and now it was right after a shift change, when there would be very few people in the locker room. He walked in, made sure it was empty, and invited Kathy to join him, hauling her equipment with her.

She didn't ask any questions other than what he was looking for.

"Blood."

"Okay," was her only reply.

Matt laid Chris' uniforms on a table for her and watched Kathy go to work. She slipped on plastic gloves and then, using a handheld light and a small spray bottle, painstakingly went over every surface of the uniforms, spending a great deal of time around the cuffs and collars. They turned off some of the lights so that the fluorescence would show better.

After ten minutes, she sat back. "Nothing."

Matt nodded.

He opened one of the three other lockers at random, using the list of combinations kept in the administrative files—no more guessing with birthdays.

Kathy bent to her work again. It didn't take her long to pronounce, "Negative."

They went to the third locker, and Matt held his breath while Kathy searched over the raincoat first.

"Blood," she said immediately. "Small specks on the right-hand sleeve." She continued to search. "Right shoulder, right front breast pocket area."

"Okay." Matt pulled out a large plastic bag and shoved the raincoat into it. "Can you drive this over to the state lab today?"

"On a Sunday?"

"Yup. Put it in their drop-off box."

Kathy stared at Matt but didn't ask the question that was so clearly on her mind. "I take it that this is a rush job?" she asked instead.

"Yup."

They searched the remaining locker and uniforms, just to be sure, but the result was exactly what Matt had expected: negative. Still, he gathered up all the uniforms to take with him. No point in showing his hand any earlier than necessary.

"Thanks, Kathy."

"I guess I should keep all of this to myself?"

"Please do."

"Is it going to get…messy around here?"

Matt just nodded, and Kathy left without asking any more questions. He stepped outside the locker room, tore off the sign, and went to his office.

Of course, he thought, *of course*. He'd had a pretty good idea, but still… He wondered what Angela was doing and decided to give her a call.

Sunday, April 23, 10:45 a.m.

He was waiting in the hallway when Kathy got back from the state crime lab. He watched her prepare a fingerprint sample for the database, then stop when her phone rang.

"This is Kathy," she answered, peeling off one of her gloves. "What? Is this a joke?" She listened, an angry look on her face. "Okay, yeah, I'm coming," she snapped, slamming down the phone and hurrying out the door.

He'd been pretending to read the bulletin board as he waited for her to leave. The locker search had been pretty clever, but he had a way of checking on things—and it required a visit to Kathy's office.

The second Kathy disappeared down the hallway, he walked in, casual as you please, and reached for the clipboard that was always hanging next to the door. It held the log for trips to the state crime lab. Matt may have taken a lot of uniforms from the locker room to throw him off the scent, but he was betting Matt hadn't sent them all to the state lab. He scanned the list quickly and found the entry for that morning.

He was surprised how calm he was when he hung the clipboard back up and snuck out of the office.

Maybe he'd always known it would come to this. It was time to put his backup plan into action. He couldn't trust his partner now, couldn't be sure he hadn't been feeding Matt information. He could rely on his woman for help, but he couldn't tell even her everything. No, he'd have to put things in motion on his own.

Like always. At the end of the day, you can only trust yourself.

Sunday, April 23, 11:00 a.m.

Diana liked to take a long run on Sundays. She was going to cut this one a little short because she needed to get ready for lunch with Sean, but she still wanted to get in a bit of cardio.

It was a beautiful day. The air was cool and relatively clean for a big city. That was one of the things she liked about Atlanta: the trees. They hadn't gotten around to tearing them all down like they had in so many other places. She thought about Sean as she ran. Everything was happening so quickly, and in the past that had always spelled bad news. He seemed different, but then, hadn't her previous lovers?

Hadn't each one of them seemed different? Was she making the same old mistake?

The first half mile or so was always the most difficult. She felt as though she were running through molasses, but she knew it would get better.

By the time she reached the entrance to her apartment complex, her arms and legs had found their rhythm and her breathing was coming easier. She turned right out of the complex, heading toward a business park about a quarter of a mile down the road. There were endless low buildings there, and square miles of asphalt and neatly planted trees in little islands of grass and hedges. On a Sunday morning like this there were usually few cars out, and Diana could get a welcome bit of quiet while she ran.

She didn't see the car until it screeched to a halt directly in her path and the man in the mask got out, pointing a huge gun at her.

She stood stock still, trying to think, as he screamed at her to get in the car.

Diana had imagined what she'd do if someone pointed a gun at her, but she couldn't really be sure how she'd react. In that moment, she found out. She froze, surprised by her own inertia. She couldn't seem to go forward or to turn and run. She was fully and completely incapable of movement.

Diana was also completely unprepared for the terror. It had flitted through her mind, the way it flits through every woman's mind, that one day she might be confronted with a physical situation: a rapist, a robber, a killer. But in her daydreams, she was always in control, always cool under pressure. But now, even her Judo training failed her. She just couldn't move, couldn't react.

"I said get in the fucking car!" the man screamed again. Still Diana didn't move. But he did, and quickly.

He twisted her arm behind her back and used his knee to push her to the ground. She was so horrified that she didn't even think to scream. *Frozen stiff.* That term kept flying through her brain. *Frozen stiff.* She understood it now.

He was very powerful, and she could smell his aftershave as he leaned close to her and whispered in her ear.

"What's the matter, Ball Breaker? Nothing to say? Where's your bullshit now, huh, bitch?"

He yanked her arm up further, and she did cry out then. She began to fight with her free arm, but it was already too late and she knew it. He grabbed her other wrist and pinned it. She couldn't believe how strong he was. The panic started to rise in her throat, a heaving, uncontrollable panic that nothing could stop.

The handcuffs appeared out of nowhere. He snapped them around her wrists so tight that she could immediately feel her pulse throbbing in her hands.

Fight! some part of her brain called out. *Scratch, roll, jump up and down, do something!*

But the man on top of her seemed to understand; he was ahead of her. He stood up, raising her arms behind her back by tugging on the handcuffs. The pain was excruciating.

"What's the matter, bitch?" His tone was almost conversational now. "How come you didn't try to stop me? Jesus, you were always balls to the wall in the courtroom. I guess it was all just talk, huh?" He yanked on her arms again, and even though she didn't want to cry out, didn't want to give him the satisfaction, she had to scream. Then, to her humiliation, she began to cry.

He lifted her and half-walked, half-dragged her to the car. Pulling the door open, he dumped her unceremoniously on the back seat. She couldn't brace herself and landed hard, half on the seat, half on the floor.

"Nice ass." He whacked her hard on her rump. "There's some good mileage there."

He climbed in on top of her, and she was instantly terrified he would rape her. He grabbed her ponytail and yanked her head back so hard she thought her neck would snap.

"Take your hands off me, you fucking bastard!" she finally yelled.

The pulling stopped for a moment.

"Well, well. Looks like lawyer bitch finally found her vocal chords." He viciously yanked back her head again until her cheek was pressed against his. She could feel his chin stubble and smell his sweat. She wanted to gag.

"Picked a bad time to open up to me, though," he said, reaching around to cup one of her breasts.

Suddenly, she was angry. She squirmed in the seat, trying to break free of his grip. She struck out with her elbows and tried to get her feet around to kick him; she even tried to bite his face. He recoiled from the sudden attack, but only for a moment. In a few seconds he'd regained his composure and was using his greater strength and weight to push her face down on the seat. He pinned her there while she screamed and flailed and swore.

Suddenly, he swept a cloth up to cover her face. She screamed then, screamed with everything she had, with every ounce of air left in her lungs.

"Shut the fuck up!" he snarled in her ear. But she kept screaming, trying to take a breath through the cloth, praying that someone would hear her, that someone would stop this.

When the butt of the gun struck the back of her head, it was so unexpected and jarring that for a moment she didn't realize what had happened. She saw colors erupt, but they weren't really colors; she heard an explosion in her head, but there was no real sound. Her body went loose and she felt something warm and wet on the seat.

In a remarkably detached way, she wondered if she'd been shot.

No, silly, she realized. *That's pee. You pissed your pants.*

She knew she didn't pass out because she could still hear noises, but she felt herself sliding toward something, something far away…

Sunday, April 23, 12:15 p.m.

Sean was beginning to worry. It wasn't like Diana to run this late. He tried her number again.

"Hey, it's Sean. Again. Give me a call. I'm starting to wonder if you're okay. Talk to you soon. Bye."

He hung up the phone and leaned back in his chair. The restaurant was swarmed with people, but his mind was somewhere else.

By half past noon, he was convinced something was wrong. He threw five dollars on the table and headed to his car. He drove to Diana's apartment complex, found her car and then her building. He knocked on her door but didn't get a response. Standing at the door, he looked around. Her car was here, but she wasn't. He pulled out his phone and dialed her number again. No answer; straight to voice mail.

"Hey. I'm, uh, outside your apartment. Are you okay? I'd love to hear your sexy voice." He wasn't sure how to end the message, so he just pressed the button to hang up.

What now?

He couldn't think of anything else to do, so he began the drive back to his apartment. He realized that he didn't know any of her friends to call to see if they knew where she might be.

When his phone rang and he saw that it was her number, he let out a long sigh.

"God." The relief was rich in his voice. "I was so—"

A badly distorted voice cut him off. "I sure like Ms. Baker's body."

"What?"

"Diana Baker. Haven't you been balling her? I can see why. Nice tits. Nice legs. You've got good taste in women."

"Who is this?"

"None of your fucking business!" the voice screamed, then, after a moment, settled back into a calmer tone. "I've got your whore with me right now. I'm afraid she's a little worse for wear, but she's still alive."

"I don't believe you."

"Yeah, Mr. Lawyer, I didn't think you would." There was a muffled sound and then he heard the voice order, "Talk to the man, cunt."

Sean pressed the phone against his ear, straining to hear every sound. He nearly collided with another car.

"Sean," Diana whimpered, and his entire world fell apart.

"Diana? Diana? What's going on? Are you okay? Who—"

"That's enough love talk," the voice barked. "You know what I'm thinking about?"

"No."

"I'm thinking about cutting this bitch's fingers off, one by one. That's after me and the boys have some fun first. You know what I mean? She looks like she'd be hell in the sack. But then I guess you already know about that, don't you?"

"Why are you doing this? What do you want?"

"What do I want? I want to know about your little investigation; you know, the one where you're trying to ruin some reputations to build up your own. I want answers, idiot, and if I don't get them, it's bye-bye Diana. Understand?"

"What investigation are you talking about?" Sean tried to buy some time.

He heard a slap and then a scream that sent a knife through his stomach. *Oh, God, oh, God.*

"Wrong answer, shyster. You know goddamn well what I want to know. Who's your main suspect?"

"I don't know," Sean said, then said it again, afraid the man would hurt Diana worse. "I really don't! Matt went through some lockers, but he hasn't told me yet."

"Bullshit! You and that fat slob share everything. You're trying to tell me that he won't tell you who the main suspect is? Do I need to get little sweetie back up here so you can hear me have some fun?"

"No, don't hurt her. Honest to Jesus, I'm telling the truth. He wanted to do the locker search by himself. He was going to tell me tomorrow if he found anything."

There was a pause. "Then tell me what you do know, shyster, and don't lie, or I'll make you listen to this bitch getting kicked to death."

Sean gulped. "The last time we spoke was last night. I helped him write up some warrant applications."

"Have you spoken to anyone in your office about this? Are you reporting to anyone?"

Sean hesitated.

"Answer me, goddammit!"

"No! They're leaving me alone. I haven't been reporting to anyone. The last time I spoke with Shepherd was last week."

There was a silence. Sean strained his ears to hear anything in the background, but he couldn't make out anything distinct.

"Here's what you're going to do," the voice said, and Sean listened closely to the instructions.

After he hung up, Sean immediately dialed Matt's cell phone.

"He's got Diana! He's gonna kill her!"

"Whoa. What are you talking about?" came Matt's reply.

"Whoever did all of this, he kidnapped Diana Baker, and he says that he's going to kill her if we don't do what he wants."

"Okay, okay. Meet me at the police department. We need to talk about this in person. Have you called anyone else?"

"No. He told me not to."

"Okay, let's leave it at that for right now."

"But he's got Diana!"

"I get that, but we need to talk, and I don't want to do it on the phone. Get over here fast."

Even driving faster than the speed limit on a quiet Sunday afternoon, Sean still encountered enough traffic to make the drive take twenty minutes. In that time, he couldn't help but run everything through his mind. He thought back to making love with Diana and the preliminary hearing where he'd first seen Tommy Resnic and about that little thing that had been pestering him, that little tidbit that had stuck in his brain and refused to go away. He thought about lemonade and Mrs. Resnic's phone call to her neighbor.

And then, he had it.

Sunday, April 23, 12:45 p.m.

Matt's phone rang, and he answered immediately, expecting to hear Sean's voice.

"I have something for you," said the thickly accented voice on the other end of the line.

"What? Who is this?"

"It's Lev. I have package for you."

"What are you talking about? Are you involved in this thing with Diana Baker?"

"I don't know who that is, but maybe you come out to parking lot. Come now. I'm by the trees. I don't want to get much closer to building."

"Lev, I don't have time for this."

"Make the time. I have something for you. Something you want to see. It from Gregor."

"Gregor? What are you talking about?"

"Come out. No more talking on phone. We talk face to face where walls don't have ears. You feel me?"

Matt agreed and hung up. He checked the time. Sean would be there soon, but something about Lev's call made him think it was almost as important. He sidled out the back door of the precinct building and walked between it and the building that housed the firing range. He stood for a moment, surveying the parking lot. He didn't see anyone, at least not at first. As he scanned the lot again, though, he saw someone briefly step out from behind a tree and then back behind it. Matt's hand went to his service weapon, but he didn't draw it.

Instead, he walked as though he were heading for his own car and then angled toward the edge of the parking lot where he'd seen the man behind the trees. When he got close enough, Lev stepped out again, showing himself and holding out his empty hands to prove he was unarmed.

Matt stopped about ten feet away. "What's this about, Lev?"

"I don't want to go inside there. I don't trust none of those bastards."

"Okay."

"Come over here, behind trees. I have to show you something."

"Why don't you just show me right from here?" Matt's hand slowly brushed the handle of his Glock.

"Matt, what the hell? I not here to shoot you. I here to show you package. From Gregor. Insurance. That's what he call it. Insurance."

Despite himself, Matt was intrigued. He stepped closer and Lev backed up a little, looking through the branches of the trees to make sure they couldn't be seen by anyone in the parking lot.

"Why not just call me and ask me to come to your apartment?"

"Because I don't trust fucking cops! Maybe someone follow you to my place. Maybe they kill me like they kill Gregor. I tell you Gregor was paranoid. That the word, right? Paranoid. Think people want to kill you?"

"That's the word."

"He was right. People did kill him. Cops! Cops fucking kill him." Lev stooped down to pick up a small package Matt hadn't noticed before. Matt drew his weapon but kept it aimed at the ground. When Lev straightened up, he saw the gun.

"Christ on crutch! I tell you already. I not here to kill you! I here to give you this." He gestured with the package.

"What is it?"

"I tell you already. Insurance. Gregor, he send to me. I get it a couple of days ago. Not sure what to do with it. What the hell." Lev opened the flap and fished out a note. He handed it to Matt. Still not holstering his gun, Matt took the note in his left hand.

"It's in Russian."

"Oh, right." Lev took it back. "It say, 'My friend, Lev. I send this to you…uh, as security, uh, insurance. Fuckers giving me bad feeling. If I'm wrong, I come for this in couple of days. If not, then you know what to do.'"

"What were you supposed to do?"

"Shit, I don't know. Gregor never tell me about this. He never say shit about package or what to do with it. So, I think for a few days. I don't know anyone in police I trust. But I trust you. So, I think to bring to you."

Matt didn't bother to point out that he was also a police officer. Making up his mind, he holstered his gun. "Let me see the package."

Inside was a cell phone and some notes. He noticed that the writing was in big block letters, almost like a child's.

"What does it say?"

Lev told him.

Sunday, April 23, 1:00 p.m.

"Head puzzle!" Sean shouted as he rushed into Matt's office.

"What?" Matt was still holding the yellow package Lev had given him.

"It's Lee, isn't it?"

Matt sat down at his desk, not saying anything.

"I was in your office the other day, and Lee came by," Sean continued. "He used the term 'head puzzle.' You found blood on Lee's uniform, didn't you?"

Matt didn't seem very pleased. "Yeah, Lee. What made you put it all together now?"

Sean sat down next to Matt and explained. "I had some time to think while I was driving over here. My brain was going ninety miles an hour, and I suddenly remembered that, when I was talking with Mrs. Jenkins, she used this term, 'head puzzle.' She said it was something her husband used to say. It's how he described that thing you can't remember but you know you should."

"Okay." Matt was obviously lost.

"Well, have you ever heard someone say that before?"

"No, can't say that I have."

"Right. Lee heard it the same place I did, at Mrs. Jenkins' house, probably as he was sipping some lemonade.

"She must have used the phrase when he was there, too, and it stuck with him just like it stuck with me. Only he made the mistake of saying it to me when he came by your office just after Neeka was killed. He was setting up his alibi. His partner had Neeka call you when Lee would be sure to have the greatest alibi in the world, talking to you. Unfortunately, you had already walked out and he was stuck with me, but still, he can put himself at the PD when she was killed."

"That's a lot to get from 'head puzzle,'" Matt observed.

"But I'm right, aren't I?" demanded Sean.

"Yeah. Kathy found blood traces, tiny ones, on Lee's police raincoat. After that, I went to his patrol car. More traces on the front seat, driver's side. It'll take a while to get the blood checked against Mrs. Resnic's, but—"

"But that doesn't matter because he's got Diana and he wants all the evidence brought to him or he'll kill her."

"He wants what, now?"

"Everything. He told me to get you and for us to bring it all to him or he'd kill her. He means it, Matt. He's gonna kill her."

"Okay." Matt still seemed confused. "But why her? Why not kidnap you? Or me for that matter?"

Sean just looked at him, anguish clear in his face.

"Ohhh," Matt said with dawning comprehension. "Your new woman, the complication you were telling me about. It's her. You're sleeping with the defense attorney in this case, aren't you? Are you out of your mind?"

"You can tell me I'm an idiot later. But for now, her life is in danger. And I, uh, well, she means a lot to me."

"You're in love with her." Matt's matter-of-fact tone brokered no argument.

"Yes! Okay? Yes. And he knows that."

"Exactly. He knows that, and he's using that against you. He's making it so you won't think straight."

"It doesn't matter. I don't care if it ends my career; I just don't want her to die. He was hurting her, Matt. I could hear it."

"All right. We need to think."

"We don't have any fucking time to think!"

"That's exactly what he wants. He doesn't want us using our brains. What else did he say?"

"He said he'll call back and tell us where to bring everything. We'll hand it over, and he'll let Diana go."

"Just like that?" Matt scoffed. "There's no way he's gonna do that. He's gonna get us out somewhere remote, and he's gonna kill all three of us."

"You don't know that!"

"Yes, I do. He's already killed Gregor. He's going to death row if he gets caught. He knows that. They can only kill him once, so he's really got nothing to lose by killing the rest of us too."

Matt thought things over. "I know Lee. He's a patrol cop. He doesn't know anything about forensics. He thinks he's smart, but his inexperience is showing. He knew about the locker search. Maybe that clued him in. He might have figured out that I sent his uniform to the crime lab. That could have been enough to set him off. But I wonder. Did he find out something else?"

"Did you do anything else today?" Sean's mind was whirling.

"Remember when I told you that the rifle used to punch open the back door of the armored car was a .50 caliber?"

"Yeah?"

"Well, if somebody was firing that rifle without the proper ear protection, it would damage their hearing, at least temporarily. So I asked for Lee's personnel files. Everybody in the department got a hearing test just a few weeks ago. I wanted to see his test to see if he'd had any hearing loss since his last one. But there was something…" Matt stopped.

"What? What for Chrissake?"

"The girl in records. Judy. She said Lee's file was missing. But there was something about the way she was acting. I was busy with other stuff, so I didn't pay particular attention. She said the file had probably been misplaced and that she'd find it for me later. I said it was no big deal, that I just wanted to confirm a suspicion, but…"

"But what? Do you think she was lying?"

"I don't know. I mean, I've seen her talking with Lee, but I didn't think there was anything between them."

"Who is this lady?"

"Name's Judy Pontus. She's worked here for about five years."

"You're thinking that she called Lee, warned him?"

"Well, she's blonde. And a blonde woman cut off the armored car, remember? Gave the men in the vans time to block it off from behind and open fire?"

"You think it was her?"

Matt shrugged. "I'll be shooting at shadows before this thing is over." He tucked the yellow package in his top desk drawer. "Come on. We'd better check it out just in case."

They went to the secretarial cubicles. "I'm looking for Judy," Matt told a woman.

"Sick, honey. Went home just a little while ago. She looked it, too. White as a ghost."

Matt thanked her, and they went back to his office.

"I get that she's blonde," Sean began, "but what makes you think—"

Matt took out his recorder and put it on the desk between them. "Who do you suppose transcribes these notes I make?"

Sean paused. "You don't mean...?"

"Yup. Judy. That's how Lee's been ahead of us this whole time. I've been dictating, and she's been transcribing them for me. But she's been making two copies: one for me and one for Lee."

"Okay, so that's how he's known about everything. But what do we do now? He's got Diana, and he's going to hurt her."

Matt pondered for a moment. "We need a plan, and we need reinforcements." He thought for a few more seconds and then looked down at his tape recorder. "Hmm. How about we turn the tables on Lee, using the same trick he's been using?"

"You said reinforcements." Sean got up and started pacing. "What about Jimmy? We both know he's in the clear now. Do you think he'd help?"

"Jimmy? Busting a dirty cop and helping save the day? He'd jump at the chance." Matt nodded. "Yeah, it's coming together. We're going to turn this thing on its head."

♦ Chapter Twelve ♦

Sunday, April 23, 8:30 p.m.

Sean parked the car and turned to Matt. He was staring out the windshield, studying the cabin in the fading light. Almost every trace of dusk had gone. They'd been told to park fifty yards away, but Matt had told him to pull up closer. Matt had also made sure the headlights and interior lights were off, so they wouldn't be easy targets when they arrived.

They sat and listened.

There was an oil barrel standing upright about twenty yards in front of the cabin, with holes punched in the side for ventilation. Someone had been using it to burn things; a single finger of smoke was rising from the interior, straight as a line in the windless night.

They both had guns, but Sean felt stupid holding his. He'd never come close to shooting any living thing, let alone a human being. *Let alone a human being who'll be shooting back*, he thought.

"Look at me." Matt seemed to sense Sean's thoughts. "If it comes to shooting, just think of the gun as an extension of your arm. Line up the sights and squeeze the trigger. Don't yank at the trigger. If I'm anywhere near where you're aiming, then you don't shoot. Got it?"

Sean just nodded.

"Got it?" Matt asked again, sharply.

"I've got it. Try not to shoot you. Try not to shoot myself. That's about all I can guarantee."

Matt sighed, and his face betrayed serious doubts about the situation.

When the cell phone on Sean's lap rang, it startled him so badly he almost banged his head on the car's roof. Matt looked at him and rolled his eyes. Sean answered.

"Get out of the car," the distorted voice instructed. "Get out and stand together where I can see you."

Sean relayed this to Matt.

"No way," Matt shot back, reaching for the phone. "Listen up good: I'm not standing out there like a target and letting you take shots at me. We brought the stuff you wanted. Let's get this over with."

Matt listened, then handed the phone back to Sean and opened the passenger door. He hunched down behind the open door and looked around.

Sean put his ear to the phone and listened.

"...the one calling the shots here," the electronic-sounding voice was saying. Sean wondered why Lee even bothered with the distortion device. He must know they'd figured out who he was. Why keep up the pretense?

"...you listening to me?"

"He gave the phone back to me," Sean replied. "I don't think he wants to talk to you."

"FUCK HIM!"

Matt looked over; even standing outside the car, he'd obviously heard that. Better, both he and Sean had heard it through the phone *and* faintly from the direction of the house. Sean could see a slight smile on Matt's lips.

Matt reached in and handed Sean his recorder. He remained crouched behind the door, listening. Then he turned to Sean. "Get the stuff."

Sean pulled the plastic bundle from the back seat. He opened the car door and hunched down beside it, following Matt's example.

Just then, two sets of high-wattage work lights came to life, blinding him. The lights were the halogen type, two bright bulbs on a T-shaped rack. One set was aimed directly at them. Sean held his hand in front of his eyes, dazzled by the brightness. The other set of lights was aimed at the far end of the cabin's porch.

"Son of a bitch!" Sean shouted.

Diana was silhouetted in the light shooting at the porch, handcuffed to the last wooden column. He could tell she was still alive by the way she flinched and turned away from the brightness. She was wearing a T-shirt and jogging shorts, and there was a dark patch on her right shoulder.

Dried blood, Sean thought and felt a surge of pure hatred rushing through his body. "That fucking bastard."

"Just remember the plan," Matt reminded him. "Okay?"

"That son of a bitch is going to die for this."

"The *plan?*" Matt looked hard at him. "He put her up there for a reason. You're playing into his hands."

"Yeah, yeah, okay." Sean struggled to calm down. "Do you see him?"

"No. He's not on the porch. He could be inside that last window with a gun on her."

Sean shuddered to think what had been happening to Diana in the last few hours. He heard the phone squawk and uncovered the mouthpiece. "What? Say that again." Sean listened, barely able to control his anger. He wanted to scream into the phone but said nothing.

"He wants us to put the stuff in the barrel and light it," Sean relayed to Matt. "Both of us."

Matt shook his head. "No way." He thought for a moment, then grabbed the plastic bag. "You stay here."

"He said for both of us to go."

"If we both go, he'll kill us."

The phone squawked again. "He says he'll shoot Diana if we don't do as he says!"

"Give me the phone," Matt ordered. Sean hesitated. "Give it to me, Sean."

Sean handed it over.

"Just how stupid do you think we are?...Go ahead, shoot her. One less lawyer in the world."

Sean turned to Matt, panic rising.

Matt covered the mouthpiece, hissing to Sean, "Trust me, he won't. He'd give his position away." He stood up quickly, rushed around the front of the open door as fast as his bulk would allow, and threw the plastic bag on the ground near the oil barrel before hurrying back behind the open car door.

"There," he shot into the phone. "There's your evidence. There's your raincoat and the complete file, including all of the originals. Now, why don't you take the gimmick off the phone and talk in your normal voice? *Lee.*"

Matt checked his watch, then covered the mouthpiece and said to Sean, "Get ready."

Sean wanted to ask how exactly he was supposed to get ready when his knees felt loose and rubbery and he was sure he was going to throw up at any second. He decided to keep his mouth shut.

"What's the matter, Lee? Cat got your tongue? This isn't up to your standard, is it? Hiding in a cabin, using something to disguise your voice. I'm disappointed in you. I thought a real man would take us on face to face. After all, I'm old and fat, and Sean here is a lawyer. A big man like you can't take us?"

Matt patted the seat. Sean handed him the recorder. Matt punched the PLAY button and arranged the phone on the seat so that it picked up his voice speaking out of the recorder.

There was a continuous string of obscenities coming from the cell phone, but Matt wasn't paying attention.

And then the lights went out.

◆

Lee listened, wondering what had happened to the lights. Had the power gone out on its own? Or had they somehow managed to cut it? Lee peered through the cracks in his hidey-hole but couldn't see anything. The light he'd aimed at Diana for effect had also dazzled him a little. It was going to take a minute for his night vision to come back.

Matt was still talking, so he must still be at the car. As loud as he was speaking, Lee would've been able to hear his voice moving toward the cabin. "Come on, Lee," Matt was saying through the phone. "You gotta know that I've put it all together. You want me to lay it out for you?…"

Trying to talk me down, Lee thought. *Can't move that big gut too fast, can you, old man?* He lifted the cell phone to his mouth and was about to tell Matt what a big, fat, out-of-shape bastard he was when something made him stop.

The lights. *If someone did cut the power, then who?* Matt and the shyster were still at the car. Then the answer dawned on him.

They've got help. They must have brought someone else. Someone else had cut the power. Damn it, he'd known that bastard Matt wouldn't follow his directions! He scooted over to look out the sides of his hiding place, but he still couldn't see anything.

"Come on," he muttered, praying his eyes would adjust to the darkness. *Listen,* he told himself. *Feel. I am the hunter. I am death. Come on. Show yourselves, and I'll put you out of your misery.*

Maybe there was more than one person helping them. Maybe Matt hadn't followed his instructions and had brought the whole fucking force. That would be just like him.

It didn't matter. His booby traps would take care of anybody who got too close to the cabin.

Time to move; time to act.

Lee reached his hand through the opening below him and used his Glock to fire off a couple of rounds in random directions.

The response, as he'd known it would be, was instantaneous.

From inside the cabin, he could hear the automatic in Judy's hands firing. Her instructions had been simple: When he started shooting, she should start shooting, too. She smashed the window out and opened up with a long burst, aimed in the general vicinity of the attorney's car.

Try that on for size, fuckheads, Lee thought with glee. He scrambled away from where Judy was firing. If they returned fire, he didn't want to get caught by some stray bullets, although he was pretty sure they wouldn't be firing into the porch roof.

I'm on top again. I'm high and dry and waiting for the prey.

He pressed himself into the sloping corner of the porch roof, just above and behind where he'd cuffed Diana to the column. He waited. Judy only had one other order if it all went to shit: Shoot the bitch. Lee moved back and forth, trying to see through the slats under him whether Judy had wasted her. After a moment, he caught a glimpse of Diana, her body slumped and partially hanging off the porch, hands still cuffed to the pole behind her. He couldn't tell if she was dead, but you couldn't hang like that for long if you were faking it.

His eyes were slowly adjusting to the darkness. He looked out the front of his hunter's blind and could see Sean still hiding behind the door of his car. The windshield and the front grill had been torn apart by Judy's bullets.

Good girl.

He tried to see on the other side of the car to pinpoint Matt. His rifle was ready, and if he could get a clear shot, he'd take Matt first.

Damn. I can't see the fat sonofabitch.

◆

Matt felt naked as he ran toward the cabin in the sudden darkness. *It's been twenty years since I had to run for anything but a beer. I'm not built for this anymore.*

Hunting, he thought suddenly as his feet pounded the ground. The little thing that had been rolling around in his brain had finally rolled to the front. *Lee's a hunter.* And Matt knew *how* he hunted. He immediately aimed his pistol up into the trees around him, scanning them for any signs of movement. Lee liked deer stands. He could wait for hours in a tree with a bait trap below. He liked the elevated position, firing down.

No, no. This time Lee's quarry would be firing back. Lee would need some protection, some cover. Matt lowered his gun and pressed himself gratefully against the side wall of the cabin he'd finally reached, sidestepping the pile of leaves he now realized could contain a trap.

Think, old man. Think. But instead of thinking, his mind suddenly tossed up a picture of Angela. Not their wedding day or anything like that. Just a day last year, when he'd climbed out of bed and peeked around a corner to see her standing on the back porch in her bathrobe. Her hair had been a mess, and she would've hated him even looking at her, but there was something about the way she was standing there, looking at the early morning, smelling the breeze... She'd seemed perfectly happy, perfectly content. He'd been glad they'd moved out there, glad that she could have a peaceful place of her very own. Before she could see him, he'd stepped back.

Angie, you'd call me a damn fool for being in this position. And you'd be right.

Matt turned to the porch roof, refocusing. Lee would want height, and he'd want cover. Matt leaned over and peered up at the porch's ceiling.

Gotcha.

♦

Lee kept darting from slat to slat, trying to see if anyone was approaching. When he'd picked this spot, he'd known he was leaving himself vulnerable to a rear attack, but he had a few surprises for anyone coming up behind the cabin.

Judy's firing stopped suddenly, and Lee froze. She must have exhausted the clip. She would reload in less than three seconds; he'd spent a good part of the afternoon showing her how. She'd be opening up again in no time.

In the sudden silence, Lee realized Matt was still talking on the cell phone. He moved over and pushed the barrel of his rifle through one of the holes he'd made earlier.

Come on, old man. Show your bulk. Show me something.

But there didn't seem to be anyone on Matt's side of the car, even though he was still talking in the cell phone, smoothly and calmly reciting how he'd put the whole case together against Lee.

Something was wrong. Lee knew it instantly. Why was Matt still talking? Nobody, not even Matt Burton, kept right on talking calmly through a firefight.

Oh, shit.

Lee began to move, but it was too late.

"Nice and easy, Lee," Matt's voice ordered from below him. "I've got a clean shot at your balls, and if you do anything stupid, I'll cut you in half."

Lee was in the wrong position to move quickly. Lying prone on the wooden slats, he was facing outward, the barrel of his rifle pointed at Sean's car. Matt was below and behind him, pressed into the wall between two of the porch windows.

"Drop the rifle through the opening," Matt instructed.

Lee hesitated.

"Do it now, Lee." There was something in Matt's voice that Lee didn't like.

"Okay," Lee said in defeat. "Okay." Then he drew in a huge gulp of air and screamed, "Ju-deeeee! I'm hit! I'm dying!"

♦

Matt heard the front door fly open and caught the impression of a small blonde woman rushing through the opening, a large automatic rifle in her hands. Even in the dark, Matt could see that her eyes were wild. He swung his gun around to point it at her.

"*Leeeeee!*" she screamed and turned toward Matt, the automatic already spitting out bullets.

The first bullet caught Judy in her side and the second one, fired at almost the same time, cut through the back of her skull. She fell like a tree, bounced on the edge of the porch, and slid down the three steps to the bottom.

Sean approached slowly, still pointing the gun at the woman with the rifle in her hands. "Oh my God."

Matt swung his pistol around at Lee, who was scrambling in the darkness.

"I'm gonna kill you, Lee," Matt said in a matter-of-fact voice, "if you do anything stupid. I won't have a choice. Drop the gun. Put your hands through the opening. Both of them."

Lee froze.

"I mean it, Lee." His soft voice was even more frightening coming in the sudden silence following all the shooting.

"Lee," the woman at the base of the steps moaned. Sean jumped back from her, aiming his pistol at her again. "Lee!"

"Get the rifle away from her," Matt ordered Sean from the porch, his gun still pointing at Lee. "Come down Lee. You know what I'll do if you try anything." Matt kicked Lee's rifle off the porch and into the darkness beyond.

Lee slid slowly through the opening and landed unceremoniously on the porch with a heavy thud.

"Hands!" Matt shouted, stepping away a few paces, his gun pointed at Lee's chest.

Lee held up his hands. "I'm not carrying anything. I'm clean."

Matt fished out a pair of handcuffs and slid them toward Lee. "Cuff yourself. Nothing funny. I'm in the mood to kill you, son."

For a moment, Lee studied Matt's face. "I believe you," he replied, picking up the handcuffs and snapping one manacle on his left wrist.

"Stop. Put your arms around the column. Then cuff your other wrist."

Lee did as he was told. The second Matt heard the other cuff snap into place, he rushed forward and planted a knee on Lee's back. Lee let out a *whoof*—whether of surprise or pain, Matt didn't care. He searched Lee thoroughly, starting from his head and going all the way down to his shoes. The spare handcuff key was tucked into Lee's belt.

"Cute."

"Lee," the woman coughed from the base of the steps. "Lee. Leeee. Where are you?"

◆

Sean lifted the rifle out of Judy's hands and threw it behind him. Following Matt's example, he inexpertly searched her. When he found nothing, he ran to Diana, lifting her from her slouched position. Matt was at his side in an instant, unlocking the cuffs.

"Diana?" Sean pulled the duct tape off her mouth and felt for a pulse. "Diana! Diana!" Oh, God, there was fresh blood on her face. "Oh, Jesus. Diana! Diana!"

"I'm here," she croaked, "I'm okay."

"The blood. Oh, the fucking blood. Are you hit? Are you shot?"

"No," she said softly, "splinter, from the column, scratched my neck." She paused. "Hurts."

Matt produced a flashlight and aimed it at her. He placed his fingers on the cut; it was a nasty one, a bleeder, just under her jawline.

"Put some pressure on it," Matt said to Sean, showing him how.

Jimmy, his gun pointing at Judy, stepped out of the shadows and asked, "Did you get the rifle?"

"Yeah," Sean replied. "I threw it over there, by the car." Jimmy went straight into the cabin. As he went, Sean noticed that he was limping. After a few minutes, Sean heard him call out, "Clear!"

Sean held Diana in his arms and whispered to her that everything was going to be okay. He was relieved when she wrapped her arms around him in turn and held on. He looked over her shoulder at the woman lying at the base of the stairs. Which shot had been his? He'd fired at Judy when she'd come through the door. Had he killed her? She was bleeding profusely from the wound in her side, but the skull wound looked even worse.

"Is she going to live?" Sean asked, nodding his head at her. Matt stepped over Lee's legs and walked down the steps to investigate.

"Lee," Judy moaned, her voice growing weaker. "Where's Lee? Is he okay?" She gasped slightly, as though speaking was causing her pain. "Lee? Lee? Did they get you?"

Lee was staring into the distance, ignoring her.

Matt turned to look at him, then lashed out with his flashlight, striking Lee on the side of the face. "Answer her, damn it!"

"Yeah," Lee snapped. "I'm here. Shut up."

"Lee..." she whispered. "I love you... I've always..."

Lee turned his head away in disgust. Jimmy, emerging from the cabin, leaned over and felt the side of Judy's throat.

"She's dead," he announced, straightening. There were engine noises in the distance, and Jimmy turned toward them. "Good guys are coming."

"You okay, Jimmy?" Matt asked, seeing the limp.

"Yeah. Bastard had a bear trap set under a pile of leaves. Fortunately, the spring malfunctioned. Probably would've taken my foot off otherwise," Jimmy replied.

Sean studied Matt as he stared down at Lee, not saying anything.

"Don't blame me," Lee said, trying to get into a more comfortable position. "It wasn't me. It was her. It was all her. Judy. She's the one who did it all. I came here tonight to stop her."

"Shut up," Matt ordered.

"I had no idea—" Lee began again.

Matt turned to him and pressed the barrel of his gun into Lee's face. "Shut up. You can talk all you want to later, but don't say another word right now." He left the gun there for a moment longer, as though considering pulling the trigger anyway.

Lee swallowed hard, and Matt lowered the gun. Sean watched Matt walk over to where he and Diana were crouched on the ground.

"Ambulance will be here shortly," Matt told her. "Are you feeling okay?"

"A little woozy; feel like throwing up."

"You've probably got a concussion. Just stay put and let the pros take care of you."

After the ambulance arrived and the EMS people began checking

Diana over, Sean walked the few paces to the dead woman. The medics had only spent a few seconds with her, confirming that she was dead before moving on to Diana. Jimmy had refused medical attention for the moment.

Sean stared down at Judy. She looked broken and used up, like a doll no one loved anymore. Jimmy returned from putting Lee in a patrol car and stood next to Sean.

"Why did she do it, I wonder?" Sean asked. There was a different question he really wanted to ask, but he didn't think he could say it out loud.

"She was a fucking psycho," Jimmy offered.

Matt appeared next to them.

"Wacko," Jimmy repeated. "Right, Matt?"

Matt looked at the body for a moment. "She loved him. She would've done anything for him. He knew it, too. He knew she'd come out if she thought he was hurt. He used her; he treated her worse than a dog."

Jimmy didn't seem to know what to say to that. He looked at Sean and Matt, who were still both staring down at the dead woman. "Like I said, fucking wacko." He stalked off, still favoring his right leg.

"I don't think *you* killed her." Matt turned to Sean.

"You can't know that."

"Ballistics will tell for sure, but I'll bet I'm right."

"How do you know?"

"I had a better view than you did. You'd have been lucky to hit the cabin, let alone a moving woman firing a gun."

"I had to have hit her, though. Two bullets did. One from Jimmy; the other one from me."

Matt shook his head. "You're right about the two bullets, and one probably was from Jimmy. I'll bet it was the one that caught her in the side. He's a good shot. But you didn't shoot her in the head.

"Look at the angles. The second shot came from up there." He pointed at the porch ceiling.

Sean was confused for a moment. "You're saying…no. He wouldn't."

Matt nodded his head. "He would. And he did. He knew he was cornered. Probably realized it the second the lights went out. He didn't call her out to kill us. Hell, he probably thought the place was surrounded by SWAT sharpshooters. He figured she'd be cut down in less than a second, but he had to be sure."

"Sure of what?"

"That she wouldn't talk. So he shot her when she came through the door. Aimed at her head to kill her."

Sean digested this slowly. "Jesus."

"I know. The hell of it is that she probably would've gone to death row before she'd turn on him. She was that type."

"All because she loved him."

"Yeah. He counted on that in the short term, but not for the long term. A man like Lee couldn't understand a woman's loyalty. He didn't understand that she'd never betray him."

The medics brought up a gurney, and Sean turned to Diana. "I'm gonna ride in with you," he told her.

Matt stopped him for a moment. "You remember what I said about a woman's loyalty, now."

Sean looked at him, then followed after Diana.

Monday, April 24, 10:30 a.m.

This time when Holloway's secretary called Sean to meet with the DA, there was something different in her voice. He couldn't tell if that was good or bad. When he walked into the reception area, she waved him directly into Holloway's immaculate office.

Sean stopped dead in the doorway. Holloway was there, sitting comfortably, but so were Shepherd, Chief Black, and Matt.

"The prodigal son," Holloway announced and motioned for Sean to sit down.

Sean sat. No one offered him coffee this time.

"Can we even count how many rules you broke in this case?" Shepherd began.

Sean didn't respond.

"You had express instructions on how to handle—" Shepherd continued, but was cut off by Chief Black.

"Yeah, and thank God he didn't follow any of them. If he had, this whole thing would probably be a complete nightmare and all of us, including you, Bill, would be looking for another job."

Sean was surprised by the support.

Holloway leaned forward and picked up his cup of coffee. "Unconventional. True enough." He sipped. "But in the end, the truth came out and we weren't caught with our pants down. How's the 'little man fights the system' angle working, Bill?"

"They're going with it big time. The focus has been on Matt, of course. 'Brave cop takes on corruption,' and that sort of thing," Shepherd muttered. "There's even some national news people who want coverage."

Holloway waved that away lazily. "They can wait a bit. This whole thing is going to blow over with the next scandal that comes along. The important thing is that Church is in custody and we have a solid case."

"You won't be prosecuting it," Shepherd told Sean.

"I don't want to. I'm not even sure I want to work here anymore."

Holloway put down his cup. "Now, Sean, let's not get hasty and start making rash decisions. From my point of view, despite some of the irregularities in the case, you did a fine job." He looked around. "A fine job. Wouldn't you all agree?"

"I think the DA's office needs more men like you, Sean," Black said in his deep voice, nodding.

"Yeah. But I'm still not totally clear on everything about the other man involved, and how the file disappearances tie in," Shepherd added, a sour look on his face.

Matt jumped in to explain—even though Sean suspected Shepherd already knew and was just trying to make it appear as though Sean hadn't delivered a thorough report. "From all accounts, Gregor the Russian was pretty paranoid, and he must have suspected something was up with his pal, Lee, so he sent some materials to a friend of his. A little package. The note was written in Russian, so we had to get it translated, but there was also a burner phone, and we didn't need to translate the numbers.

"That led us to Rick. Turns out Rick and Lee have known each other for years, back from when Rick worked for the department before becoming a DA investigator. In addition to attempted armed robbery and full-fledged murder, he was also in on some scheme with Lee to make certain police files disappear—for a price. Lee would identify the marks, Gregor would make contact, and Rick would make the cases disappear from the DA database. Rick rolled on Lee so fast it was kind of disappointing. I think he even cried a little at the end."

"Well, it sounds like all the loose ends have been tied up. Good work, both of you." Holloway gave an approving nod.

There wasn't much left to say after that, and the meeting broke up.

In the hallway, Matt fell into step with Sean as they walked in the general direction of Sean's office.

"Boy, that was an ass-covering extravaganza," Matt said. "Before the end of the day, they'll have themselves convinced they knew all along that you were the perfect choice to handle this sticky assignment."

"How do you deal with this crap, Matt?"

"I try not to. The political stuff, anyway. I just work the cases. I try to get results; try to put the bad guys away. It's really that simple."

They stopped in the hallway, and Matt extended his hand. As they shook, Matt smiled. "Stop by headquarters later and look in on S&P. It'll be worth the trip."

"I'm going to see Diana."

"Good for you. She's a fine lady. Still, you might find a quick stop at S&P very interesting…"

Sean nodded and went to his office to pick up the bouquet of flowers he'd purchased earlier. When he turned, Tom Delaney was standing in his doorway.

"I heard what happened. Wow."

"Don't start thinking this is typical for the DA's office," Sean warned. "It isn't. In fact, this is the most bizarre thing I've ever been involved in."

"Did the Russian thing help?"

"Yes, it did. It helped clear up a little mystery we've had here for a while. I'll tell you about it later."

◆

Sean drove to police headquarters and walked over to where the S&P offices were housed. He was surprised to see Bernie sitting behind a desk, looking thoroughly miserable. Katie came out from the back office and gave him a big smile.

"I thought you were through with this," Sean said, surprised.

"It has its privileges." Katie smiled. "They wanted someone to help clean house. And I wanted to clean this particular house very badly and in my own way." She raised her hands, as though displaying her kingdom.

"Well, congratulations. And let me know if I can be of any service. Taking down dirty cops is apparently what I do now."

"Thanks! Say, Bernie," she said, not taking her eyes off Sean, "grab us some coffee, will ya?"

"Sure thing, boss." Sean couldn't help but smile at the acrimonious look on Bernie's face.

◆

Sean frowned when he saw that his bouquet of flowers wasn't the largest or even the prettiest. At least the hospital room was empty of other visitors when he walked in. Diana looked terrible. She was lying on her back with a large bandage on the side of her neck. She had dark circles under her eyes, and her face was still unusually pale. His heart constricted when he saw her. He stayed there in the door for a moment, wondering whether he should go in. Her eyes were closed, and he thought she might be asleep.

"Hey," she said, slowly opening her eyes.

"Hi. How are you feeling?"

"Better. They want to keep me in here for a day or two, just to monitor the concussion. They're probably just doing it so they can stick it to the insurance company."

"Now that sounds like a liberal defense attorney if I ever heard one," Sean joked, moving to stand next to the bed.

"Stick it to the man." She gave a weak smile.

"I brought you something." He fished a folded piece of paper out of his pocket. "The judge signed it today. I told him I'd deliver it personally."

"Such service. I see our tax dollars are being well spent." She took the paper and opened it. "So, the case against Tommy is dismissed. I'm glad."

"I contacted the jail before I came over here. He's being processed out right now."

She nodded her head.

"You're tired. I'll come back later."

"No." She reached out and took his hand. "Stay."

"Okay."

"Did you get into trouble? With your boss, I mean."

He shook his head. "It's ugly, but they're making do. They're playing up the bad cop angle pretty heavily. Holloway is talking about seeking the death penalty against Lee. It's still a black eye for the police department, but the press is playing up the 'courageous man takes on the establishment and wins' story."

"You being the courageous man?"

"No, Matt. He makes a better symbol."

"But they should be talking about you, too."

"That's all right. I'm just glad it's over. And Matt really played the biggest part."

"No, he didn't. If you hadn't gotten this thing started…" She sighed.

"Shush. It's okay. Really. I'm kind of glad to be left out of it."

"But people should know."

"No, they shouldn't. If I get my face plastered all over the news, I start stepping on some other egos in the office. And then," he mugged for her, "I become Mr. Big Head. Look at the size of that head! You can't fit it down a hallway. They'd make Japanese horror movies about me."

She laughed a little. "You wouldn't get like that."

"Don't be too sure. Matt can handle the attention a lot better than I can." Sean watched her for a moment. "Besides, I'm through thinking about Lee Church. I've got another big project in mind, and it's going to take up a lot of my time."

"What's that?"

"It's the Diana Baker Project. There are several steps. I've made meticulous plans. Would you like to hear about it?"

"Yes." She looked up at him and smiled. "I want to hear all about it."

www.ingramcontent.com/pod-product-compliance
Lightning Source LLC
Chambersburg PA
CBHW061941170626
46813CB00006B/2487